# EXPIRED REFUGE

## LAST CHANCE COUNTY - BOOK 1

## LISA PHILLIPS

Publisher: Lisa Phillips

Cover design: Ryan Schwarz

Edited by: Jen Weiber

Created with Vellum

# 1

According to intel, this was where it would go down. Police Lieutenant Conroy Barnes watched the feed on his laptop, which was sitting on a folding table in the janitor's closet of the high school. Low light meant it was hard to see what was happening. But he could make out enough.

The undercover was about to make the sale.

He could hear her every breath through the microphone. The second his officer made the exchange, cash for drugs, he was clear to move in.

Conroy watched as the dealer reached into a pocket. Even behind the door, he was ready to pull his weapon and step in. His officer was also armed and wearing a bulletproof vest. Not a foolproof plan, but she understood the risks, and they had been over all the contingencies.

The department was big enough they could have brought in several officers as backup, or even a couple of detectives. Each of them worked as part of a SWAT team when it was necessary. But tonight's operation had to be done discretely in order that word didn't get back to anyone that the police had snatched up this guy.

The drug dealer, who conducted business under the moniker

"Iceman," pulled a small baggie from his pocket. "You got the money?"

Conroy held his breath, watching the screen as he waited for the right words. He didn't like being the one on the other end of the video feed. He much preferred the front lines, but he also had a high profile in this town. His officer was new, which meant few people knew she was a cop.

So he'd put her in as an undercover.

And she was turning out to be seriously good at it. Though, with her history, he wasn't entirely shocked. She impressed him, but she was also his underling and barely twenty-four. He was creeping towards his thirties.

"Got it right here." Her voice was steady which shouldn't surprise him given everything he knew about Jessica Ridgeman. She might be green, but she was also proving to be a serious asset.

With just enough desperation in her voice, she said, "It'll be a good weekend."

That was the signal. Conroy shoved open the fire door and led with his weapon. Cold night air hit him like being slammed with a thousand ice picks.

"Police! Hands up!" He approached the suspect they had been surveilling who was still standing with Officer Ridgeman.

Iceman whipped around. Conroy saw him realize this had been a setup. He released the cash and pulled a knife.

"Drop it!" There was no way he would be so stupid as to hurt a cop just because he was about to be arrested. Then again, smart criminals didn't usually get caught this easily.

Dollar bills hit the ground. Iceman swiped the knife toward the customer, Jessica Ridgeman. She reacted with the reflexes of a police officer trained and, evidently, completely comfortable working undercover. Conroy had never seen someone under his command so cool in the face of a weapon. This newcomer to Last Chance County was going to fit in well.

She swiped at it with a flat palm, connecting with Iceman's

wrist. The knife dropped.

"Hands up." Conroy held his gun aimed at the man. "You're under arrest."

The drug dealer grunted. Then he made the choice so many of them did when faced with poor odds.

He ran for it.

Iceman took off across the quad toward the field and the neighborhood behind the high school.

His officer took a half step back, shook out her hand, and said, "Ow."

"You okay, Jess?"

"I will be if you go arrest that guy, Lieutenant." She pulled her gun. "I'll get the car."

He took that as a green light and took off after the drug dealer. Iceman's real name was Simon Petrov and he seemed, by all accounts, a low-level guy. The man on the street dealing hand-to-hand with townspeople hooked on destruction. Not the boss.

Conroy wanted to sit Petrov down in his interview room and ask him to testify against the person who supplied him with the drugs. Whether that meant just straight testimony, or if it involved Petrov being put back on the street to get Conroy evidence on the one who got him the supply—a supply he then divided up and sold off for a cut. Conroy didn't mind either way if it got him the boss in cuffs.

Petrov made it all the way to the far end of the field. He went right through the break in the fence and took the walking path that ran along the back of the neighborhood.

Conroy pumped his arms and legs, his hiking boots pounding the salted path. Snow had been shoveled off the sidewalk for dog walkers and kids going to school, but he was going to send the landscaper a gift basket if he managed to get all the way to the end without slipping or sliding on the ice.

Petrov disappeared at the end of the path, turning into the neighborhood. Mostly larger family homes at this end, he didn't

4 | LISA PHILLIPS

figure anything good would come of Petrov breaking into one. The last thing Conroy needed was to spend the night working a hostage situation. Or a homicide scene. He'd worked exactly one murder in the last six months, and even a ratio that low didn't sit well with him.

One of his plans if he became the chief of police was to work on reducing violent crime. This town—affectionately known to all who lived here as Last Chance County—was supposed to be a safe haven, a place people could live their lives peacefully and quietly.

He'd grown up here, and during those years, as well as his years as a cop, Conroy had seen the best and worst of this place. He never wanted to be anywhere else. And except for the odd vacation in Hawaii during which he complained about the heat nearly constantly, driving his sister, her husband, and their kids crazy, Conroy was going to stay here until the day he died.

His earpiece crackled. Officer Ridgeman's voice came through loud and clear. "You copy me, Lieutenant?"

"Heading down Aspect now, about to cross Herrin Ridge."

The center of the neighborhood had a huge roundabout, grassed over in the middle with a kids play area where his niece and nephew loved to spend their time.

Petrov vaulted over a downed tree trunk and ran across the road to the center of the roundabout. Most of the snow here had melted, except for what was rolled into snowmen that now were nothing more than mounds of dirty, white stuff. Remnants of facial features and buttons—carrots and pieces of charcoal from someone's barbecue—lay on the frosty grass.

"He's on the north side of Aspect."

"Copy that," Ridgeman said. "I'm almost to Charmer."

That street ran along the top end of the neighborhood, a busy main road with strip malls on either side. A grocery store, a library, and the gym he worked out at. Plenty of potential spots for Petrov to come across another innocent bystander and make this situation more complicated than it already was.

"We need to cut him off at the light."

"I'm stuck behind a semi." And she sounded exceedingly irritated about that.

Conroy heard her use the sirens and knew she would have lights flashing. Ridgeman was a city girl, accustomed to employing defensive driving tactics just to change lanes. "Hurry it up, officer."

"Copy that."

She might have only been here two months, ever since her grandfather had gotten sick, but she was solid. Only on the job a few years, when he had been doing this for nearly twelve. Still, Ridgeman was going to be an asset to the team. It was that way with all the people in his department. He could tell who would fit, who would stick it out, and who wouldn't last.

Conroy picked up his pace, knowing the end of this foot chase was in sight.

It had to be.

The alternative was innocent citizens in danger.

Petrov had started to slow. Winded, maybe not sure where to run next considering he had a bullheaded police lieutenant right behind him.

Conroy called out, "Give it up, Petrov. There's nowhere to go."

But he didn't. Petrov glanced left, and then right. After that second of indecision, he raced toward the grocery store parking lot. What was he going to do, steal a car?

Conroy passed the chain-link fence that separated the neighborhood from the grocery store parking lot. A vehicle came out of nowhere. The driver slammed on his brakes, which locked and squealed as he started to slide on the icy asphalt toward Conroy.

He jumped out of the way and hit the ground, rolling as his mind flashed back to that night. The screech of metal and the sound of the impact. Blood, everywhere.

"You okay, boss?"

He could hear the sirens now, and not over the comms.

"Lieutenant?"

"Yeah." He picked himself up off the ground and allowed the sound of approaching police sirens to relax him in the way it always did. Help was almost here, even if he was practically the boss now and she was only one of his officers.

He said, "I'm okay."

"I see Petrov. He's running past the front entrance."

"Let's cut him off."

Conroy ran toward the front doors of the grocery store and saw Petrov. A customer came out cart first, loaded with bags. She was a slender woman in skinny jeans and a huge, green coat. Her boots were edged with fluff that matched the collar of her jacket and her hood was up.

"Stop!" He yelled as loud as he could, both to Petrov and as a warning to the woman. "Police!"

She shifted immediately. There was a split second of decision-making before she rammed the shopping cart into Petrov's hip. He cried out and went down to the asphalt in a heap.

The woman didn't move. She just held onto the handle of her cart and watched.

Ridgeman pulled up in the car, lights flashing. She got out and held her weapon on Petrov while Conroy put the cuffs on.

"That was nice." He hauled Petrov to his feet and moved the guy toward Ridgeman. Conroy was breathing hard, harder than he would have liked. "Now I don't have to hit the gym on the way home. I already got my run in for the day."

Petrov said nothing.

"You good to take this one in, Officer?"

"Sure thing, Lieutenant." Ridgeman smirked, took hold of Petrov's arm and led him to the back of her black and white patrol car. She loaded him inside, glanced once back at Conroy with another smirk he didn't get, and then drove away.

Conroy turned to the woman. "Thanks for your help." Never mind that it had been dangerous. It also should never have been necessary for a civilian to get involved in the take-down of a suspect. He was still grateful, and it couldn't be denied that no one had been hurt.

"I'd say 'anytime' but that would be a lie." She squeezed the handle of her shopping cart and shoved it forward.

There was something about her that... "Hold up one second. I'm going to need you to sign some paperwork."

It was lame, and he didn't really need her to do it, but that was what had come out of his mouth. No taking it back now.

She turned and he saw her face in the yellow glow of the grocery store lights. A nasty gash ran down the side of her face in front of her right ear. "No, I really don't."

His jaw tightened. *Mia.*

It had been years since he had seen her last. And with all those images and sensations fresh in his mind, thanks to that car, the past rushed into the present and everything just kind of got blurred. Fear. Anger. Hurt. Why was she here?

He closed in on her.

Fury that she would put herself in danger like that almost overwhelmed him. "Then why get involved?"

"Reflex." Her eyebrows lifted. "One I will be seriously reconsidering in the future."

He stared at the injury on the side of her face. "How did you get hurt?"

"None of your business." Mia shoved at her shopping cart again. She headed for her father's truck parked in the center of the lot under a streetlight. "Good night. *Lieutenant.*"

Conroy should have gone over and offered to help with her bags. He also should probably have apologized for getting in her face.

He did neither of those things, instead opting to head back toward the high school to pick up their equipment.

As he turned, he spotted a car across the lot. A man sat inside.

Watching Mia.

# 2

Mia slammed the front door so hard the windows rattled. She winced, not just at the sound that screamed of potential for more home repairs on her father's tiny lake cabin, but also at the state of her shoulder, tweaked and still not healed.

She sighed to the quiet, empty home and then wandered across the threadbare rug to flop on the couch. Another wince.

She toed off her running shoes. Nothing wrong with her legs. She'd figured going for a morning jog wouldn't exactly hurt. Except that it did hurt. A lot.

She leaned her head back. Eyes closed.

The whole place smelled like her father and his old dog that had passed away. She breathed deep, her body covered in sweat despite the frigid temperatures outside.

Yeah, she wasn't doing so hot.

Infection? No. More like burnout plus injury, plus stress, plus emotional strain. The idea she might need to take *another* nap was the worst part of it. Every time she closed her eyes she saw Conroy and that look of confusion and surprise on his face.

Not that she minded the surprise. It was fine to throw a guy like that for a loop when the opportunity arose. She just didn't want to have anything to do with him.

Not now. Not ever.

Especially not now.

Her phone rang. Mia pushed aside that thought and answered it. "Tathers." The screen was cold against her good cheek.

"It's Hudson."

Tate Hudson. Calling back already? "That was fast."

"Best private investigator in Last Chance County."

"You should put that on your business card." Hesitation made her pause. "What did you find?" Mia didn't like her tone. Entirely too hurt, which happened constantly with regards to information about her sister.

"Train wreck, this kid. Wasn't hard, since I only had to follow the wake of destruction back to the source."

"And?" Her sister was only three years younger, so twenty-four. Hardly a kid, but for a man in his mid-forties, she figured anyone south of thirty was basically a child.

His turn to pause. "I almost want to give you this one for free, but I got a mortgage I'm paying extra on."

"Just tell me."

Mia half wondered if her sister was dead. A longtime junkie with a rap sheet, no one would have been surprised. But they would have grieved. All that light she'd had as a child, all that potential, gone now from the world.

Her father chose to bury his head in the sand. Case in point, the fact he was off hunting right now while she was here recuperating. No, she didn't need him to "take care of her," but she wouldn't have minded the company.

"I found her."

"Hudson—"

"Currently shacked up with a local dealer. A guy with a whole lot of muscle and a stable of ladies of which your sister appears to be the queen bee."

Great. A "stable." She didn't even want to think about what that meant. "You saw her?"

"Talked to some acquaintances of mine...a few of his guys. Got the scoop. She's up there, living the high life."

"I'm sure." Just as Mia was sure it wouldn't look anything like the high life she might have chosen for her own life.

Mia squeezed the bridge of her nose. It was tempting to leave her to it, let Meena live her life however she wanted. But there were things left unsaid. "Thanks, Tate. I appreciate it."

"That's it? You're not planning on making the approach yourself, are you?"

She said, "You'd rather I pay you to do it?"

"I'd rather you didn't go in there without backup. You flash that badge of yours around, let them all know you're a federal agent, and you'll wind up full of more holes than you already have."

"I regret telling you about that." A long time ago now. And nothing to do with any of this.

Tate's sigh was loud enough she heard it over the phone. "I'm coming over."

"No, don't." He would end up seeing what a mess she was in. She'd have to take a shower to be presentable since she had just run four miles and now wasn't even sure she could get up to answer the door. Her legs were still shaking from the exertion of her run.

She shifted on the couch and planted her stocking feet on the coffee table. If he did come over, he could make her a sandwich. That would be fair.

"You even think about making a move, you tell me. Do *not* go in there without backup. This guy is a bad guy, Mia."

"It's sweet that you care."

He chuckled. "I just want my paycheck. After that, I'm not paid to worry."

She huffed a laugh out through her nostrils and smiled at the empty room. "I should go."

"Don't make me regret this."

"I won't do anything without calling you. I promise."

"Like you promised to pay me for mowing your lawn when your dad gave you the money and left for work?"

"I was twelve. I wanted to go to the movies." He'd been in his twenties, home from college for the summer. Doing odd jobs.

And he'd never once taken his shirt off when he mowed the lawn.

Tate groaned. "I went to the church and said a prayer of thanks when you swore that oath as an ATF agent. Finally landed on the right side of the law."

She had been kind of…precocious as a teen. Not as much as Meena, but more than her older sister Mara. Then Mara had been killed. After that, getting her way didn't seem to matter so much.

She said, "You mean like the prayer I uttered when the football captain went off to college? Or when he was sworn in as an FBI agent?" Not that she had prayed, considering church and all that wasn't really her thing. Not with the way she'd grown up. But that wasn't the point.

"Yeah, like that one." She could hear the smile in his voice.

"Life is funny that way." Too bad she was so busy working cases lately that she didn't have time to live it.

"Like a bad pun."

He'd wound up blowing out his knee, retiring, and becoming a local private investigator. She'd always figured there was more to the story, but since they were only friends—and not even good friends—it wasn't her place to pry about the real reason.

She decided to lighten this entire conversation. "Ain't that the truth?"

She figured she needed to either laugh about it or wind up crying. One dead sister and one as good as gone. Her career had stalled out while she stayed home and recuperated during the investigation of what had gone down. Everyone said she'd be cleared back to full duties, that the shooting had been justified.

Mia touched the scar in front of her right ear. Self defense.

Now she was here, wallowing in her dad's cabin. Trying to distract herself from the fact she was stuck here without a thing to do while someone else decided her fate. The alternative? She didn't even know where to begin, but she could start by figuring out what she would rather be doing with her life. Being a cop, even a federal one, was the only thing that had ever made sense to her.

"How about you do what you should be doing? That's resting, by the way." He paused long enough she wasn't sure he'd continue. Then he did. "I'll make the approach, see how Meena feels about meeting up with you and let you know what she says."

"What about this guy she's all shacked up with? He's going to be okay with that?"

Tate said, "I know what I'm doing."

"Sure you don't want backup?"

"I'll let you know. But I don't have the budget for a deputy, so don't get any ideas." He hung up.

Mia tossed the phone on the couch beside her.

Above the mantel was a framed picture. Herself, age nine. Standing between Meena, six, and Mara, eleven. Behind them was a Christmas tree. Last one they'd had that actually looked good, far as she could remember. The year before her mom took off. Before her dad realized he had to raise three girls on his own, with no idea how to do that.

Mara had died the summer before her senior year.

Mia descended into a tailspin after that, hitting junior year with a vengeance. It was a tailspin she'd managed to pull out of by reinventing herself in college. Thankfully she'd never run into any trouble with the law. That would've made becoming a federal agent problematic. Now she worked as an ATF agent out of the Seattle office, and it was widely known that if any of the agents ran into a teen through the course of an investigation, they should send Mia to talk to the kid.

Mostly she figured the guys just didn't want to deal with drama.

Her sister Meena, on the other hand, had hit rock bottom right before ninth grade and never pulled herself out of it, despite Mia's attempts to convince her to turn her life around.

She knew where her sister was now. Shacked up with some local bad guy.

Mia just didn't know what to do about it. If her dad was here, or anywhere there was cell signal, then she would have talked with him about it. Which, according to him, defeated the purpose of "getting away from it all." He had a right to know where Meena was, and if he didn't know, then surely he at least cared about her enough to want to check in.

He parented like he did everything else. In "his own way." Which most of the time made no sense to anyone with no Y chromosome and part of the time seriously ticked her off. But she didn't want to spend her vacation—recuperation—time stewing over family stuff. She should have stayed home and gotten a hotel room until they were finally done dealing with the mold in her apartment building.

Mia shoved out of the couch.

Shower first.

Then food.

After that, she'd figure out what to do next.

Mia had wet hair and was assembling a sandwich when someone knocked on the door. A cop, if she wasn't mistaken. No one else rapped on a door like that.

And she only knew one cop in Last Chance County.

She pulled the door open and smiled sweetly. "Lieutenant, how nice to see you."

"Liar."

She shoved the door closed. Conroy Barnes put the toe of his boot between the door and the jam. Any other day she'd have fought it, but she didn't have the strength to go at it with him. Not with a messed up shoulder. "Move your foot!"

"I just wanna talk to you." He sounded tired.

She pushed the door against his foot and peered out through the tiny gap. He hadn't slept. She worked with enough alpha male cops to see he'd been up all night. Hopefully doing paperwork. She also hoped it had been mind-numbingly boring. "So talk."

He shook his head. "Inside."

"I'm not letting you in. We have nothing to say to each other." After what he'd done to her and to her family? "You have some nerve coming here, asking for time."

Not to mention whatever else he wanted.

"Mia."

"Don't do that." She knew all about him. "Don't put this on me. I don't care if your case got screwed up for whatever reason. It is *not* my fault."

His eyes narrowed. Piercing blue. She'd never really understood what that was supposed to look like. Until now. They were the color of that bright blue sky, so rare in Seattle. He even wore a suit. Dark blue tie with tiny gold dots.

He said, "You don't seem surprised I'm a cop."

She shrugged one shoulder and took inventory of her own state. At least she'd put on her good sweatpants when she got out of the shower. The sweater was thin and fitted, zipped up far enough it still gave him a view of her collar bones—which she'd always thought were her best asset.

*What is wrong with you?*

She'd gone crazy. Or this was some kind of torturous nightmare.

"Mia."

"What?" She snapped at him, mad at herself for finding him attractive. "Move your foot and then leave. I'm busy."

"Doing what? I heard you're ATF now. Is this time off? Because you should know your dad isn't back for another couple of weeks."

She was so surprised she let go of the door. He got his whole foot in, along with a leg. Now she wanted to slam the door on him for reals. Ouchie. "Why do you know my dad's hunting schedule?"

He shrugged, looking pretty pleased with himself that he knew something she didn't.

"Get out of my house."

"Not your house." The accusation was clear. She didn't belong here. "Your dad's house."

"The police chief is going to hear about this."

A shadow crossed his face.

She ignored it. "Get ready for a fight, because you're inviting a world of hurt down on yourself and your precious career. *Lieutenant.*"

"Don't bother the chief."

Sore subject. That was interesting. "Then leave."

If he didn't want her to call his boss, then he could end this right here. Before things got ugly.

He shook his head. "Not before we talk."

Talk? He was all grown up, pretending to be some good-guy police officer, and he wanted to talk to her?

"You and I." She wanted to scream and rage at him. "We have *nothing* to talk about."

"No?" He folded the arms of his jacket across an expansive chest. Had he been that big in high school? "Meena?"

She nearly choked. "Planning on killing another one of my sisters?"

He frowned, but not at her. Conroy Barnes tore through her house to the back door and what amounted to her dad's yard beyond it. "Call 911. There's a prowler outside!"

Mia closed her eyes. She did get her phone, but she didn't call emergency services. Not when it was likely nothing but a deer outside.

Instead, she sent Tate a one word text.

Traitor.

# 3

Conroy stepped onto the frosty grass and winced. Wrong shoes. Coming to Mia's dad's cabin, he'd stupidly made the mistake of wearing his nice shoes. Something he wasn't about to think on, at least not overly much. It had nothing to do with her.

He held his gun loose in his hands and scanned the area. Beyond the grass and the half-height picket fence was the lane that led to the main road. The back of the house faced the lane where his silver, unmarked Jeep was parked. The front of the house faced the lake, with big, wide windows that Rich told him had been the selling point on the house. Mia's father had put all his money into buying the house at its exorbitant price, now fixing it up bit by bit as he had the cash to do so.

Conroy had even helped with the bathroom tile since he'd done his own only a few months before.

Shooting the breeze. Two single guys hanging out, chatting. Conroy's parents lived in Arizona now and came to visit in the summer. When they did that, Rich tended to be absent as they didn't exactly get along. But sure enough, when it came time to return home to their retirement house, Rich showed back up.

That the father of the girl who'd died was the one who felt

he had to retreat never sat well with Conroy. But he and Rich had made their own kind of peace with it. Between the two of them, they'd figured out how to move on. Something his parents hadn't yet made the effort to do to get past the death of a young woman they had loved, who had been so closely tied to their son.

He kept walking, circling the house back to the front yard and the lake shore. Eight houses were tucked in this corner of the lake, nowhere near the dock located down the shore or the neighboring occupants. Summer parties. Speed boats. Other activities that went on at the party side. Rich kept to himself, and he liked the quiet here at this end of the lake.

Conroy spotted a dark figure, same jacket he'd seen just moments before. Just a flash of color and movement between two trees. It was gone so fast he wondered if he imagined it. Conroy stared at the spot but saw nothing else.

He walked to the front door and tried the handle. Locked. Had she shut him out, or shut herself in?

He rang the bell.

Mia opened it. Her wet hair hung straight over her shoulders. The depth of her eyes was so dark brown the color bled into her pupils. Same as her sister's, that olive-skinned, exotic beauty none of them even realized they had—that was, until Meena figured out how to use it to her advantage. Mia's sweater fit snug against her volleyball-player figure, over dark blue sweatpants with white letters down one leg.

"Yes?" She had her phone in her hand.

He sighed. "Did you call it in?"

"A prowler? It was probably a deer."

He didn't give her the chance to shove the door in his face this time. Conroy pushed it open and stepped between her and the door. He holstered his weapon and folded his arms across his chest. Suit. Tie. His nice shoes.

Conroy dismissed the idea he might have been trying to make a good impression. It had nothing to do with last night, or the fact she seriously reminded him of her sister Mara. Not in a weird way, like he was trying to get back what he'd lost when Mara had died. More like he remembered the way life was then and that junior high kid he'd known, the one who had clearly had a crush on him.

Now Mia was all grown up, though she seemed not to have grown out of her gangly phase. She was still all arms and legs. Almost as tall as he, and that was in bare feet. He figured the guys she worked with teased her for being a "girl," and all treated her like their kid sister.

She looked at him, her expression like, "*well?*"

"It wasn't a deer."

"I'm not sure I care what it was."

Conroy said, "That guy you took down last night was a low-level drug dealer. We're working to get him to roll over on his supplier. I'm poking the bear, and I doubt I'll manage to pull this off without some form of retribution. So you need to keep your gun close…" He realized she didn't even have it out. "Where's your weapon?"

"In my backpack…I think." She shrugged one shoulder.

"Did you call your people at the ATF?"

"No." She blinked. "Why would I?"

Conroy said, "Get your gun. Keep it close, Mia. These people don't wanna go down, they want to keep making money and don't care who gets hurt in the process."

"Is that why you came here, to warn me about that guy you took down last night?"

"No." He'd received a very interesting call from Tate Hudson. "You wanna talk to Meena, that's fine. But be smart. Don't go walking in there without backup."

He didn't want to know what would happen. He would wait about ten minutes max before going in after her if she did try it. Mostly he figured she'd wind up going in there…and never coming back out. Sucked into a life she didn't want. A life she shouldn't even know about, but probably already did, what with her experience as a federal agent.

"My relationship with my sister has nothing to do with you."

He winced. "I know this town, and I know the players involved in this. You don't want to get caught up with them."

She studied his face for a second, those dark eyes assessing him. "Is it this 'boss' you're trying to take down?"

"I have no evidence to back up my theory but, yes, that's what I think."

"It's *my* sister we're talking about."

"I know. I just want you to be careful."

"Why do you care? I'm a grown woman and a federal agent. Also, last time I checked, I was a free citizen of this country."

"Last Chance County is my jurisdiction. Unless you're working a case." Which he knew she wasn't since Tate confirmed she was home on leave. Recovering. He saw it in the way she moved. "You're hurt. This is not the time to stir something up. You need to be on your A-game for that."

Mia moved to the kitchen area, about ten feet from the entryway. A sandwich sat plated on the counter.

"You should eat. I should go." His stomach rumbled, probably because he'd only had coffee so far today.

"I don't need protection." She lifted her gaze. "But thanks for the warning."

He'd have said "friendly warning." She probably didn't think that was what this had been. Truth was, he cared about her. It had to do with his connection to her family, but also because of his job.

"Like I said, my jurisdiction." He looked at the back door, where he'd seen someone moving around outside. "If you hear or see anything, call it in."

There had been a man outside. Whether that had to do with Iceman's boss, he didn't know. Whether it was or not, it wasn't worth the risk of Mia being caught injured and off guard.

He pulled out a business card from his wallet and moved to

her. "My cell is on the back. Please use it if you think you've seen someone. You have cop instincts, and I'm going to trust those. But I want you to call."

She didn't take the card.

Conroy tossed it on the counter. "You need a reference? Fine. Your father called me…about six years ago now. Someone slashed his truck tires. I helped him through that and caught the kids responsible. They'd been gearing up to more serious crimes. Namely, putting your father in the hospital."

"What. Why?"

Conroy said, "Dispute over stupid stuff—road rage escalated. Your dad pushed it and they didn't back down. Then they turned it back on him. So he called me."

"And you helped him. Caught the kids who were responsible."

That was what he'd said.

"And he let you."

Conroy said, "Yes."

She planted her palms on the counter. "Probably figured you needed to earn his trust back, so he gave you the chance when there was nothing big at stake." She swiped his card off the counter, turned to the cupboard under the sink and tossed it in the trash. "I don't need your brand of help."

"This could be serious. Someone was outside."

"Who?"

"I didn't get a good look at him. Dark jacket, hood up."

"Probably one of those kids you saved my dad from."

"It wasn't." They were all in county jail.

"I don't need your problems coming around here. I have enough going on."

She'd been hurt. That much was clear by the scar down her face, an angry red scratch. Now it was light, he could see it wasn't as bad as he'd thought last night. But it was still bad. "Tell me what happened."

She jerked her head back. "It's none of your business. Just leave, Conroy."

Not "lieutenant?" Now he was Conroy, and she looked like she was about to cry. Which, considering the alternative, might be good. He'd rather that than her screaming at him. He could try and help her, and she might accept it instead of him having to leave.

Conroy needed to accept she was more than just a citizen to him. This was more than just him doing his job.

"If there's something going on with you, I might actually be able to help."

"I don't need anything from you."

"Mia—"

"Don't." She shook her head, eyes squeezed tight. "Even if there was someone outside, it was probably nothing. Just a nosy neighbor. Leave it alone, and leave me alone while you're at it." She opened her eyes and pinned him with a stare. "I'll be talking to Tate about being overbearing. There's nothing more I need from *either* of you."

Conroy pulled out another card and laid it where the first had been.

"I don't need to be kept safe. I can take care of myself."

"Good." She might need it. "Keep your eyes open and your gun close."

Conroy turned and headed for the front door.

"Whatever."

He pulled the door open and hauled it shut behind him. The slam rang out across the lake. A neighbor, unloading a leashed dog from the back of his truck next door, looked over. A puppy, by the look of it. But when it was done growing, the thing would be massive.

Conroy pretty much stomped back to the lane and his Jeep. He didn't have the filter to not let frustration bleed into his walk. Why did she have to be so infuriating? Sure, it was clear she hadn't forgiven him, but he'd been there to do her a favor. He could've worked on making amends. If she'd have let him.

He beeped the locks on his car.

The world flashed orange and Conroy was hit by a wall of heat. The force of the blast threw him through the fence and onto the grass of Rich's back yard.

Conroy hit the ground and everything went black.

# 4

Mia raced out the back door. She dropped to her knees on the ground beside Conroy, who lay face down. The entire car had blown up like a fireball. Flipped end over end, landing on the roof.

She clutched her phone in one hand and rolled him to his back. "Conroy." She patted his cheek. "Conroy, can you hear me?"

"Is he okay?"

She looked up. Her dad's neighbor ran over. "I'm not sure." She checked Conroy's pulse. "He's alive."

"Thank God." He shook his head. "I have to get back to my family. They're freaking out. Want me to call it in?"

She shook her head, already dialing. "I've got it."

He raced away again, leaving her alone. Conroy's chest rose and fell. She couldn't see any visible injuries. Hopefully he wouldn't have a concussion.

"911, what's your emergency?"

"Lieutenant Conroy Barnes's car just exploded outside my father's house." She gave the address.

The dispatcher, an older man by the sound of it said, "Is Con okay?"

"He's unconscious. You should send an ambulance."

"I'll call Dean. He'll be closer."

"Does this 'Dean' person have medical training?"

"Sure does. Former Navy SEAL." The dispatcher said, "He'll get Con sorted out."

"Great. He can give Conroy a ride to the hospital, where he can be seen by a medical professional. Not just someone trained to patch up bullet holes and other field injuries until the person can be transported to *an actual hospital.*"

Conroy groaned.

"Who are you?"

Mia ignored him. "Conroy. You with me?"

"Your father." The dispatcher muttered something, and she thought she heard the clacking of a keyboard. "Mia Tathers... ATF. You're a federal agent?"

"Aren't you supposed to be making a call?" Mia hung up on him. She tossed her phone on the grass. "Conroy, can you hear me?" She patted his cheek.

His lips puffed apart and air escaped.

Mia pulled his eyelids up, one at a time. "Wake up, Lieutenant." She used her command voice, but he still didn't rouse.

She twisted and looked around. His truck was a mess, still smoldering. Hopefully that dispatch guy would send a fire truck as well. She didn't want this turning into a blaze that got out of hand. She could hardly fight it with her father's out-of-date extinguisher.

Movement beyond the car caught her gaze.

"Hey!"

She was up and running before she even realized what she was doing. Around the Jeep, the heat bleeding off flames that licked at the underside, Mia stepped on something. She yelped and hopped a couple of paces, but kept going towards the movement. A man, wearing jeans and a dark blue jacket.

The prowler?

She didn't want to think Conroy had been right, but things were different now. He'd been targeted in an attack.

Asphalt changed to grass. Dirt and rocks, sticks and crusty snow. She nearly went down, wincing as she caught herself. Her muscles wrenched as her body fought to stay upright. She gritted her teeth and stopped.

He was gone.

She didn't have shoes.

As soon as Conroy was taken care of, Mia planned to gear up—with shoes and a coat, and her gun—and search for the prowler.

A truck pulled down the lane, going pretty fast.

She moved back around the Jeep and sprinted back to Conroy. His eyes were open. "Hey." She knelt again, her pants wet now. "Don't try to move, help is here."

A big man raced over, moving faster than she'd have thought he'd be able to, carrying a huge duffel bag. "Conroy?"

"He's awake."

The man knelt, digging in the duffel. "And you are?" He pulled out a pen flashlight and glanced up at her. She was a newcomer, and as far as he was concerned, that was cause for suspicion.

Mia wanted to be difficult. Instead she said, "ATF Special Agent Mia Tathers. This is my father's house." She explained what had happened.

He did those medical things, assessing Conroy. She should probably take some kind of training so she knew what it all was. So she'd know how to do more than the basics—apply pressure, or get a tourniquet on. Maybe that was what she should be doing now that she was "recuperating" from work.

"You're Dean?"

He nodded, holding Conroy's wrist and staring intently at the diver's watch on his own. "Dean Cartwright."

"The dispatcher said you're a SEAL."

"Was." He studied Conroy's face. "Wake up, Bud. The day's

a wastin'." He patted Conroy's cheek a lot more vigorously than she had.

She said, "Easy."

Another car pulled up. A marked police car, and though the driver was a woman, she wasn't the same one from last night. Mia was having trouble keeping all these people straight.

This woman wore jeans and a fitted, red-checkered shirt. Badge on her belt, dark hair pulled back into a ponytail. "Dean."

"Van."

Conroy moaned. He blinked and tried to sit up.

Dean planted a huge hand on his chest and didn't let him move. "You landed hard. Knocked the wind out of you. And your car is toast."

The red shirted woman leaned over. "You okay, boss?"

"Wilcox?" Conroy looked around. Everywhere but at Mia.

"Yeah, boss."

"There was a prowler. We need to find—"

Dean shoved him back down. "*We* aren't doing anything. The ATF can take the lead on this one, considering it's an explosion and all."

Someone who actually understood federal jurisdiction? That was new in Mia's experience. "I only caught a glimpse of him, but I'll get on the search." She rocked back and stood.

Then nearly fell over.

"You okay, ATF?"

"Yep." She forced her legs to straighten. That run had been a seriously bad idea.

"Mia Tathers?"

She looked at the other woman. "Yeah."

"Savannah Wilcox." She held out a hand, an assessing gaze on her face. "Detective."

Mia shook her hand. The woman's grip strength was killer, but she held back a flinch even though she was sure the woman just crushed a couple of bones in her hand. "Special Agent Tathers. Mia is fine."

"Savannah." Not "Van" as this Dean guy had called her.

"I should put shoes on."

"Don't go *anywhere*."

She ignored Conroy's comment and headed for the house.

There was a shuffle. Conroy said, "No, get off." Pause. "Mia!"

She turned around, already at the back door. He was sitting up now. "I need to change, Lieutenant. And you need to see a doctor."

"No, I don't." He got up. Steadier on his feet than she was, or so evidence indicated. "I just got the wind knocked out of me."

Dean stood, a clear six inches taller than Conroy. He started feeling around the back of Conroy's head. "Hold still."

Detective Wilcox smirked. "The women will figure out who did this, and we'll catch them. You go get your boo-boo looked at."

Conroy glared at her. "I will write you up for insubordination."

"Suspend me. I'll go on vacation."

Conroy was about to say something but closed his mouth.

"Good call." She traipsed across the grass toward Mia and caught up to her just as Mia stepped inside. "He only thinks he can fire me." She smirked. "His other detective quit a month ago. I've got sixteen open cases on my desk, and he's out running down drug dealers?" She shook her head. "The Lieutenant should be in the office, finding me a partner. Or at least taking some of my cases."

"But...he isn't?" Because he was working undercover with that officer. And following up at her father's house. "Does he shirk protocol like that often?"

"Oh no. You're not one of those by-the-books, my-way-or-the-highway feds. Are you?" She looked at Mia like that might be the worst possible thing that could happen. "And here I thought we could be friends."

Mia shook her head. "I'm not the one you need to be worried about."

"Mmm. Heard about you." That assessing gaze was back. "Rich talks about you...how he's so proud of you."

He does? This was the first Mia had heard of it, but she was not super surprised her dad had failed to communicate his feelings so that she could hear.

"But that's not what I'm talking about." Savannah waved a hand.

"I really should get changed." She heard a fire truck pull up outside, took a look, and saw another police car as well. Firefighters spilled out. A uniformed officer spoke with Conroy. "We should get on with the search."

Savannah nodded "I'll wait right here."

Mia worked on focusing, so she could change into different clothes as quickly as possible. She pulled on her favorite black cargo pants and a blue polo shirt over a long-sleeved running shirt that she often wore during training. About the most "federal" clothes she could put on considering she hadn't brought a suit. Holstered gun on her belt along with her badge. Boots. She put her hair up in a ponytail and pocketed her cell phone.

The hairstyle made it all the more obvious that an angry scratch ran down the side of her face. The collar of her shirt disguised the fact it went farther down than was obvious to anyone.

"And the transformation is complete."

She shot Savannah a look and snagged her jacket.

"I feel the same way. Clothes for home, clothes for work. Cause when I'm off, I'm *off* this job. This life? It does *not* exist." She shook her head. "Know what I mean?"

Mia said, "Let's just get moving." The longer they waited, the farther away this guy was going to get. "Someone tried to kill Conroy."

"I know. It burns, right? Seriously, he's like the *nicest* guy I've ever met *in my life*."

Did she really talk like that all the time? Mia had never met anyone this passionate in her entire life. It was weird. Savannah said, "Why would anyone even want to kill him?"

Mia said, "Could it have something to do with the guy he brought in last night, the drug dealer?"

Savannah whirled around, hauled the door open, and stormed outside. "You and Ridgeman brought in a drug dealer last night?"

Dean got in her face.

Savannah said, "Move it, Spud."

He didn't. "Calm down." Dean folded his arms. "He's got a headache. Doesn't need you shouting at him."

Savannah said, "I'll do more than shout unless someone explains this to me."

Conroy said, "I'm your boss. I've gotta explain myself?"

Savannah blustered. "I—"

"Cool it. You knew we went out." Conroy's words were measured, as though he was talking through the pain. "I was gonna brief you this afternoon, but I didn't get into the office yet."

Mia figured the coast was clear. "I'm going to get started looking for this guy. Anything specific?"

"Male, white. Blue jacket."

She waited. "That's it."

"My car exploded in my face."

"You should go see a doctor." She looked around. "Where's the ambulance?" There didn't appear to be one, and the spray from the firefighter hose was freezing.

"I don't need one."

"I'll call if I find him." She started walking.

"I like this girl." That was Dean. Or, "Spud" as Savannah had called him. She wondered what that was about, but not enough to backtrack and ask.

These people weren't her people. They would never become her friends. She was better off being professional, and maintaining that until it was time to leave home and go back to work.

This wasn't where she wanted to be. Even if it was home, and where she lived didn't mean much to her except a place to crash, she didn't belong here. She could barely even stand being in Conroy Barnes's presence.

And nothing would change that.

"Hold up."

She didn't, regardless of what Conroy wanted from her.

"Mia. Wait up."

She sighed and slowed so he could catch up to her. Then she spun and said, "Should you be walking around?"

"I just got the wind knocked out of me, that's all."

"Yes, that's why you were unconscious for minutes. Because you *got the wind knocked out of you.*" Great. Now she was starting to talk like Savannah. "Can we just look for this guy?"

It was probably a serious long shot, but she had to do something. Her yard was crawling with first responders, all of whom clearly thought she was more of a spectacle than the smoldering wreckage of a Jeep.

"Fine. But you shouldn't go alone." He clutched her elbow, his blue eyes intent as they darkened to denim. "Someone in town is out for blood, and he's targeting you."

## 5

"I don't see why I had to come here."

Conroy pressed his lips together and waited for her to enter the police station. Her face was paler than it had been earlier. They'd walked for a while, sweeping the area around her dad's house with the help of a few locals—friends he'd called in—and a couple of his officers.

"Except I can have that conversation with the chief now."

The receptionist looked up. Dark skin and a round figure. White blouse, gold buttons. She always wore pants and black flats. Her hair was dark brown with a purple tint, and she had on even more makeup than Mia's younger sister had worn.

"Kaylee Caldwell," he said, "meet ATF Special Agent Mia Tathers."

Her perfectly-manicured eyebrows rose and her red lips moved succinctly when she said, "Rich's daughter?"

"The one and only." He leaned on the front counter. "And if you could find us some Ibuprofen or something, I'm guessing she'd be as grateful as I'd be."

"Heard you got blown up." She eyed him, only one brow raised now.

"I'm okay. But it's sweet that you care."

Kaylee smirked. "I suppose you want me to find you another vehicle."

"You're a peach."

She buzzed them through the door into the main area of the police station, the bull pen. The early shift had twenty minutes left, and the afternoon shift was here already. He'd always loved the buzz of this place. Now it was his. He claimed it despite the fact he wasn't chief. Yet.

Savannah lifted her chin, phone tucked between her ear and shoulder. The desk opposite hers was unoccupied, so he had Mia sit there. Conroy asked his detective, "Did I get my call back yet?"

"He left a number." She handed him a piece of paper, then shifted the phone. "Yes, this is Detective Wilcox." She kept talking. Conroy tuned it out because Kaylee wandered over with a bottle of pain pills and two waters.

She handed him one.

"Thanks."

"Sure thing, boss." She turned her round figure to Mia. "You okay, hon?"

"Yes, ma'am." She twisted the cap off the water and downed four Ibuprofen. Conroy took three.

His head still hurt from being hurled across her yard, but it wasn't too bad. He was tempted to thank God for it not being a concussion. Problem was, that would only lead him to asking why it had to happen in the first place.

Mia shot him a look as soon as Kaylee's back was turned. Then she glanced around. "Nice house."

She liked his police department? He pressed his lips together to hold back the smile. "We try."

"Is the chief in?"

Conroy worked his mouth. She was going to find out sooner or later, and if she kept pushing, it would be sooner. He figured there wasn't much point dragging it out.

He walked to the window of the chief's office and looked in.

Officer Ridgeman looked up from the novel she'd been reading. She gave him a tiny wave of her fingers. His best undercover officer must be having a good day, if she was smiling. Or, more likely, her grandfather was.

Beside her, in the hospital bed they'd brought in, the chief lay still.

He opened the door. "How is he today?"

She shrugged one shoulder. The twenty-four year old former NYPD officer and current Last Chance County officer, when she wasn't here taking care of her grandfather because the nurse was off, looked older. Not worn or world weary. Just older than she was. Life had dealt those cards to her. She said she didn't mind, but he still felt the need to make sure she was all right from time to time.

"Hey." Mia nudged his side so he'd get out of the way, allowing her to step inside the room. "You're the officer from last night, right?"

"Jess." She closed the book in her lap.

He said, "Officer Ridgeman is Chief Ridgeman's grand-daughter."

"It's uh...good to meet you." Mia shifted her stance and stuck her hands in her pockets.

"Did he eat?"

The old man was slowly deteriorating, and the nurse had told Conroy last week that she didn't think it would be long.

He wanted to talk to Jess about moving the old man to the hospital, or home hospice care. But if he did that, wouldn't everyone think it had nothing to do with honoring the old man's wishes? Conroy wanted him to be in a better situation. Where he had a full medical staff, instead of around the clock care by people who cared but weren't trained. He'd have to assume the chief's job then, in the interim. People would figure him ousting the chief from his office was about that, not about doing what was right for the old man.

Jess shook her head at his question. "I heard you guys had an eventful morning. Did your car really blow up?"

He nodded.

She chuckled. "I'd have paid money to see that."

"Nice." He grinned. "I'm fine, thank you."

"I know." She waved off his comment. "I saw Dean at the diner eating lunch."

Conroy's stomach rumbled.

"There's half a sandwich in the fridge if you want it."

He led Mia out and shut the door so the chief could have quiet.

"Cancer?"

He glanced at her. Those dark eyes stormy. "Pancreatic. It spread quickly."

"How old is he?"

"Seventy-four."

Her eyebrows rose. "My dad is sixty-eight already."

He nodded. "My parents are mid-sixties." He saw the question in her eyes and said, "They live in Flagstaff most of the year, except for a summer visit to see the grandkids."

"Cassie?"

He nodded. "My nephew Brendan is six, my niece Leora is four." He knew from her father that she'd never been married and didn't have kids. Her dad also said she'd never had a serious relationship with a man. Just a couple of dates here and there. As though he'd even asked that about Mia.

"Have you…ever been married?"

He looked at her in surprise.

"Come on." She shot him a wry smile. "Can't a girl be curious?"

"Not much to be curious about. I've lived here all my life, went away to college, and came straight back. Joined the police department."

"That doesn't exactly answer the question."

He felt his cheeks flush and reached up to squeeze the back of his neck. "No. Never married."

She shrugged. "Me either."

"Lieutenant, there's a call for you!" Kaylee hollered across the bull pen. "Line two."

"I should take this in my office." Especially if it was what he thought it was. The returned call he was waiting for.

"I can make my own way home."

"Stay." Why he said that he wasn't sure. "Please? Why don't you sit in when I interview the guy from last night?"

She frowned.

"I want to see if he knows you. Then we have a shot at figuring out who blew up my car."

She didn't look super impressed with that idea but headed for the desk across from Wilcox.

"I'll be back in a second." He shut the door to his office but didn't glance back through the glass. Conroy didn't want to know if she and Wilcox were in quiet conversation, probably about him. "Barnes."

"Lieutenant. It's *Sheriff* Alvarez."

"Sal." Conroy slumped into his chair and let out a groan. His head was still pounding. The pain meds had barely taken the edge off.

"Does this have anything to do with how rough you sound?"

"Mia Tathers. ATF." Conroy didn't need Sal asking about what was happening. He didn't live close, but he would be all about helping if it came to it. They were old friends, having met years ago when Sal had been a US Marshal on his way through town, transporting a fugitive to Denver. They'd hit it off and stayed in touch ever since.

Sometimes Conroy just needed someone with no personal stake in his town to run things by and ask for advice.

"Yeah, I talked to my wife about her."

Sal's wife was former ATF. "And?"

"She's by the book. Not in an uptight way, more like just

professional. Detached. Doesn't take things personally, unless it's a kid. Otherwise she keeps to herself."

Conroy stared at her through the window. "Okay."

Deep pain, like losing her sister at a young age, could explain that. But it didn't tell him a whole lot.

"As far as why she's there, Allyson heard it was a rough takedown. The team served a warrant. House was full of people. Suspect made a run for it in the confusion and Tathers raced after him. She cornered him and there was a fight. Sounds like it was nasty. In the end she had to use lethal force. Allyson dug a little and found out she'll likely be cleared. It was justified. But the guy put her in the hospital, and she's on leave until the doctor clears her to be back."

"Tell her I said thanks. I appreciate her digging."

"Sure." Sal's voice had a sardonic tone. "Happy to pass on federal gossip to an old friend."

"Liar."

Sal chuckled. "Not much else happening around here."

They chatted for a little longer, and then Conroy excused himself. He hung up, then called the officer in holding. "Get me Petrov, stick him in number two."

"Copy that."

He grabbed the file on his desk, and along with Mia, headed for the interview room. Petrov was already at the table.

The officer who brought him there said, "Lieutenant," with a nod and then left.

Conroy watched Petrov. In the daylight, Simon Petrov seemed kind of...regular. Just another guy selling drugs on the streets. Petrov's gaze strayed to Mia, but there was no recognition there. He spotted her badge, which was curious to him. That was it.

Mia leaned against the wall. She didn't look as tired or in pain as she had earlier, but he didn't know if that was due to the meds and the protein bar he'd found, or if she was faking it for Petrov.

He stared at the guy. "Got you dead to rights on possession with intent." Conroy pulled out the chair across from Petrov and sat down. "What happens next is up to you."

"I'll be sure and discuss that with my lawyer when he comes back." Petrov smirked. "Which is why I have nothing to say to you right now."

"Did I ask a question?" Conroy glanced at his smartwatch. "Due in fifteen, right?"

Petrov shrugged. "If you say so."

Conroy shoved the chair back and turned to Mia. "You okay with waiting? I wouldn't want to take up too much of the ATF's time."

He was banking on the fact Petrov hadn't gotten a good look at her the night before when she'd hit him with her shopping cart.

"I guess you'd better make it worth the wait then."

Tough as nails. Professional. Except for the pink, sparkly toenail polish he'd seen this morning—which he figured no one she worked with had ever gotten a look at.

He said, "That's what I'm counting on. After all, Petrov here will have a hard time in prison when his boss finds out that he spoke at length with us. Imagination is more powerful than the facts sometimes, so when that boss hears about how Petrov spent *hours* in here, then who knows what he's going to think?"

He heard Petrov shift in his chair and turned like he was surprised the guy was still in here with them. Like maybe he'd forgotten, or at least said too much. Problem was, he needed Petrov to name his boss so that he could be sure he had his sights on the right guy.

"No. No way." Petrov shook his head. "Ed won't believe you. He knows I'd never talk."

"Ed?" Conroy lifted his brows. "Ed Summers?"

Petrov leaned forward. "I'm not sayin' nothin' and you can't press me into flipping on him. No one does that to Summers. Not if they want to live to see tomorrow."

Sensational, but accurate. Conroy had seen the aftermath of Summers' work—the remains of the last person who had crossed him. He just hadn't been able to prove Ed Summers was behind it.

"What did you say?" Mia pushed off the wall and closed in on him. "Ed Summers? That's who's behind this?"

Petrov glanced at her. He was about to speak when Mia reached across the corner of the table and gripped a fistful of Petrov's collar. She hauled him out of his chair and slammed him against the wall. "Ed Summers is your boss?"

"Special Agent Tathers." He didn't know what to say to calm her down. "Stand down."

She got in Petrov's face. "Summers. That's what you said?"

"Mia—"

The door to the interview room flew open and Petrov's lawyer stood there. "What on earth is going on here?"

# 6

Mia shoved off the drug dealer guy. "Guess your lawyer is here."

"Yeah. Guess so."

The lawyer said, "And I'll be filing some paperwork with the judge by end of day. You can be sure of that."

She almost didn't want to go because he would see her badge, but she was no longer needed here. Mia turned.

"A fed?" The lawyer's face turned smug. "I'll be needing your badge number."

She lifted her chin. "I'll leave it with Kaylee."

Mia strode out of the interview room and headed for the closest exit door. That had to have been why Conroy asked her into the interview room. To prove to her how much of a "bad guy" this bad guy drug boss was.

Ed Summers. She'd hoped to never hear that name again for the rest of her life.

"Mia."

He caught up to her just as she opened the front door, which he grabbed hold of right out of her hand. She stepped through without saying, "thanks."

Mia headed for her car. Her shoulder hurt despite the meds.

The whole side of her face stung. That suspect had probably thought she was unhinged, and no doubt his lawyer's assessment of what had happened would reiterate that exact sentiment for her boss's reading pleasure.

She gritted her teeth. If she didn't get fired soon, she'd be surprised.

"At least meet me later. Maybe for dinner? We should talk about this."

She whirled on him. Why meet later when they could talk now? There was no reason to drag this out.

"All I did was ask a private investigator to find my sister. That has nothing to do with whoever is targeting you." Despite the fact he'd seen someone outside her dad's house, or that his car exploded. Obviously they'd been there because of Conroy. "Was it a bomb?"

"That's what my people think."

Whoever his "people" were, she hoped they knew what they were talking about. The ATF investigated explosions—both explosive devices and arson. She'd never had the patience for the science of it, or the repeated experiments to try and reach a workable theory on what had been used and how it worked.

She said, "Who did you make mad enough they would want you dead?"

The skin over his nose shifted, kind of like a small shrug. "I don't think it has anything to do with Petrov, it's too early for retaliation."

She figured he was right. If Summers wanted to be sure he hadn't talked, then he'd be targeting Petrov and not a police lieutenant. "What about your other cases?"

"I have no idea."

"Why is the police chief here and not at home?"

"Twenty four hour on-call care. There's a full time nurse, and Officer Ridgeman slips in and out when she's on shift. And when she's not."

There was more to it than that, but he seemed to be very

diplomatic about the whole thing. Unconventional. Was that how he ran things? Or did no one have the heart to tell Ridgeman to take her grandfather home?

"Meanwhile," she said, "you're running the whole department and working cases, and no one knows you're juggling all those balls in the air?"

He did that nose-shrug thing again. "The chief's wishes were clearly spelled out. Doesn't matter if I like it or not, or if I think it's the right thing."

"Ed Summers is really a local drug kingpin?"

He nodded.

"You're trying to bring him down, aren't you?"

He didn't answer.

This whole thing was just strange. Not just that Ed had chosen that path, given Conroy was on the opposite side. They'd been friends. Apparently there was a whole lot of water under that bridge, as it seemed Conroy wasn't too pleased with what his former friend was currently up to.

Conroy hadn't been surprised to hear Summers's name. She figured he'd been after Petrov to roll over on his boss, and provide testimony—if not actual physical evidence—that could be used to convict him. He wanted to take the guy down, and he seemed determined to do it. Something that, if he could at all help it, would happen without her interference. No matter that she was determined to find her sister and talk some sense into her.

He took her keys and beeped the locks.

"I know what you're doing." She folded her arms. "Trying to get me to back off finding my sister. You know I'm a fed and you aren't even going to utilize my skills. All you're going to do is tell me not to get involved because he's *dangerous*."

"Please get in the car." His expression gave away nothing.

"Because I need you to drive for me? You'll be stranded at my dad's house with no way back here."

"I want to make sure you get home, and I can bet you won't

meet me later to talk." He shrugged and opened the passenger door, holding it for her.

He wanted to give her a ride home? She wanted a reason why he looked basically fine, while she felt like she'd been hit by a semi. Truth was, Mia was too wrung out to put up a fight. Who cared if he had to call a rideshare to get back here? She climbed in the front seat, and he shut the door.

It occurred to her too late that she should have sat in the back seat. That would have been much better.

He climbed in and must have seen it on her face. "What's funny?"

Great, he'd caught her smirking. "Nothing." She buckled her seatbelt and pushed out a long sigh. She'd known him years ago when he'd dated her sister Mara in High School. Conroy the high school boy. Her sister's true love. He'd actually calmed Mara's otherwise wild nature. This guy driving her car? She knew nothing about him. What you saw was *not* what you got.

And she had no interest in having a puzzle to solve.

Mia leaned her head back and closed her eyes. *Wow.* That was so much better. She actually felt her body start to relax. Two weeks she'd been home, and she hadn't felt like this even once.

She wasn't going to acknowledge that it just might be because she was under his care. Making sure she got home safe and sound.

Or how long it had been since anyone cared enough to do that.

She didn't need it. She was strong. Independent.

Then it all came rushing back. Her sister Meena, shacked up with a local bad guy. She'd put money on that being Ed Summers, which was probably the real reason Conroy didn't want her going over there.

He was a big time drug dealer now, and Meena was queen bee up at his house. Did she even know who Ed Summers really was? How could she not? Ed Summers had been driving the car when it flipped over, killing her sister. Conroy had been in the backseat, and Mia had never understood why.

Now Ed was this big-time, bad guy. So bad that Mia shouldn't go in without backup. Because she'd have figured out quickly who he was. And she'd have lost it, just like she had with that drug dealer.

"Question." She opened her eyes and turned to Conroy, already on the road to the lake. "Were you just trying to prove your point about this drug dealer guy...that his boss was such a bad guy...all so I didn't go see Meena without knowing everything up front? Or did you bring me into the interview room so I *would* go ballistic on him when he mentioned Summers's name?"

Either way, she figured she wasn't going to like his answer.

"I brought you in there because I wanted to see if he knew who you were." Conroy gripped the wheel. He turned a corner, even using his indicator. Some cops didn't care about rules because they could get away with whatever they wanted. She didn't operate that way, and it was becoming clear Conroy didn't either.

Too bad this man was as wicked in her mind as Ed Summers—both men had equal responsibility for what happened to Mara. Mia had no intention of softening toward Conroy. After all, she would leave in a couple more weeks, and she didn't plan on coming back. Ever. Her dad was *way* overdue to visit her. He would just have to deal with flying.

Mia wanted out of Last Chance County.

Just thinking about Ed Summers rolled through her, bringing up memories of the worst things she'd seen. "Meena has to know who he is and what he did. There's no way she doesn't know."

She didn't want to think her sister was a chump. Being played while everyone knew it. She hoped Meena at least had her eyes open.

Ed had been convicted of drunk driving and vehicular

manslaughter. He'd been sent to juvenile detention, and Mia knew the records were sealed. She'd looked it up.

Conroy glanced at her. Seemed like he wanted to... She actually didn't know what he wanted to do. Squeeze her hand, maybe. "I don't know if she does or not. Summers and I aren't exactly friends right now."

"You used to be close with Summers."

He said, "You know what happened."

She pressed her lips together. "Now look at you. Opposite sides of the law."

"It's taking too long to bring him down. I can't pin charges on him just because of what he did. Ed served his time for Mara's death. This has to be by the book, not just because I hate the guy."

"Except that he destroys lives. Apparently, he's made a career of it." She looked out the window. "If he knows you're looking more closely at him now, then he could have set that charge in your car while you were at my dad's house to try and force you to back off."

"It won't work."

"And if he pushes it?"

"I don't care. I'll do what is necessary to bring him down." He gripped the wheel and turned down Lakeside Lane. "No matter the cost."

He pulled up at the curb, right where he'd parked before.

It seemed kind of hypocritical of him to go after Ed Summers so hard, considering his own culpability in her sister's death. She should probably be looking at both of them. And would have, if she'd been at full strength.

Maybe this was all a ruse, a way to play off the fact he worked with—or for—Summers, and Conroy was nothing but a dirty cop. Perhaps by bringing her into it, he could convince his officers that he wasn't corrupt.

Could be he even planned on pinning cooperation with Summers on her. After all, with her sister Meena being a part of

Summers's life, there wasn't a big leap from Mia to the drug trade.

Mia was in a vulnerable position just by being here. Especially considering she wasn't on her game.

Was Conroy playing her?

"That's why I need your help."

She twisted in her seat, which took the pressure off the back of her shoulder and allowed her to look straight at him instead of twisting her neck. "You're not entitled to receive anything from me."

He winced. "I know that doesn't sound good. But I promise you, my intentions are good."

"Would that all life was measured on good intentions. But it isn't." She leaned in on that word. "It's about results. So if you want to bring Ed Summers in, then find the evidence to get a judge to issue you a warrant for his arrest. I'm not your girl."

She grabbed the door handle and was halfway out when he said, "Mia."

She climbed out.

"Mia!"

She bent to the open door and looked at him. "What?"

"It's been good to see you."

Really?

She said, "Because I remind you of Mara?"

Maybe this was nothing but nostalgia, and he only saw her sister when he looked at her.

"A little, I guess. But that's not all of it."

She didn't even know what to say to him or what to make of his soft expression. Mia just slammed the door to her car. Another sigh. How many times would she do that before she got home? This trip to recover was turning out to be more frustrating than her usual work. She was going to call the management company for her apartment building and find out when they were done fumigating.

Conroy didn't pull the car away. Instead, she heard the engine shut off and his door open. Creak. It slammed shut.

"There's more to say."

"Is there?" She strode to the corner of the house. The neighboring family was out, and the kids looked worried. One called out the dog's name.

"Plus you need your car keys."

She ignored him. "What's going on?"

The husband and father, same guy who'd run over to check on Conroy when he was hurt, called back, "The dog got out earlier. Have you seen her?"

Mia shook her head. "Sorry."

Conroy caught up to her while she was distracted. "I also want to make sure you're safe inside. While I give you your keys."

She glanced back at him as the tiny path curved around the corner. He wasn't waiting inside for his ride. No way.

"Because it occurred to me that the prowler was here, and my car blew up here. So while you may be right about this not having anything to do with Ed Summers, or Petrov, it might have something to do with you."

She was about to argue with him when a brown body, low and moving fast, raced at her across the yard. She shoved Conroy away and braced like she did during dog training with the team's canine. Except she was usually decked out in protective gear during those times.

The father yelled, "*Daisy!*"

The dog snarled, building even more speed as it raced to her.

Jumped.

Teeth sank into the skin of her forearm. One of the kids screamed.

Then again, maybe that was her.

## 7

Mia's scream echoed in his ears. Even two hours later, it was like his ears got stuck and he couldn't stop hearing the sound of it.

Conroy threw the lever into park outside the vet's office. He leaned his pounding head back against the driver's seat of Mia's car. If it didn't quit that incessant thump, he was going to have to talk to his doctor. Yes, he'd been unconscious for a few minutes this morning, but no one needed to know he was still suffering. Unless, of course, it didn't quit and then he'd have to let the doc know.

Right now, the guy was stitching up Mia. And probably giving her a tetanus shot. After everything she'd been through—most could be assumed from the scar on her face and the rest Alvarez had briefed him on—he figured she didn't need this as well.

Whatever was going on, he'd figure it out. That was what Conroy did.

*Blessed are the peacemakers.*

Conroy had been given that verse years ago when he was sworn in as a police officer. It was what he tried to do all day, every day. His role in this town was to keep the peace. Keep the residents safe by pouring his life into the job.

A car explosion. Now a dog attack.

This kind of targeted, personal vendetta didn't sit well with him. Regardless if it was directed at him, or at Mia, didn't matter. He wasn't going to rest until he got to the bottom of what was going on.

Conroy finished the drive-thru coffee he'd bought on the way, and then went inside the vet's office. Mia had insisted they take the dog here—once they'd subdued it. He'd bargained with her since she was bleeding and clearly in considerable pain. The family's dog had been taken there by the father, and Conroy had driven her to the hospital.

He hauled the front door open and the father immediately stood up.

"How is she?"

Conroy said, "Getting stitched up."

He could tell the guy she was a fed. Or that she was strong and could handle this. Truth was, Conroy didn't have much interest in making the guy feel better about the situation.

He pulled out his notepad. "Full name?"

"Nathan Masterson. Nate."

"How long have you had the dog?"

"Maybe four months."

"Has she ever done anything like this before?" He had an idea about what had happened, but needed to get the vet's opinion before he laid down judgment.

"No. She's usually so sweet." Nate ran a hand down his face. "Becca is freaking out. The kids are distraught. They're all headed over here now."

Great.

Nate continued, "Doctor Filks said he thought she might have been drugged."

Conroy nodded. "I was wondering about that."

"The kids are *freaked.*"

Conroy was about to say something that would have just been him placating the guy. Instead, Filks walked out of his back office and into the waiting area. "Con."

Conroy lifted his chin. "Brett."

They shook hands. Brett Filks, longtime Last Chance County vet, shook hands with Nate.

Masterson claimed his wife and his kids were *freaked*. It seemed to Conroy that he might be the one who was freaked, or at least as much as the rest of his family. He got that. Conroy was a dog person, though he hadn't had one for years—not since the yellow lab they'd had passed away when he was a kid. That had to have been tenth grade.

Brett glanced aside at Conroy. "You okay?"

"You can check me for brain injuries later, yeah?"

Brett shifted half a step closer, staring Conroy in the eyes. "Did you hit your head wrestling the dog down?"

Nate said, "Should I call an ambulance?"

Conroy shook his head, then winced. *Ouch.* "It's just a headache."

Brett slipped a tiny flashlight from his shirt pocket and shone it in Conroy's eyes. "More like a migraine would be my guess."

Conroy shoved at Brett's wrist. "I'm fine. Mr. Masterson probably wants to know about his dog." Before his family got there.

Nate nodded. Conroy was glad to know the guy was aware that a father's job was to shield his kids from any unnecessary blows. Rich let his girls swing out there, leaving them to carry the weight of life on their own. He'd left them to find their own path, creating two cynical and fiercely independent women. And yet in most ways they were polar opposites.

Conroy's dad had been the same as Nate. Determined to at least soften the landing when it became necessary for Conroy to hit the ground. But he did allow Conroy to hit the ground, and afterward he was there with a helping hand. That was what fathers were supposed to do—before they got an RV and went to live their best life in Arizona.

Brett said, "She was drugged. Daisy is out now, I gave her something to calm her down since she was pretty upset. I ran a panel of tests. When I get answers as to what she was given, I'll be able to combat that with medicine. Get whatever substance it is out of her system."

"And then?"

"We see how she is after the medicine. When she wakes up."

Nate glanced between them, still every inch the worried father. "You aren't...ordering me to have her put down?"

"Brett?" Conroy wanted his medical opinion before he went ahead and recommended a decision. Yes, he was the final authority on safety in this town, but Nate needed to make the call on the dog.

The vet scratched at the late-day stubble on his chin. Conroy had known him since it was brown, back far enough Brett had been the JV quarterback while Conroy was his counterpart on the varsity team. These days it was threaded with gray, like his hair, though he was only pushing thirties like Conroy—who fought that battle in the receding temples, rather than the color of his hair.

Brett also tended to gravitate more toward jeans and denim shirts. Conroy wore a suit six days a week and sweats on the seventh. The jeans in his closet had dust on them.

"It all depends on how she is when she wakes up. If the drug is gone, and it seems like she doesn't even remember what happened, then we can look at seeing how she does with the kids."

"Seriously?" Nate's eyebrows rose. "She could come home?"

"Don't get your hopes up. It'll be a long road." Brett said, "I'll want to talk to the woman Daisy bit. If she agrees, then Daisy will need to be herself around that woman before she'll be allowed to see the kids. But if it is what I think it was, then once it's out of her system, she should be back to normal. Though..."

"What?" Nate asked.

"It's clear she was kicked. Several times. I'm going to do an X-ray, but I'm thinking she has at least a couple of broken ribs. She has some abrasions as well. I'll also have to thoroughly clean her mouth so there's no taste of blood when she wakes up."

"She could bite someone again, though. Right?"

Brett nodded in response to Conroy's question. "I'd argue that any dog can do that at any time. Given the right circumstances."

Conroy turned to Brett. "Keep me apprised of how it goes. Every step of the process." He glanced at Nate. "Anything happens I don't like, this entire process goes back to the drawing board. My advice? Don't get your kids' hopes up. I'd hate for them to get crushed if, or when, it becomes clear Daisy could be a danger."

Nate pressed his lips together.

"I have to get back to work." Conroy said his goodbyes and got out of there.

The wife was unloading kids from her van. Becca Masterson spotted Conroy. He was about to lift his chin when she shot him a dirty look and pulled one kid onto her hip. She tugged the other one alongside her to the front door of the vet office with her chin in the air.

Conroy climbed into his car and drove to the town's small hospital. It was only two floors and not bigger than most elementary schools.

He'd just tapped the brakes to head for a parking spot when the doors slid open and Mia walked out.

He changed directions and flashed headlights.

She shielded her eyes from the glare of her own headlights. Conroy eased up to her, stopping so the passenger door was right in front of where she stood.

He leaned over and pulled the handle. She caught the door and tugged it open. "Hop in. I'll take you home."

She waited long enough he wondered if she was trying to formulate a good response.

"Just get in, Mia."

She slid onto the seat. "This is my car."

He pulled out, turning and heading for the exit. His stomach rumbled. "Hungry?"

"I'm actually not." She laid a hand on her stomach and rubbed side to side. "They gave me a sandwich and some juice, since I lost blood." Her left arm had a bandage wrapped around it.

"You okay?"

She laid her head back and shut her eyes. "I just want to fall asleep. They gave me some good stuff."

Conroy figured that was his cue to quit talking. He drove to her father's house, wondering if he should suggest she sleep somewhere else tonight. The owners of the town's little motel were always happy to accommodate whoever he brought to them at any time, day or night. Then again, they called it a "ministry" and not work. So he figured being grumpy because you were inconvenienced didn't fit.

He needed to get back to the office to check in and finish up his paperwork. Figure out what was happening with Petrov's charges. See how the chief's day had gone.

He roused Mia when they pulled into the driveway of her father's house and held his hand out for the door key. She placed it into his palm and looked over at the spot where she'd been bitten and shivered. Conroy took her right hand and they circled the house. It was dark. They'd both had a long day. She was hurt, and he still had a raging headache. He figured all that accumulated to the reason she didn't pull away from his hold on her hand.

Conroy unlocked the door and stepped inside. "Wait right here for a second, yeah?"

"I know what you're doing." She yawned. "I'm just too tired to object."

"Good." He walked through the house and even checked the shower. Every spot someone who might want to harm her could be hiding.

He found her in the kitchen. Not exactly waiting by the entryway. "You're good."

She was replacing the lid on a peanut butter jar. "Sandwich." She slid the plate across the counter toward him.

She hadn't wrapped it to go, so he ate standing up while she filled the electric kettle enough for a cup.

"Thanks."

She shrugged one shoulder, flicked up the button on the kettle and turned around. "You helped me out today. And I feel kind of bad you almost got blown up."

He swallowed another bite. "Not your fault."

"I know. Still…" She didn't say more.

Her face was soft. She was wrung out, in pain. Medication had her talking softly. Being nice.

Conroy said, "Thanks again," and took a step closer, around the counter. "Though not the way I would've chosen to spend the day with you." It had been a long one, and painful.

"We haven't seen each other for years."

"Doesn't mean I haven't thought about you."

*Talked to your dad about you. Asked around after you.*

She lifted her chin slightly. "The only thought I've had concerning you, is why you didn't stop Ed Summers from killing my sister."

He opened his mouth to speak, but she cut him off.

"This police lieutenant thing you've got going on seems to be working. Fooling everyone in town into believing you're this knight in a suit. The man for the job. Too bad I know the truth about you."

Conroy turned around and walked out.

# 8

His plate clattered in the sink. Mia stared at it. She almost wished it had broken, then she'd have something to think about aside from the blow she'd just dealt him. And the fact she actually felt *bad* about it.

What was that about?

She trailed through the house, shutting off lights as she went. It was after midnight. He'd seen her in. Checked the house to make sure no one was hiding anywhere inside. Not only was he a good police lieutenant, he was also a *good police lieutenant*. Ugh. Of course she couldn't find fault in him.

He might seem like a nice enough guy on the surface, or at least the kind of cop who cared about the people he'd sworn to protect. But it could not be denied what he had cost her. The wrong he had done.

Mia dropped onto the twin bed she'd slept in as a kid and groaned as she stretched out. At least as much as she could stretch. It hadn't been big enough even back then. Her dad had told her to use his bed since he would be gone, but that was just weird.

Her arm stung. And ached. The stitches tugged at the skin,

which still felt odd. Not painful at the time, but she'd felt each tug of her skin as the doctor pulled the thread through.

She shivered.

Would she ever be okay around dogs again? Or would she flinch every time one approached? Intellectually she knew they weren't all vicious, and they certainly weren't all drugged. She would meet nice dogs. But she knew she'd hesitate as they approached. At least at first. Maybe forever. She would remember the way Daisy's teeth had sunk into the flesh of her forearm.

That hadn't even been the worst of it.

They'd been forced to wrestle Daisy to the ground even while she still had that bone-cracking hold on Mia's arm. Working side by side with Conroy.

Ed Summers might have been driving the car that crashed, killing her sister. But she blamed Conroy. He'd been her boyfriend at the time, not Ed. Conroy had been responsible for her safety that night. And in the end, Mara, not wearing her seatbelt, had been killed. She'd been thrown through the front windshield. Alive at the scene, Mara had died two days later in the hospital.

Mia had read the police report years after. That was how she knew Conroy should have stopped it, but didn't. How he'd walked away—along with Ed—without even a scratch on either of them. Just some whiplash and that was it. Meanwhile, Mara was dead. And she'd had to adjust to life without her older sister.

She remembered him ringing the doorbell, a couple of days after. His face. *I'm sorry*. Like he had to apologize to his girl-friend's younger sister. She just stood there and screamed at him. Then she tried to slam the door in his face—only her father had grabbed it. He'd wanted to *talk* to Conroy. Mia had run to the bathroom just in time to get sick.

Mia drifted off in the midst of her swirling thoughts. She

dreamed of dogs running at her, snarling. Mouths foaming. Gunshots.

Boots racing down hallways. The thunderous sound of her team racing up a concrete stairwell until the sound echoed so loudly she wanted to scream.

Then she was alone.

Conroy's car exploded. He lay on the ground, bleeding this time.

Dead.

The dog ran at her. Then that neighbor guy. Conroy yelled, but she couldn't hear what he was saying.

Mia sat up, all the noise in her head still there. She blinked and tried to figure out why she felt so disoriented. Lights flashed under the closed door. Alarms blared through the house, even in her childhood bedroom.

She shoved the covers back and nearly tripped over her own feet as she moved to the door. She yanked it open and a wall of sound hit her. Boots. Yelling. Gunshots. More yelling. Like a scene from a war movie left playing on the TV and turned up way too loud.

She clapped her hands over her ears and tried to find the source.

It was everywhere.

In her father's bedroom...there had to be a speaker blaring in there as well. Lights flashed in the window, like someone flicking their headlights to bright. On and off, over and over. She stared out the window too long, then could only see sparks of white behind her eyelids.

The noise was deafening and blared through the whole house. Her dad hadn't told her he'd wired the house up like that, so music could play through all the rooms.

She needed her gun.

Mia flipped the light switch. Nothing.

She moved down the hallway toward her room. She had to get to a gun first, then find a way to shut off the noise.

A dark figure ran at her. The frame was bigger than hers, in a way that sent a wave of fear crashing over her head like an ice bucket.

He slammed her against the wall. She cried out as he shoved her down. Her head hit the corner of the entryway table and everything went black.

How much time passed, she didn't know. It felt like a second. "Mia."

Her shoulder moved, up and down.

"Mia, wake up." It was a woman. "Let's go, sleepyhead. Before I get worried and call for an ambulance."

Mia sucked in a breath and blinked, straining to clear the cobwebs in her head. How long had she been out? Light glared at her. She lifted her arm to block the brightness and hissed at the pain in her arm.

"There you are." Wilcox rocked back on her heels. "I was getting worried."

She helped Mia sit up.

"What are you doing here, Wilcox?"

"I was called in. And it's four in the morning, Mia. Calling me Van is fine, or Savannah."

"I work with a bunch of guys." Mia pressed her fingers to her face and blew out a long breath between pursed lips. "Surnames are nicknames. First names are a running joke."

"Well, you don't have a concussion."

Mia leaned back against the wall. "The shouting. It was so loud."

Savannah winced. "Yeah, it was still going when I got here. Neighbor dude was worried about you, so he called it in. But he didn't come over, because he figured you didn't want to talk to him after what happened with Daisy."

Mia clasped her hand, and Savannah hauled her to standing.

The detective said, "Speakers. One in each room. I shut them off."

"Except the one I slept in."

"Really?" Savannah walked through the bedrooms. "Your room?" She pointed at the last door at the end of the hall.

Mia nodded. She was woozy, but that could be the after-effects of whatever they'd numbed her arm with after the dog. Maybe she was as fine as Conroy after he got knocked unconscious.

She bent forward and tried to stretch out her back and neck. How long had she been out? When she straightened, the hallway spun. Maybe they were both stubborn and only pretending they were fine.

"You're right. There wasn't one in there." Savannah said, "Let's go sit on the couch."

She found six speakers on the coffee table. No wires. "Bluetooth?"

"And he was close enough to hit 'play' when he decided he'd wake up the whole neighborhood." When Mia glanced at her, she said, "Got calls from four houses away."

That was practically the whole neighborhood.

Mia said, "He flashed headlights. In my dad's bedroom window."

"So he sat in his car, pressed play, and flashed his lights." Savannah said, "I found an old iPhone outside in the grass. He must've tossed it."

"He was in here." She retraced everything that had happened and told Savannah everything she knew. "He ran past me, headed through the house. Slammed me against the wall."

Savannah winced. She had a notepad out and scribbled on it with the stub of a pencil.

"Were there two of them?" Mia spoke her thoughts aloud. "Then again, if there was only one then I guess he could have flashed his lights and then run in quickly enough to slam into me."

Van studied her. "What do you think?"

Mia said, "I honestly don't know. I didn't see two." It had

felt out of control, or like she'd surprised him. He'd been playing a game with her. Trying to freak her out.

"What makes you say it was a 'he'?"

Mia closed her eyes. She raised her hands in front of her. "His body…it at least *felt* this big." Shoulders wider than hers. Taller. "He smelled like a guy. I don't know, you can just tell."

She opened her eyes to find Savannah nodding at her.

Mia said, "Sorry you got called out in the middle of the night. I know how busy you are."

She shrugged. "Boss's orders."

"What does that mean?"

Van closed her mouth. Then said, "Only that Lieutenant Barnes said that if anything happens here, if he's not on duty, needs to come to me."

"So you can get woken up in the middle of the night instead of him?"

Savannah shook her head. "He nearly got blown up this morning." She looked disturbed by that. It was plain to see on her face. "So he sleeps, and I'm here."

Mia didn't know what to do with that. His coworkers respected him as a boss, but that didn't mean he was a good person. Right? It meant he was a good cop. Or at the least a boss who commanded respect and didn't accept anything less. Maybe it was just that Savannah was a nice person. Someone who wanted to make sure those around her had what they needed.

Maybe Detective Savannah Wilcox was in love with her handsome, single boss.

Bile rose in Mia's throat. What if they were dating?

"Uh…what was that?"

Mia swallowed, her throat burning. "What?"

"Your face."

"Nothing."

Savannah's eyebrow rose. "Hah. Yeah, right."

"Shame. We could've been friends, but you don't take me at my word."

Savannah sat back in the chair, smiling. "Should I?"

"Not ever."

She barked a laugh.

Mia smiled.

"What's with you and Lieutenant Barnes?" Savannah asked. "I mean, aside from the family connection. He and Rich are pretty good friends."

Mia frowned. "There's nothing with me and Conroy."

Savannah lifted her hands. "O-kay."

He and her father were *pretty good friends*. What on earth did that mean?

The detective said, "So I'll have these speakers dusted for prints, along with front and back doors. That kind of thing. Don't hold your breath on a result. It will *literally* take weeks."

Mia made a face.

"My thoughts exactly, considering it's a whole lot easier to solve a murder with DNA test results."

"I can imagine."

Savannah shot her a look like, *what are you gonna do?* "Well, I should be going. Unless you need anything else?"

"You ask all your victims that?"

"You're an ATF agent. It's not like you're actually going to need anything from me."

"Good," Mia said. "'Cause this has been very weird and entirely too personal."

"Babe, I didn't even get started yet." Savannah grinned. "How do you think I'm such a good detective?"

Mia chuckled. She glanced at the clock and groaned. "There's no way I'm gonna go back to sleep now."

"Run?"

"Probably not the best plan." Though she often literally jumped at that idea. Traversing up and down trails through state parks, either by running or hiking, was her favorite past time.

"And I need to take a small collection of meds the doctor gave me."

"Food, then?"

Mia shrugged. "I got some cereal...last night? No, two nights ago I think." She couldn't believe that was when the drug dealer had run at her and she'd been forced to ram him with her shopping cart, opening the door for Conroy to come barreling back into her life. Instead of keeping her low profile—hello, grocery shopping at midnight wasn't for sissies—and generally avoiding him and everyone else in town.

"We can do better than that." Savannah waved at the front door. "There's a diner in town. You probably remember it. New managers as of five years ago, and let me tell you, Hollis makes the *best* waffles."

The alternative—Stay here, under the radar. Lick her wounds. Drown in the unfairness of it all while she wondered when that guy was going to come back again? Her dad had actually mentioned the famous Hollis's waffles.

Mia stood. "Waffles sound great."

Savannah said, "Get your gun, babe, and let's *go.*"

## 9

"And then he yells, 'hands up!'"

Two women erupted into laughter. Mia was sitting across the booth from Conroy's detective, Savannah, at the diner where Conroy's dispatcher, Bill, had told him Detective Wilcox was currently located—clocked out for breakfast apparently. Seeing Mia there with Savannah was a surprise.

Mia wiped a tear from the corner of her eye, her face twisted with laughter. Savannah laughed so hard she sounded like she was going to be sick.

"This looks interesting."

Van twisted around and yelped.

Mia's eyes widened.

"You're supposed to be my best detective." Conroy folded his arms over his chest, aware of how his shirt tightened on his biceps. Savannah didn't notice, and that was fine by him. Mia's eyes flared. "And yet I snuck up on you. This does not fill me with confidence."

Van snorted out another laugh. Lovely. "I'm on break."

"You're still a cop."

"Party pooper." Van said, "You should put that on your business card instead of lieutenant."

Mia smirked into her coffee cup. He saw a glint and realized she had makeup on. That was why she looked head-turningly good this early in the morning after a broken night of sleep. But good in a way that was more like frosting on a cupcake. If the sponge cake wasn't good, then what was the point?

It was all about light, golden sponge underneath the decoration.

Yes, he watched too much of that British show about baking. But no one ever complained when he brought baked goods into the police station, did they? He just had to deflect questions about where they came from. He had a reputation to protect.

Conroy leaned his hip against the side of the booth and tried to push aside all that had kept him awake half the night. Despite being flat-out exhausted and desperately needing a good amount of sleep, he'd laid there thinking of her.

The guilt, rushing back up.

Mia had always been a tough nut to crack, even as a kid. Apparently, fully-grown, federal agent Mia Tathers was no different. He'd known as soon as he saw her that he'd have to work to gain her forgiveness. Her trust. He just hadn't been expecting the kickback at that moment, the sudden slap of reality. She hadn't forgiven him.

Then, or now.

He might understand a whole lot about who she was, and how she was. But the truth was that they hadn't known each other for years. They were little more than strangers.

"Kaylee sent me an email. She forwarded me your initial report." Basically a few sentences of notes reiterating what had happened to Mia last night.

Mia shot her a look.

Savannah said, "I typed it up in the bathroom."

"Nice." He turned to Mia. "Break it down for me."

She told him about waking up to loud noise, the headlights, and some guy slamming her against the wall. As though Mia was writing a report of her own. Basically what Van had put in her notes. Conroy would have to dig if he wanted more information, but if he treated her like a witness, she would no doubt realize it and shut down.

"You aren't taking my case."

He turned to Van's glare. "Because you don't have enough open cases already?"

"You aren't having this one. You have a bunch as well."

"Van."

She said, "Take one of my others. Heck, take two."

"Mouth."

"You aren't my mom."

"No, I'm your lieutenant," he said. "And that leash you have is getting shorter."

"Don't hamstring my ability to do my job."

Conroy leaned down. "Only thing I'm hamstringing is your ability to tear down this department because you went too far."

Van pressed her lips together.

"Good choice." He didn't need to say more, and she wouldn't want him to. Not in front of her new best friend, Mia. Yes, she was his best detective. That could not be denied. However, her tendency to jump in too fast with both feet often meant he had to swing in and haul those feet out of the fire before she turned the whole thing to ash.

One day Savannah Wilcox was going to find a man who could either jump in the fire with her and help to watch her back while she did her job. Or he was going to rein in her tendency to leap in the first place and Conroy's life, for one, would get a whole lot easier. He certainly would have fewer sleepless nights.

"Gotta get back to work." Van waved her hand in Mia's direction. "But you should know, I'm keeping this one."

Conroy ignored the twitch of Mia's lips. She didn't seem to object to being claimed as a new best friend. She said, "Fine by me."

He said, "Did you ask yet if Mia knows who is targeting her?"

"Mia, who is targeting you?"

Mia's eyes lit. Then she realized Conroy was waiting for an answer. "Oh, uh…how would I know?" She sipped her coffee.

Van shifted in her seat. She knew Mia was holding something back. "We have time," Van said. "The interview isn't over yet. We didn't get the check."

And yet their plates had been cleared away. Coffee cups drained and refilled so many times there was a mound of empty half and half single-serve pods at the end of the table. Someone had tried to stack them in a pyramid, but they appeared to have fallen over in the process.

He set his palm on the table and leaned toward Mia this time. "Who is targeting you?"

She looked up at him towering over her. If he looked imposing, then good. He was glad to have the upper hand, even if it was because she was seriously off her game after a rough night.

He said, "My car exploded. Then a poisoned dog bit you. *Then* you wake up to a racket, an assault, and an intruder. What is this? Because I'm starting to think it's not entirely about me."

An expression skittered across her face.

"Tell me, Mia. Or I have a bad feeling it's going to get worse."

"I…" she swallowed. "It can't be him. He's dead."

"Someone is after you. And they're very much alive."

Hollis wandered over with a to-go cup she handed him. Her full figure was covered with a salmon-colored waitress uniform. Her hair was light brown and caramel, her eyebrows thick brown. She and Conroy had been in the same grade in high school, so Mia probably remembered both her and her father. Though it had been her father who had run the diner before Hollis took it over—after he'd had a stroke in the kitchen.

"They've been here since five."

Conroy's eyebrows rose.

Hollis shot him a knowing look.

"Want me to kick them out?"

One of the women gasped at his question. He didn't know which. Hollis said, "Are you kidding me? They keep sneaking me tips."

"Always use your blinker to signal a turn." Van had a completely straight face.

Hollis groaned.

Mia grinned. "Never get dressed in the dark."

She gave him a side glance. "Enjoy your coffee."

"Thanks, Hol." He took a sip. Still the best coffee in town. His phone rang in his pocket. "The two of you—" He leaned in and spoke low. "—please, at least *try* to stay out of trouble."

Van smirked.

He caught Mia's gaze. She nodded. "I mean, it's not my fault. But I'll try."

Conroy's gaze slid across Van, and she caught his drift. Keep this woman safe. Regardless of how Mia felt about him, it was his job as a cop and as her father's friend to make sure she wasn't hurt. So far he'd not done so well. He'd have to answer to Rich for that.

Things had turned serious. This guy had targeted her and broken into her house to send her a clear message. He was still coming for her, and he could get to her whenever he wanted.

Conroy turned back at the door.

He could see the edge of fear she was trying to hide. Conroy had always liked that soft spot she guarded, like her life was a fortress hiding a precious treasure. He intended to protect it until she decided she could trust him, and then they'd have the conversation about her finally forgiving him for what had happened to Mara.

She met his gaze. Tipped her head to the side.

Conroy lifted his chin. This wasn't over. She would have to realize that, or it would get pretty uncomfortable when she figured out he was all in. No backing down.

His phone had quit ringing. It started up again.

Conroy slid the tip of his finger across the screen. "Yeah, Kaylee."

"Call for you. He'd like you to call back."

"ASAP?"

"He said no, but…"

There had to be a reason she had called instead of just leaving a paper on his desk. "What?"

"Ed Summers wants to talk to you." She sighed audibly. "It's going to be another one of those days, isn't it?"

"Probably should just clock out, get a dozen donuts, and hit the couch."

She chuckled. "You ever eat a donut in your life?"

He tried to remember. "Maybe?"

"Yeah. I don't eat one. I eat seven. So that's a no for me. But I like the way you think, boss. We should put that on the list for our Easter bash."

She never did turn down an excuse for a party. "Copy that. I'll head over to Summers's place."

"You think that's wise?"

"Just call him back," Conroy said. "Tell him I'm on my way."

She said nothing else, which was probably for the best. Rousing a house full of people who thought their personal residence meant they could do whatever illegal things they wanted, and weren't likely to welcome a police officer, wasn't on his to-do list for today. Especially when it was early enough most would probably be off their game. Hair-trigger reactions meant unpredictable outcomes.

Conroy needed at least Summers off his game. The guy was slippery and had been in high school, as well, even when they were friends. It was worse now that Ed had full access to whatever he wanted, whenever he wanted it. The guy had built what amounted to an empire out of one estate house on the edge of town. A gated residence with armed guards. Conroy had gotten a couple of noise complaints. There had been a sexual assault case about a year ago, dropped when the victim decided she no longer wanted to press charges.

He knew what was happening.

Summers thought he was above the law, and so far that was proving true. But it wouldn't be the case forever. Conroy was going to find something he could make stick.

He had to honk his horn to rouse the guy on the gate. It was wheeled back, and Conroy drove down to the main house. Summers walked out onto the porch, smoking a cigarette and drinking from a steaming white mug. Jeans, no belt. No shirt. Tattooed sleeves up both arms and over his shoulders, along with half a dozen more on his chest. His back was also covered. What was almost a beard covered his chin, and his hair needed cutting and combing about a month ago.

"Morning." Summers lifted his mug in salute.

"Not good?" Did he know about the car explosion, the dog, and the intruder at Rich's house?

"Heard there's a new girl in town."

"Yeah?"

"I need to be worried there's a fed poking around?"

"Bureau of Alcohol, Tobacco, Firearms and Explosives. Any of those in your small business plan?"

"Bro, my business ain't small."

"I'm not your bro." Conroy hadn't been that for a long time. If he ever had been.

Summers cracked a smile. "You and I, we'll always be connected."

He was willing to concede that might be true. "You know it's not just a fed. It's Mia Tathers."

Summers took a drag on his cigarette. "One of my men is missing. Tyler Lane."

"You wanna file a police report? Cause you could've just called an officer down here to take the information." He didn't need the lieutenant, his old friend. "This isn't concierge policing."

Ed's lips twitched, but not for long. "He didn't come back last night."

"And that's unusual?"

Summers shrugged.

"You need to get me his real name and a photo." DNA would be better. "I'll keep an eye open for him."

"I appreciate it." Another drag. "Mia's really back?"

"And she's gonna be left alone. Spread it wide," Conroy said. "If I hear about *any* of your people messing with her, you and I will have an even bigger problem than we already do."

## 10

M ia figured she should just print out a sign that said, "Available for Attempts on Life." Nothing else was working.

It had been three days since her breakfast with Detective Wilcox. She and Savannah had a couple of text conversations since then, but that was all she'd done except sleep and watch TV. The drone of shows she didn't care about did a mediocre job of keeping stray thoughts at bay. Her dad's house had never been a sanctuary. Now it was worse, though.

She shivered, and not just because of the cold. She needed to walk. Even if she was scared.

Her beanie itched the skin of her forehead. Mia's hair lay over the shoulders of her winter coat. She should have worn a base layer under her jeans because it was seriously cold. Her gloves weren't stopping her fingers from freezing.

She walked anyway. Down the new trail that ran alongside the highway. Right up until a car slowed alongside her.

She twisted, reaching for the gun by her side.

"Easy." Conroy rolled up the window and pulled over.

Mia stopped on the path and looked up at the thick, gray clouds hanging low. More snow tonight, she figured.

"What are you doing?" He got out and came over to her. Work shoes, khaki pants, and a black wool coat. Maybe it was dress-down day at the police department.

His badge, in the leather holder, was fixed to the lapel of his coat above the top button. She'd always thought that was cool. On him...okay, so it made him even hotter than he already was, and it wasn't like he needed help in that department.

"Well?" He waited for her answer.

"I'm trying to get him to come at me again."

"Because you're bored?"

Mia glanced up at his furious face. "I'd like to say it was nice to see you." She started to walk away.

His fingers snagged her arm. Right where the dog's teeth had sunk into her skin.

Mia let out a cry.

He released her. "The dog. Sorry, I forgot it was that arm."

She held it to her front, hugging herself, not willing to tell him it was okay when it was not.

"So you're mad and bored, and determined to get him to come at you again. So you can shoot him?"

"I'd call you. After."

He didn't laugh.

Mia sighed. "Yes, my arm hurts. I can't take more pain meds for like an hour, or however long it is until three."

"You don't know?"

"My watch is under my jacket, under my sweater, which is tucked into my glove."

He looked at his phone, then stowed it back into his back pocket. "It's two thirty."

"I have half an hour." She wanted to take the meds now, but spacing them out came before weaning herself off them. In the end, Mia preferred the pain rather than going the route so many others did by taking too long to go off them and developing an addiction.

"I'll drive you back to your dad's house."

"I'd rather walk this nice path they've put in since I lived here." It had been shoveled and salted and everything.

He folded his arms across his chest. If he was cold, he should get back in his fancy police SUV. He looked like he didn't know whether to be mad or to laugh. Instead he said, "Can we please get in the car?"

"I need to stretch my legs."

Conroy reached into his pocket. The lights of his vehicle flashed and the horn honked. "So let's go."

She said nothing.

"Lead the way." He waved up the path. "You wanted to walk, right?"

She set off. "I've realized my legs work fine. It's the rest of me that's having problems."

Conroy shook his head, looking a little exasperated.

"How about you?"

"Head still hurts." He strolled like it was June and they were at the park. "But I ruled out Summers as playing a part in what is going on with you."

Mia pressed her lips together. She'd been thinking about what he'd said, and the way he'd put it. The car exploding, the dog running at her, and the man in her dad's house. Specifically, she'd been mulling over what those things, in that order, might mean. Because it sounded awfully similar to the order of things that happened when her team served a warrant on someone's house.

How did that make sense?

She'd wondered about calling Tate and asking him to open a new case. Have him find out whether the last suspect had any friends or family who might have a bone to pick with her now. Tate had texted her after he ratted her out to Conroy. But only to tell her he wasn't sorry. Then he'd sent her a PayPal invoice. He shouldn't hold his breath anticipating a tip.

Conroy touched the back of her shoulder, thankfully the good side. Sure, she could ask the police lieutenant to look into the life of a man she'd killed on that ATF operation, but then he would know she had an idea what all this was about. Who it was causing such havoc in her life. Mia would rather solve this problem in-house. Which meant...by herself.

Conroy gave her shoulder a squeeze. She glanced over. Surely he wasn't making a move on her, was he?

"Bike." He shifted them both to the right side of the path. A mountain biker whizzed past, wearing tight-fitting pants and shirt.

Mia shivered.

She heard Conroy chuckle under his breath as he lowered his arm. "I prefer to ride a stationary bike at the gym this time of year. When my head doesn't hurt."

She nodded. "I walk."

"I see that."

"No." She shook her head. "I don't mean stroll like this. I mean, like, hiking. Vigorous hiking. It helps me clear my head."

"Lots of that in Seattle?"

"If you know where to look."

"You like it?"

Mia said, "You mean, do I like it better than here?"

He shrugged. "Do you?"

"It's where my job is; where they assigned me. Seattle is fine, and my team is all right."

"Just all right?"

"They're guys. And when I say that, I mean like the 'good ol' boys' type of guys. My friend Allyson was on my team until she married a US Marshal and they moved out of state." Mia shrugged.

"What about a local church, or friends?"

"I guess." She hadn't attended service in a while, though she'd gone to a women's group a few times before she realized she didn't really fit in there.

He was going to pressure her until she cracked. Mia could just tell. What she *should* do is walk home. Immediately. Lock her door and wait until whoever insisted on messing with her knocked. Then she could deal with it her way. No more contact with Conroy.

And yet, since he got out of the vehicle, all the fear she'd felt when she was by herself had dissipated. She'd never needed a man to make her feel better. Not once in her life. Starting with her own father who had been present but had little idea what to do with hormonal, emotional girls. He'd never been her steady foundation. He could barely stay still himself, always off doing one thing or another. Working. Hunting. Fishing. Camping by himself, leaving them in the care of neighbors or older women at church who spanked them with spatulas. Like that was how you imparted Jesus in someone.

Conroy wasn't like any other man she'd ever met.

Which was probably how her sister Mara thought of him in high school, when they'd decided to be exclusive. The king and queen of youth group *and* high school prom. Mara had only gone to church because of Conroy.

There was no way she should fall for the charm and reassurance of his presence. Especially when he had no control over it. Conroy was just this way without realizing it, and she shouldn't find herself relying on it.

They came on a park she recognized. "It's like this is a whole new town, and yet the one I remember at the same time."

"That about sums it up, considering all the city council does is argue about whether to accept the movement of progress or preserve the town's legacy. It's history."

She grinned.

He shook his head. "Don't even get me started on that."

"Not thinking of running for Mayor?"

"No way."

"Police chief?" It seemed like he was doing the job already.

He shrugged, but she could see an edge of exhausted grief in his eyes. "If the mayor appoints me to the position after Chief Ridgeman passes."

"And in the meantime you're doing it all, just not getting paid for it."

They crossed grass, moving toward the deserted playground. It was a school day, and too cold for moms with little kids to be out.

"That doesn't mean I'm not able to help when you need it." He turned to face her. "If someone is coming after you, then it's important they are dealt with so they aren't able to hurt anyone else."

"Agreed."

"Why does that not look like a good thing?"

She wasn't going to back down. "I don't want anyone to get hurt, either. But I'm a federal agent. I can do this without help."

"Sure, if it's set up perfectly and he walks right into it. You and I both know life doesn't work out like that, especially not in our line of work. You can't guarantee an outcome."

She patted the jacket over her hip. "That's why they gave me a gun."

"You didn't get to it at your house."

"I don't need you to do that guy thing where you pick apart my plan until I feel stupid."

"That's not—"

Mia shook her head. "Just don't. Okay? If I need something, I'll call Wilcox."

"Your new best friend?"

"I don't need your help."

"You mean you won't accept it. There's a difference."

"Who cares when the outcome is the same?" She turned and started across the playground. "You have enough to do, and I'm fine."

After what he'd done, she didn't want to trust him. She shouldn't by any estimation. Mara was dead. Mia didn't want to end up the same way.

No, that wasn't fair.

"Mia."

She nearly turned back. He even sounded like he felt guilty, about what though?

The fact he hadn't prevented it wasn't the same as him causing her sister's death. Ed Summers had been drunk behind the wheel. Summers was the reason Mara was dead. But that didn't remove at least a measure of responsibility from Conroy's shoulders—he'd been her boyfriend. At the least it could be argued it was some kind of criminal negligence as an accomplice to Ed's actions.

"Stop trying to protect yourself from me." His shoes crunched frosty grass behind her. "When I'm the one here to help you." He paused. "Mia."

She kept walking.

"*Mia.*"

She whirled around. "What?"

"Stay right there." He moved past her.

A man's body had been laid out on the ground at the far end of the playground. Medium height, so far as she could tell from him lying down. Yellowed, dirty jacket. Worn jeans covering thick legs. Huge, black work boots, scuffed. Dark blue beanie pulled down over his ears. Facing away from them, but like he'd been rolled against the curb separating the bark from the grass of the playground.

"Stay there."

She wasn't sure that was needed, but this was his jurisdiction. Murders weren't what she investigated. They occasionally played a part in her work, though.

"And call Detective Wilcox."

She tugged her phone out and peeled off one glove to call it in. While she spoke with Savannah, Conroy rolled the man to his back. She said, "Dead?"

He looked at her.

Mia asked, "Well, who is it?"

On the other end of the phone, Savannah said, "I'm on my way."

The line went dead.

She said, "How did he die?" She strode over to get a look at the man.

Conroy straightened from his crouch. "I'm not a medical examiner, but I'm guessing it was the gunshot to his stomach."

She sucked in a breath that got stuck in her throat. "Who —" She coughed. "Who is it, do you know?"

"His name is Tyler Lane. He's been missing three days."

"You know him?"

"He works for Ed Summers."

She took a step back. "I had nothing to do with this."

"That's a little convenient, don't you think? We just happen to stumble on the site where a body was dropped." Conroy's eyes narrowed. "And when I run his prints against what was gathered from your dad's house?"

"This isn't my fault! Don't make it sound like it is."

"And yet every step of the way, you've been right smack in the middle of it."

Mia opened her mouth then, too fast for her to hold the words back.

"Just because he was killed the same way I killed the other guy doesn't—"

Conroy got in her face then. "Start talking."

# 11

Conroy held himself still. "This man was killed the same way as who?"

He wanted to touch her but held off. He could see she was ready to bolt. That would only leave her unprotected and alone with no way to get back to her dad's house. Not without walking all the way back, and it was at least an hour's stroll from here.

No. He needed to wait until an officer relieved him at the scene or until Detective Wilcox showed up. So Conroy could drive her back, not Savannah.

And he needed her to talk.

"It doesn't matter." She lifted her chin. "I'm not going to put anyone here in danger, okay? I'll make sure of it. I'll even promise you that no one will come to harm. Your precious town and all the people here will be fine."

Her words were biting, but he saw the pain she was in around her strained jaw and in her eyes.

He wanted to tug her close and give her a hug. Not the way he'd treated her as a kid, part nuisance and part cute, younger sibling of his girlfriend. This was something entirely different, and it seemed to have come out of nowhere.

A black and white Last Chance County police car pulled up.

The officer who got out was male and had been on the job a long time—which was fine with Conroy since he was very good at his job. Basuto just didn't know that Conroy planned to get him to take the Sergeant's exam soon.

"Lieutenant." His officer was five-seven, but only barely. Dark complexion, dark eyebrows, and dark hair. But Zander had the brightest smile, and he was quick to use it. Conroy had seen him charm kids in the most terrifying of situations and have them laughing at one of his jokes five minutes later.

Conroy motioned to the body, not willing to move away from Mia. She would see that as her being released to leave. "Over there, Officer Basuto. This is ATF Special Agent Mia Tathers."

"Rich's daughter?"

She shifted to glance at his officer. "Is that a good thing?"

"Why wouldn't it be?" He stuck his hand out. "Zander."

"Mia."

Conroy said, "You should start processing the scene."

Basuto snapped to attention. "Yes, boss."

Conroy didn't laugh. Mia coughed to cover her chuckle. They went over the scene and checked the guy's ID, which was in his pocket in a wallet stuffed full of old receipts. "Ed Summers's boy. Tyler Lane."

Mia frowned down at the body. A movement alerted her peripheral. She snapped out of it and glanced past Conroy's shoulder. Her expression changed. "Hey, Savannah."

"Mia."

Good. Wilcox was here. "Basuto, Wilcox, you guys process this scene. I'm going to take Mia back to her dad's house."

Only that wasn't exactly a safe place for her to be alone. And it seemed to occur to her also.

He wanted to hold her hand but instead put his hand on her jacket over the small of her back to lead her away from Basuto —who looked amused—and Wilcox—who frowned.

"Keep me posted." He waited for Wilcox to say something. "Detective?"

"Yes, Lieutenant. I'll keep you posted."

He led Mia away from the scene.

She twisted and bolted away from him. Conroy spun around. "What—"

"Stop! Police!" She screamed the words as she raced across the grass, leaving footprints in the frost.

Conroy tore after her.

His head pounded, but he pumped his arms and legs and prayed he didn't slip. Most of the time he was a capable guy. Pretty adept at handling just about any situation. But when it counted, he called on God to kick in. Like now, when losing his footing and landing on the cold, hard ground would be a bad thing—bad for either of them. Both had enough injuries already.

The man ahead of her raced toward a car. He'd been between two trees, hiding and watching them. Blue jacket, hood up. Conroy hadn't thought it was malicious. He also didn't know the guy, but could admit he hadn't gotten a good look at him either.

Mia gained ground.

Was it the killer?

She stumbled and her knee went down. He gasped, moving too fast to ask if she was all right. Of course he wanted to help, but she would want him to keep going and catch the guy.

But her stumble had cost her ground. The man ahead of her ran, faster than either Conroy or Mia. They weren't going to catch him. He headed for a beat-up, sea green, compact car on the side of the road, climbed in, and roared the engine to life. A cold engine. It whined as he revved it up and sped away.

Conroy studied the license plate and got the first three characters.

He turned back, reciting them out loud so he would remember, and got to Mia in time to hold out his hand and help her up. She clasped his wrist, not his hand, and stood. "Thanks."

He recited the first three characters of the license plate.

She said the last three.

Conroy's eyebrows rose.

Mia said, "Everyone reads right to left. So with license plates, I trained myself to look at the right first and work my way backward. That way if someone gets half, then I get the other half." She smiled. "Like right now."

"I don't know what to say." He was proud of her. That was really smart, considering she was absolutely right. She'd taken steps to fill in the gaps. "Your team probably sees you as a serious asset."

A frown darkened her expression.

"They don't?"

"No one has ever really reacted to something I did. Not the way you do." She went to say more but shut her mouth and shook her head. "Most of the time it's completely infuriating when you go all 'cop' over a situation I can handle. The rest of the time it's nice."

"You're welcome. I think." He chuckled, hoping she would too.

He got a smile.

"Was that him?"

She frowned. "I don't know who that was. That man was a stranger."

"So what made you chase him?"

She opened her mouth, then closed it again.

"Cop instinct, otherwise known as your gut."

"Intuition." She nodded. "Thanks, that is what it is."

But she wasn't used to anyone understanding when she reacted like that?

She turned and headed back toward Wilcox. Conroy fell into step beside her. "I'll have my officer go grab the vehicle. Then I can get you somewhere you can sit down."

She winced. Yes, he'd noticed the slight hitch in her stride. She'd landed on her knee on the hard winter ground. They both needed about a week or two of recovery time to get back to being fighting fit.

"How about somewhere we can run that license plate?"

He glanced aside at her. "You wanna hang out at the police station?"

She shrugged.

Was she scared to go home? He'd thought as much. Just as he'd considered alternatives, like the town's bed and breakfast. Or his house.

*Nope.*

The temptation to pull her in for a hug—or something else —wanted to override his good judgment. He was the police lieutenant, the ranking officer in town. She was a victim as well as a federal agent. There was no way he should go there.

And even if he did, she wouldn't even be thinking about that. He would end up blindsiding her and then things would get all weird. She didn't forgive him. She'd said as much. She also didn't trust him, at least any further than his badge would go.

Cop to cop, he figured they could work together. Personally? That was another thing altogether on her part.

Cop to cop, she seriously intrigued him. Personally she could say the same. The preteen girl he knew from years past had grown up into a capable woman he respected.

Could he show her he was worth the chance she would be taking on him? It would have to start with trust. Personal, real trust. Then she would have to forgive him for his part in her sister's death. Which was, far and away, easier said than done.

He had no doubt she would be worth the chance of being shot down.

He'd have to tread carefully, though, and sacrifice a whole lot of pride. If it worked, then the gain could overwhelmingly outweigh the cost of convincing her he was worth staying in town for. A place she'd left as soon as she could. What would it take to persuade her to stick around this time?

"We'll find somewhere you can go to hang out." He tugged on her good arm before they got within earshot of Wilcox and his officer. "Are you worried about this guy?"

"If there's something to be worried about, then yes. Otherwise, no."

Logical, but not exactly decisive. She was reserving judgment.

Mia gave him a smile and rolled her eyes. "After always jumping in because of my gut, I'm stepping carefully on this one."

"Officer Basuto!"

Mia jumped. Zander straightened, a camera in one hand. "Lieutenant?"

Conroy tossed the guy his keys. "My car is a mile up that way." He pointed. "Please retrieve it for me."

"Sure, boss." He reached up over his head. "My back is aching from photos." Basuto handed off the camera and set off at a jog. Definitely going to be taking the sergeant's exam soon.

"You okay, Mia?" Wilcox had wandered over.

Mia jerked around. So deep in thought she hadn't noticed Savannah was right there. "Hey."

"Okay?" Wilcox's blue gaze flashed to him, and then back at Mia.

Conroy didn't have the chance to reassure her. Mia wasn't fine, but she would be if he had anything to do with it.

"Sure." Mia shrugged. "I just need to take more meds. For my arm." She hugged it to her front again.

"Get her home, Lieutenant." Wilcox took a step back. "Or I'll think that you don't trust me to work a murder scene."

"You qualified to make that call, Detective?"

"You can read all about my findings in my report, *Lieutenant.*" She waved at Mia. "Get her somewhere she can take her meds and get some rest."

Mia twisted to the detective. "I was kind of hoping you'd let me hang at your place."

Conroy was about to offer some kind of response when Wilcox cut him off. "My place is a little crowded. And the natives are rowdy. You'd be better off at Conroy's." She twisted to face him. "Actually that's a great idea. Grab her stuff and park her at your place."

He stared down at the tiny, blonde detective. Wilcox only smiled that knowing, crafty smile. "It's a great idea."

"Oh, well…"

That was all Mia had to say? He cleared his throat. "My place is fine. I have a guest room if you want to take a nap."

Maybe since she'd spent a couple of nights at her house since the intruder, and those were without incident, she would prefer to head home.

Conroy studied her. "What do you think?"

She turned to him with a smile. He didn't believe she meant it in the slightest. "Sure, your guest room sounds good."

"Everything is going to be fine."

"He's right," Wilcox said. "We'll catch the guy who did this, and the guy who broke into your house. If it's the same guy, then great. Only one man to find—" She clapped her hands together and Mia jumped a little. "—and case closed."

Basuto pulled up in Conroy's police vehicle. He left the engine running.

"Let's go."

Mia moved with him. But Conroy couldn't shake the feeling that she was walking to her death.

And she knew it.

## 12

H e didn't let her drive. Then again, she didn't expect to. Mia squeezed her eyes shut and tried to push away the errant thoughts.

"Have you thought about calling in?" Conroy shoved the car in park outside her dad's house.

She half expected her dad to be back. Called home by some previously unexplored fatherly instinct that let him know she was in trouble. Then she realized that was just ridiculous, and she wasn't sure why she cared where on earth her dad was.

"Mia?"

"Huh?" She twisted to him. Her arm hurt. Her knee ached. She needed coffee something fierce and probably some sort of comfort food like chili and a baked potato. Something hearty that would sustain her, a meal that weather like this just seemed made for. Frosty trees, and low gray skies.

"You're miles away." He cracked his door. "Let's get you inside. You can pack a bag and get your meds."

"You know, *you* could be the one packing a bag."

"I have a guest room. And this place—" He pointed through the window at the house. "—is where he found you. That's not going to happen at mine, where I have an extensive security system."

"Nowhere is impenetrable."

"That's true. But we go where the odds of survival are best."

Mia pressed her lips together.

"Did you call your team lead, or someone else you work with? They probably need to know you're in danger, and that it's connected to one of your previous cases. The death's been escalated to murder now. We need to—"

Mia got out of the car. She rounded the hood and strode toward the side path where Daisy had run at her. She held her arm to her front. Probably should have accepted the sling.

"Hello!"

She saw the little girl coming. Pig tails. Her mom trailed behind her, walking fast with long strides while the girl raced toward Mia holding a plastic food storage container.

"Mands!" The mom didn't exactly sound scolding, just exasperated.

"She's home, Mama. We have to do it now." The little girl stopped in front of Mia, cheeks flushed red. "These are for you. Because Daisy bit you." She held the container out and tears filled her eyes.

"We're all very sorry about that." Though, it seemed Mom didn't exactly mean it. "I'm Rebecca, and this is Amanda. We know your dad, and we like him."

"Grandpa Rich gives me caramels and—" The little girl gasped. She whirled around to her mother. "Uh…"

Rebecca grinned, but it was shaky. "You're fine, Mands." The mom lifted a paper. "The kids also drew you this."

Mia was still stuck on *Grandpa Rich*.

Conroy leaned in front of Mia to take hold of the container and artwork. "Thank you, Amanda."

She basically curtseyed, beaming under the full force of Conroy Barnes's smile. "You're welcome, Mr. Conroy." The girl glanced between him and Mia. "But they're for Miss Mia."

He grinned. Both the women, mom and daughter, practically swooned. "I know." He glanced at her, then said, "Miss Mia says, 'thank you.'"

The little girl frowned. "Does she hate us because Daisy bit her?"

Conroy shook his head. Before he could say something, she cut in.

"No."

The little girl flinched, and Mia realized she'd been too loud.

"Sorry." Mia continued, "I know Daisy was sick. It wasn't her fault, and it wasn't any of yours." She paused. "I hope she'll get better."

"She is." Rebecca nodded.

Amanda said, "She woke up, and mom says we can see her tomorrow."

"That's great. Thanks."

Before she got dragged into any more conversation, when she should be taking meds she was due to take an hour ago, Mia headed for the front door and let herself inside.

There was a hitch of breath as she realized someone could be inside. Then her brain decided it was more likely the inside would've been ransacked if that was the case. The house was quiet. Everything looked like it was where it should be.

She still entered slowly.

Conroy strolled by her, all the way to the kitchen. He set the container on the counter. "Water or milk?"

"Milk." She got the meds from her backpack, one handed.

He stood in front of her, a concerned look on his face.

"You really need to stop doing that." She set the pill on her tongue and swallowed half the glass of milk.

"Doing what?"

She took another drink to make sure she'd gotten it down. Then she wiped her mouth with the back of her hand. "Caring."

Mia swiped up her duffel and walked to the bedroom. He

stood in the doorway while she grabbed a few things, averting his gaze when those things got personal. Bathroom stuff. A towel. Did he even have good towels, or was he a bachelor at home?

She glanced aside at him, in the bathroom now. The man dressed well. That could not be denied. He leaned against the wall in the hallway. Most people would have their phone out right now. They'd preoccupy themselves because nothing else was going on. Outsourcing their brains to an electronic device designed to illicit an addiction in the user.

For the most part, ATF agents stayed clear of social media. No one needed their face out there for bad guys to see. On top of that were the ways she'd seen it used and abused. People were torn apart and hurt every day online. The whole thing left a bad taste in her mouth, except that she could deposit a check in her bank account using her phone. And see what the weather was whenever she wanted.

"Ready?" He gave her a small smile.

She sighed and looked through her bag one last time, thinking about how these last few days had really turned things upside down for her. He had to be feeling as she did right now, namely that this whole situation between them was bizarre. He'd dated her sister back in the day. His actions, or lack thereof, had caused Mara's death. Mia had shown the information to her friend at the DA's office in Seattle. Her friend only explained about the conviction, the time Ed had served. And the inner workings of a local town police department. Like she hadn't already known about that.

Now Mia was the one in danger. She knew the reality she faced all too well. And Conroy seemed to understand this reality, too.

He was determined to make it okay for her. So determined that after they left her dad's place, he took her to his house. His extremely nice three-story condo in the middle of what appeared to be urban development, close to the ski area north of town where the snow never really melted until April. Not too close to town, and not technically within city limits. She wasn't going to lie—it made her feel taken care of. He parked her in his guest room and even offered to make dinner.

Mia said, "Only if I can help."

Conroy hauled out fixings for a salad and set them on the counter in front of her. He pulled a package of chicken from the refrigerator drawer and tossed it in a glass dish.

"This is a really nice house."

He looked up, hands full of paper towels he was using to pat the chicken dry. "Thanks."

"How long have you lived here?"

"Six years. When the economy took a dive, the units were going for nearly nothing and they never really recovered. I had a down payment saved up. Never thought I could get in here. There's a running path, a gym, and a pool. Instead of not being able to afford it, the down payment ended up going further than I thought."

She looked around, not recognizing anything from his parent's house. Didn't everyone have at least one piece of furniture that was hand-me-down from their parents? "It's really nice. Like a model home, but you've made it yours."

He gave her a small smile, then turned away. While he was at the cupboard pulling down a collection of spices and herbs, she said, "So…what's with Wilcox's living situation?"

He turned around. A flash of hurt on his face disappeared almost as fast as she'd seen it. Was he worried she would rather be there?

He said, "It's like a boarding house," and shook salt on the chicken. "Small one-bedrooms, and a shared dining hall."

"Huh."

"It's over on Lomax by the elementary school, you know?"

She shrugged, given the general area he'd described.

"The chief said it started as a shelter for women and children who needed a safe place to be. Now they accept applications on a case-by-case basis."

"And Wilcox?"

"She was a detective before she came here. I don't know much about her. Other than that she had a Louisiana assistant district attorney vouch for her." While he spoke, he shook spices and herbs over the chicken, flipped both, and then did the same to the other side. "She needed a place to live, and that's where she chose."

She chopped a head of lettuce. "You aren't worried about people getting the wrong idea about this when it gets around that I stayed the night?" She knew what this town was like.

He set the jar of smoked paprika down. "You'd rather be at your house? Or at the bed and breakfast where you put all the other residents—and the owners—in danger along with you?"

"I didn't say it was going to be a logical argument. Besides, what people believe about others and the world is rarely logical." Usually it was clouded by their own issues and experiences, which could be good or bad.

"My car will be here all night. As will you. I can head to the office, watch over the chief, and give whoever is on rotation the night off."

She got the feeling he'd done it before. Maybe even often. She didn't want to soften toward him, so she concentrated on chopping the vegetables for the salad. He'd also given her cracked pepper and an unlabeled jar that looked like balsamic dressing.

A patio door slid open. She glanced over and saw him step outside. She hadn't even realized there was a back deck.

When she'd assembled the salad, Mia filled two glasses with water. Thick blue glass with swirls in it. She'd have called them "handsome" like the rest of his decorations. His couch invited you to sink down and probably wind up taking a nap. It looked that comfortable.

She found stoneware plates and had located the silverware in a drawer when he came back in.

"Ready?"

"Yep." She glanced over. The smell reached her before he did. "Grilled chicken?"

"It's one of my specialties." He forked it onto two plates, and Mia dished up the salad. "Every time I go to Cassie's house, she and Jack rope me into manning the grill."

They settled at the dining table. "Your sister is married?"

"She met Jack in college. They have two kids now. Brendan is six, and Leora is four." His eyes flashed, and she knew he loved them. "They're so busy, and loud, but I love it."

"And you…you said you never married?"

He shook his head. "Never even came close."

"Oh."

He gave her a look that held the same question.

Her mind blanked. She didn't want to go there, so she changed the subject. "I would've thought you'd have just taken over your parent's house when they moved out of town."

Instead, he was in a gorgeous townhouse that made her apartment look like a…she didn't want to know what. That would hit too close to home.

She lifted her water glass to her lips.

He shook his head. "It blew up."

Mia choked. He started to get up, but she held up a hand and coughed. "I'm okay." When she'd composed herself, she said, "It really blew up?"

"Gas leak." He grinned. "Mom was devastated over all that hideous art she'd collected and all those angel curios. Completely destroyed. Dad thought it was the best thing that ever happened to him. She heard and accused him of purposely blowing up all her "collector's items." They worked it out. Now they have a condo in Scottsdale and a motorhome they illegally park at the lake every summer for four months."

Mia laughed. "I'll bet the grandkids love that."

"Yep." He chuckled. "They're living the dream."

Seemed like he thought that was a pretty good dream, too. Maybe even one he wanted for himself, where he was married with two kids. She looked around. If Mara was alive, would she be sitting here across from him instead?

Would they be married, two kids? Busy, and loud. A life that was like a dream it was so good. Full of life, and love.

Mia picked up her plate and headed to the kitchen. Alone.

Like the rest of her life, it was nothing resembling that good kind of dream.

# 13

Conroy saw her shut down. He didn't know why—if it was something he'd said or done. He carried his plate to the kitchen and placed it in the sink. She finished rinsing her own, then did his. He loaded them in his dishwasher.

She didn't even look at him.

"Dinner wasn't good?"

She shot him a look mid-eye roll. "That chicken was amazing and you know it."

He grinned. "Thanks."

"And the company, too, for the record." She dried her hands on the dish towel his sister had hung on the front of his oven.

"Thanks." He leaned a hip against the counter. "I know things aren't all the way smoothed out between us, but I can honestly say I'd like them to be."

He knew she essentially blamed him for her sister's death, but he was tired of stepping around it. Conroy decided to lay it all out there. "I know it will take time. I'm actually hoping that while I keep you safe, you'll finally realize you can trust me."

He wanted to say he was the same guy she'd known years ago. Maybe that wasn't such a good thing. Before Mara's death, she'd hung with them some. More than just an irritating little sister of his girlfriend. He'd thought Mia was interesting, even if the junior high crush she had on him was obvious.

She'd never been that hilarious, no-worries kid who joked around. None of the Tathers sisters were. Mia had been thoughtful and intelligent. She'd also been driven enough to know she needed good grades in order to get a decent ticket out of Last Chance County.

Go where she wanted.

Make something of herself.

"Do you like Seattle?"

Mia's lips shifted. Telling enough in itself. It took her a minute to answer. "I like my job, for the most part. I like my apartment. For the most part."

He knew they were going back over ground they'd covered already. But he was trying to get to the bottom of why it seemed like she wasn't proud of all she'd accomplished. "What about being back in Last Chance County?"

"Not as...bad as I'd thought."

He smiled. "You were determined to have an awful time?"

The edge of a return smile curled up her lips. "I was in pain, and I couldn't distract myself with work."

"That would frustrate anyone." It would definitely frustrate him.

She said, "It's been...interesting."

He had to chuckle.

"Not just your car, and the dog bite." She winced. "It hasn't been bad, exactly, seeing you and getting to know Savannah. I'd planned on staying under the radar to avoid talking to anyone. Mostly because I was in too much discomfort to be human instead of a jerk."

"How did you get hurt?"

"We served an arrest warrant. The guy got out, and the K-9 that's attached to our team went after him. I went after the dog. The guy got bitten." She swallowed. "So he stabbed the dog."

Conroy started to speak.

Mia lifted both hands. "She had surgery, and she's recovering. But I don't think she'll be a cop dog anymore."

"And you?"

"The dog's blood was everywhere. I had a guy with a knife, and he was going to stab her again. I tried to shoot him in the leg, but I missed. He dropped the knife and launched at me. The dog was between us. We landed with me on the bottom, my shoulder hitting a rock on the way down." She winced. "In the end there was nothing else I could do. He was choking me. I still had my gun. I got the dog out of the way and fired up into his stomach. There was no room to do anything else."

"You don't have to convince me. Your life was in jeopardy, and the guy presented a serious threat to others, as well as you."

She nodded.

He moved half a step closer. "I'm sorry you got hurt."

"Because you're hardwired to protect people." She was certain of that, he could see it on her face. But it was edged with the grief she still felt, over the loss of her sister so many years ago, and the fact she'd taken a life.

"I did everything I could to try and save Mara. In the end…" He shook his head. "I'll regret that for the rest of my life."

Her father had forgiven him. They were even friends now.

She turned away, half a turn, and said nothing. He'd known it wouldn't be that easy. He couldn't simply state his peace and be instantly absolved of the guilt she'd piled on him since the night Mara's heart stopped beating.

Earning her forgiveness wasn't what his focus needed to be right now, anyway.

"You think this is about retaliation for that incident?"

She shrugged one shoulder. "I still don't know if the guy had family or friends who might feel strongly enough about his death to come after me."

"If you give me his name I can have an officer look into it. But I should be getting that information from your boss."

"Good luck with that." She looked at the screen of her phone. "No one has called me back. Or even emailed. Maybe my boss saw my call and ignored it because I'm supposed to be on vacation, not asking about cases."

"And when he knows you're in danger?"

She just shrugged again. He could tell now that she'd injured the other shoulder, though she wasn't obvious about it. Still private. Independent. Intelligent.

She was the kind of woman who would stand by a man's side. Fight *with* him instead of making him fight on her behalf while she did nothing. Or complain when he did what he had to do.

With a team member who didn't know how to switch off, he could see ignoring a single call. But only because repeated calls, with no message or little time in between, meant there was something wrong and Conroy should pick up.

All that could be solved by simply reading an email.

Conroy didn't think much of her boss now, even though he knew it wasn't her intention to give him that impression. "I thought agents were supposed to step up when their colleagues were in danger."

She said nothing.

"You don't need them to keep you safe." He moved in front of her. "I have a whole department. We can find out who is doing this and make sure you're protected."

"Just make sure no one else gets hurt."

He nodded as he edged closer. "I have a vested interest in keeping you from harm."

"Because of Mara?"

"That's part of it." It was also because of his respect for her dad. If she didn't know he was attracted to her, she would in a second.

Conroy touched her hand. He threaded his strong fingers through her slender ones and watched her eyes widen.

He shifted closer. Forced himself to go slow. "I'm also going to make sure you're safe because it's you. Just because it's you, Mia."

Conroy leaned in, planning to press a quick kiss to her lips. A light touch. No demands. No expectations. He couldn't say he would brush her off if she responded, turning it into something more. But he had no intention of giving her more to stress over than she already had working behind those knowing eyes.

His phone buzzed across the kitchen counter.

Conroy tucked his chin and saw her smile as she turned away.

"You should get that." She looked amused. Or maybe even pleased with herself.

He'd shown her his cards, and she had the upper hand now. She knew it. The balance had been tipped in her favor.

His secret was out. He was attracted to her.

Conroy gave her hand a squeeze and went to get his phone. "Barnes." He kept his back to her, knowing she probably needed a minute to herself in order to process the shift he'd just orchestrated. It wasn't a ruse. He wanted her to know his intentions were more than just to do his job. Conroy hadn't met anyone like Mia in…years.

Wilcox didn't sound happy. "We didn't get much from the body, but we've confirmed for sure that it is Tyler Lane, the guy who works for Summers. How is Mia? She okay?"

He turned then, his gaze locking with hers. "She will be."

"Can you look at something for me?"

"Sure." He trailed down the hall and unlocked his office. The keypad was because of his niece and nephew. Precocious kids didn't mix with computers, surplus SWAT gear, and his gun safes—even if the dangerous stuff was locked away.

He left the door open and pulled up his chair to the desk. "What is it?"

While his computer woke, she said, "Some guy named Alvarez called back. He passed Kaylee the information he got from somebody named Allyson…" Her voice trailed off.

"Yep. What is it?"

"A name. And the name of a brother. The guy—Alvarez— also wanted to know if you need help. Apparently, Kaylee said she was sure you'd ask for it if you did."

Conroy chuckled. "Good."

He wouldn't be asking. Alvarez and his wife, Allyson, were both former federal agents. He was a sheriff now and she worked at a bookstore/coffee shop. Not that they wouldn't be useful, but he had a whole department of capable people he worked with every day instead of bringing in a ringer.

She gave him the name, *Thompson Stiles.* "The brother's name is Anthony Stiles. Seems like he's been all over social media, posting about the female ATF agent who murdered his brother."

Conroy said, "It was justified."

He heard an intake of breath behind him and twisted in his seat to see Mia in the doorway. He waved her to sit in the armchair he'd dragged in here when he got the new couch set.

She curled into it, pulled her knees up, and tucked her feet onto the seat. Her face was pale. She looked like it was time to take a nap, which meant he should head to the police station.

He typed the name into his system. "Armed robbery. Resisting arrest. Possession of a weapon and drugs."

"And that's just the brother," Wilcox said. "The one Mia didn't take out is evidently ten times worse."

Conroy read down Thompson Stiles' rap sheet and blew out a breath. Then he went to the brother, Anthony. The one that was here. Coming after Mia.

It was Savannah who said, "Animal cruelty charges that occurred when he was eighteen, finally tried as an adult. Before that there's a hefty, but sealed, juvenile file. Post-eighteen, two counts of attempted rape. He beat one of them into a coma. Criminal stalking. Harassment that put one of his victims in the psych ward."

Conroy blew out a long breath. He'd left her alone at her dad's house to rest, not knowing any of this.

He squeezed the bridge of his nose.

"There's more."

"What?" His voice was thick. Conroy didn't look at Mia, even though he could see her attention on him out the corner of his eye.

"The last woman he psychologically tortured?" Even Savannah's voice sounded like she had to fight back emotion. "She killed herself. Philadelphia PD were investigating. They liked Anthony Stiles as their main suspect for it, but he disappeared. That was two months ago."

Conroy stared at the image on his monitor. Was this the man he'd seen in the parking lot outside the grocery store? Back then, he hadn't known what it meant. Who'd been following her. Why. How big of a threat this guy was, or would turn out to be.

Now he was kicking himself that he'd walked away, more concerned with his own hurt feelings.

He printed out the guy's photo. "Get this image out to everyone."

"Uh…"

"Yes, I mean *everyone*. Got it?"

Wilcox said, "All hands on deck?"

"Yes."

"Wow."

He ignored Wilcox's comment. "Just do it." There was no way he was taking chances with Mia's safety. Not when this town had a core of seriously highly-trained resources he could call when he needed a favor.

He saw Mia frown out the corner of his eye but figured there would be time later. He'd explain about some of the people who lived in this town now. Though, she'd met Tate Hudson. The PI was a character enough, but she probably figured he was an anomaly and not the general rule these days.

"Okay, I'm back to work."

"Don't be there all night," he told her. "I'll come by soon, so leave me something to do. Yeah?"

"Sweet. I'm not gonna turn down an offer like that." Wilcox hung up before he could change his mind.

Conroy set the phone beside his computer.

"You guys seem friendly."

He said, "She's a good woman and an excellent detective."

"There's what, a few years between you?"

He shrugged. "She's mid-thirties."

"Have you ever..?"

"Goodness, no. She and I wouldn't last a minute before we drove each other crazy. It isn't a disaster at work only because I can tell her what to do, and she knows it." He leaned back in his chair and stretched.

"So you've never...with anyone you work with?"

"Never." He decided to give her the truth, hoping she would do the same. "I haven't really had much in the way of a relationship since Mara. It hit me hard. Only maybe two women have caught my eye up until now. Didn't really go anywhere though. There aren't many who understand the life we lead."

She nodded. "I always thought that would be an asset." Her head dipped to the side, and she gave a long exhale. "That two cops could make something work."

Conroy was smart enough in his field to read behind the lines, and he could tell there was plenty Mia wasn't saying.

Her lashes lowered. She'd taken her medicine. She had food in her stomach. She was safe, and the day was catching up with her.

"You were involved with someone in your department once?" Conroy guessed. "Tell me what happened."

She sighed again, and her eyes drifted closed. "Not quite involved. I thought there was something there, but I was stupid to have thought that. He thought it was a joke that I would think he would ever be attracted to someone like me." She paused a second. He almost thought she wouldn't say more. "I guess I wasn't his type." She smiled ruefully, eyes still closed.

Conroy frowned. His smartwatch buzzed. He glanced at it and sighed. Time to head to work.

Leaving her alone again, while he tried to find this Stiles guy. He didn't want to just leave Mia right as she was opening up to him, but he couldn't keep his officers waiting and she'd fallen asleep.

Conroy made a call so she wouldn't be alone. Then he set up his security system. He couldn't take any chances with Mia's safety. Not with a man like Anthony Stiles after her.

# 14

Mia's entire body tensed. She blinked, still sitting on the ratty armchair in Conroy's command center, which he probably called an office. The chair smelled like pretzels.

Her arm hurt. And her shoulder. Her knee. She pushed out a breath, not entirely ready to stand up yet. That was only going to hurt more. Even if it was the fastest route to more meds.

He was gone. A lamp by the desk had been switched on, casting a white glow across the room. Mia had no idea what time it was, and had no recollection of what they'd been talking about. Where had Conroy gone?

Then she remembered. He'd kissed her. Conroy had told her he would keep her safe because of her. Just because of her. Then he'd leaned in.

She let her eyes drift shut and pictured his face in her mind. The look in his eyes when he leaned in and gave her the lightest of lip touches had been like nothing else. A kiss. And yet, what a kiss could be was so much more. Or so she'd heard.

Mia's relationship history was abysmal. Now Conroy had come along, and everything he did showed he cared about her. Maybe even *liked* her. Enough to kiss her and tell her he would protect her. Just because it was her.

She hardly knew what that meant, and yet her brain was happy to invent all kinds of reasons. Maybe she'd read too many sweet romances. Her dark secret. One she'd deny to her grave if anyone ever found out. Mia loved...love. Only problem was, she tried to actually be realistic in life. Now everything in her wanted to leap for joy at the idea that a handsome, strong man was attracted to her. Her. Just when she'd given up on the notion that anyone would ever find her attractive.

A man who was everything she thought a cop should be. And nothing like the guys she worked with—definitely nothing like the one she thought she'd have a chance with.

Mia tried not to think of her sister, but the truth was that when Mara fell for him, Mia had been right there. She'd known exactly why he was worth falling for. Now? The man was even more potent. She'd been trying to separate her feelings. Stay professional. He made it hard to do that.

If he wanted to "protect" her because he was attracted to her? Well, that was fine because Mia had always liked him. More than like. She'd had the biggest crush on him back when she was a teen, watching him treat Mara like she was the loveliest thing he'd ever come across. She'd seen how they'd looked at each other. That became the standard by which Mia had measured every guy. Probably not fair to the unsuspecting men she met, but she'd also never settled for less than what she wanted. Which was why she wasn't locked in a loveless marriage by now.

The door was now open. Did Conroy really want to step through it? She could hardly believe she might be the woman he made so lucky. How he had remained unmarried all these years was a mystery in itself.

Mia figured there was no point delaying the inevitable. Plus, she wanted to see where Conroy was. She hauled herself up from the chair, hissing out a breath as she did.

On the computer keyboard was a sticky note that had been

scrawled on with what looked like a man's handwriting—no cute loops, no hearts dotting the i's, no pink gel pen.

AT THE OFFICE. WILL CALL.

It was signed simply, "C." But just the sight of it made her heart flutter. Then she rolled her eyes. Heart flutters, really? She needed to figure this out, or she was going to wind up in some kind of romantic delusion.

Considering there was a man who appeared to be trying to get revenge on her, she didn't figure being distracted by her attraction to Conroy would help. Right now she needed to stay safe. Wait for whatever he came at her with next so she could be prepared.

The computer chimed.

Right after, the screen illuminated. A map loaded, along with a red, flashing dot. She recognized the area. Her dad often hunted up there.

Mia hovered the mouse over the red dot. A string of numbers appeared in a tiny window. Her dad's phone number.

This was her dad's GPS location?

She took a step back. Strode to the kitchen, tugged the meds from her purse, and got a glass of water. She downed the whole thing along with the pain pill.

Her dad's GPS. It could mean nothing, except that Conroy was keeping tabs on him. He knew where her father was. Presumably her dad knew this, and maybe he'd even asked Conroy to have the information. After all, every year during hunting season, people went missing. If her dad was out there alone then there was every reason to be worried and give someone information as to where he was. It was just a safety thing.

No reason to think much of it. Except that it was her father, and it was Conroy. Two men who should have been at odds over what had happened to Rich's daughter, who, at the time, supposedly had been under her boyfriend's protection. Conroy should have looked after Mara but he hadn't, and now she was dead. And now, not only was Mia having sweet, romantic delusions about Conroy, he and her father were "friends." They were a part of each other's lives.

Mia reached for her cell phone. Was he tracking her too? That could be how he'd found her when she'd been walking down that path. He'd pulled up beside her and acted like he stumbled across her randomly. It wasn't like she and her father were on the same phone plan, but maybe he'd known where she was all along.

A shiver rolled through her. She needed food or her stomach would have issues with the medicine.

*Just because it's you, Mia.*

She'd asked him, straight out, if all this was because of her sister. He'd kissed her. But now that she knew he had her dad's GPS location, and he might have hers as well, things felt different. Conroy had a bent to protect her family. An imperative, born out of the fact he'd failed once before. Now he was keeping her dad safe. He was keeping her safe.

He probably figured he owed her family after what he'd done. Or not done.

And if she fell for him for real, that would keep her closer. It would reduce the likelihood she might take off. He probably figured if feelings were involved, then she would stick with him. Trust him.

She didn't want to forgive him if he was only playing her. Pretending he liked her so he could do his job more easily than he would be able to otherwise.

Anthony Stiles was out there, looking for revenge for Thompson's death. Meanwhile, Conroy intended to be the one who stood between her and Anthony's next attempt.

If he wanted her to forgive him for Mara's death, then saving her life was poetic almost. The perfect scenario for her to come to the realization that he was *such a good guy* after all. Not someone she should hate, but someone she should trust and forgive.

Life had taught her more than just what she'd learned from losing her sister.

Mia had lived more years since then. She'd worked. She'd allowed her emotions to sweep her up. She'd been torn down.

A car explosion. A dog bite.

The dead guy could be completely unrelated, except for the gunshot to his abdomen, but the other two things? The cynic in her wanted to see it as Conroy trying to force her to trust him. Taking the opportunity to prove to her that he was "good" by manufacturing scenarios where he saved her life. A true knight in shining armor to a single woman recovering from a serious situation. She could have died, and she had been injured. Alone. Fighting for her life. Now Conroy was here. Strong, and determined to protect her.

Maybe, like the teammate she'd fallen for, it was all a scam. Conroy could be staging things so he was the one who was there to protect her. The person who just happened to be *right there*, exactly when she needed saving.

Sure, it was seriously cynical to think Conroy was behind the explosion. Or the dog being poisoned. She didn't really believe it. But she couldn't help the fact she'd thought of it, and now that she had, her brain wouldn't let the idea go.

She'd been tossed aside too many times. Manipulated, and then laughed at.

There was no way Mia would allow anyone else to do that to her.

Not again.

She walked to the patio door and looked out over the valley behind his house. The scenery was amazing, but the beauty of it didn't take away the sour taste in her mouth.

She called her father, considering he had a cell signal right now. Conroy's computer wouldn't show his GPS signal unless his cell was in range of a tower.

"Yeah."

"Dad." Her voice broke. She sounded choked up. "How's hunting?"

"That really why you called?"

"No."

They were honest with each other. Probably too honest sometimes. But Mara was gone, and Meena never told the truth about anything. Her younger sister had played them both. All of it, Mia's education of a cynic.

"So say it."

"Conroy thinks someone is after me." She told him about his car exploding, and the dog bite. Followed by the intruder. "One of Ed Summers's men was murdered. Maybe it's connected, maybe not. But I saw a guy running away from the scene."

Anthony Stiles.

"He keeping you safe?"

She watched a rabbit hop at the end of what should be Conroy's yard but was just an expanse of grass. "Why does Conroy have to do it? I can take care of myself."

He said, "I know you can." Like she was a hormonal teenager he was trying to placate.

"I was doing just fine, Dad."

"Is that true?"

She pressed her lips together. "When will you be back?"

"When I'm back."

She pushed out a breath.

"Thought you didn't need anyone."

"Conroy moved me into his house." She waited. "No opinion about that?" She wasn't going to tell him about the kiss. "He killed Mara."

She heard her dad's sigh blow across the microphone. "If he wants to help, maybe you should let him."

"After what he did to us?"

"You're all fired up to protect yourself, but it's okay to lean on other people."

"I'd be leaning on you, but you're not here," she pointed out.

"Because you can take care of yourself, remember? Also when you're in pain, you're no fun to be around."

"Reminds me of someone else I know." She turned back to the kitchen, considering she still needed to eat something. "Remember when you broke your ankle?"

"Don't remind me."

He'd been a bear. Uncomfortable. Calling every day to complain, even though the older church ladies let themselves in his front door twice a day, bringing food. Taking care of him until he was sick of it, griping about how he couldn't get a second alone. But he didn't ask her to fly there and take care of him herself. He'd just wanted to be miserable because he hurt.

Was that what she was doing?

Mia pulled open the refrigerator, chuckling about those church ladies. Most of them single and searching. Then she saw the contents. "All he has is liquid egg whites, every green vegetable you can imagine, and heavy whipping cream. Who eats like this?"

Her dad chuckled. "I'll text you the number for the pizza place in town. They deliver."

"Tha—"

Two arms banded around her. One squeezed across her diaphragm and cut off the air in her lungs. The other snaked across her shoulder, and a hand covered her mouth.

A male body. Every instinct in her fired, and she knew only one thing. Get away. Run.

Mia tried to breathe but could only choke. He swung her around, and she saw the open patio door. She hadn't even heard it slide open, too distracted by her conversation with her dad.

Hot breath puffed over her ear. "Now you pay."

Her phone fell to the floor, and she heard it shatter.

## 15

"You like her." The old man's eyes glinted in the lamplight, shimmering with the edge of pain. Constant pain. His voice was barely audible.

Conroy leaned forward, his full attention on the chief. "Yeah, I do."

The nurse had told him when he got to the office that the chief didn't have much longer. He'd ordered Jess home so she could get some sleep.

The old man shot him a knowing look. "It wasn't good. Your relationship with the sister, and all that had happened. Was it?"

Conroy didn't especially want to talk about Mara. She was coming up a lot lately considering how hard he'd worked to put her and what had happened behind him. To leave it in the past.

"Drives you."

Conroy said, "You should rest. Try to get some sleep."

The old man chuckled.

Conroy didn't need to be told what he already knew. Namely, that the tragedy between him and Mara *did* drive him and his need to prove himself. He just said, "Alan."

"Don't chide me, son."

"That's not my intention. You're the chief. I'm not sure I could ever see you as anything else." He'd been someone Conroy respected before he ever even thought about putting the badge on. Becoming a cop was another thing that drove Conroy. Since the night Mara died.

Alan Ridgeman had been a Lieutenant back then. He'd shown up to the scene first and stayed to the end. His work as a cop at the accident was what made Conroy want to do this job. Follow in his footsteps.

"I'm tired."

"I know." Conroy knew what the old man *wasn't* saying, as well.

"Take care of Jessie."

Officer Ridgeman would likely object to being taken care of, despite the fact she was one of his youngest officers. Still, Conroy nodded.

"Find happy." The chief's eyes closed. "Convince her."

Conroy squeezed the old man's hand. He had to stand up so he could dig his cell from the pocket of his dark blue jeans. Rich was calling?

Conroy said, "Barnes."

"We were on the phone." Mia's father sounded flustered. It definitely wasn't the normal, relaxed-but-exhausted demeanor he was used to hearing while talking with Rich after ten days of hunting.

"What?"

"Mia. We were talking, and then she dropped the phone or something. I heard her cry out."

Conroy let himself out of the chief's office. "Are you sure?"

"Boy, would I—"

"Okay, okay, dumb question. Sorry." He squeezed the bridge of his nose. "I have a friend in the neighborhood. And I'll call someone to stay with the chief and get home. See what I can see."

"Make it fast. He said she would pay. If someone took her…" Rich's voice trailed off.

Conroy knew what he wasn't saying. He'd been at plenty of major crimes, always after the fact. He just couldn't imagine it from Rich's perspective. Hearing his daughter's voice.

He quickly told Bill, the dispatcher in the corner office, what was happening. The other officer in the building nodded when Conroy asked him to sit with the chief. Then Conroy told Rich. "Hudson is outside the house."

"Good. Now tell me what is going on."

"I will," Conroy said. "After I locate Mia and ascertain her situation." He winced as he hung up on her father, but there was nothing else he could do. Right now Conroy had to be the police lieutenant and not a friend of the victim's father. Later he could tell Rich all about the Stiles brothers, and what they thought was going on.

He grabbed his keys and made a phone call on the way out the front door.

"Hudson." Tate Hudson, local PI and former FBI.

"Where is she?" Conroy climbed into his truck and fired up the engine. It was after midnight. He hadn't been gone but a few hours. A little work while Mia took a nap in his chair. He'd planned to return in the morning with coffee and breakfast. Now that idea was out the window.

He'd dearly wanted to try for another kiss. Maybe a longer one this time.

After they talked it over, of course.

Tate Hudson, local PI, had the radio blasting in his ancient beater. The car he swore up and down did better on icy roads than any new vehicle. "Headed west on Francesca."

"You wanna tell me how this happened?"

"Apart from your WiFi sucks?" Hudson had a tone. Then again, unless he was talking to a pretty woman, he *always* had a tone. And a scowl on his face. "Feeds cut out. Then she was on the phone in the kitchen."

"Her dad heard the whole thing. He's sure she was taken."

Conroy assumed as much at least, even though the last thing he wanted to think about was her being hurt. Or killed. "He hauled her out. I caught up to him loading her into the back of his tank."

"Tank?"

"One of those three-row monstrosities."

"An SUV."

"I guess," Hudson said.

"And you didn't stop him?"

"I'll tell you why if you quit asking me dumb questions."

Conroy pressed his lips together. He drove through town, headed toward Francesca Drive which ran all the way out to the edge of his jurisdiction. He had time, but not enough to inspire prayer that Anthony Stiles didn't get her out of his area. He'd have to use his time in pursuit to call state police and the county sheriff.

What a nightmare that would be.

"I was too far away to intervene, so I followed. Been behind them since he left your yuppie village."

"Great. You get a look at his face?"

"Your guy....Tony Whatever?"

"Anthony Stiles."

"Yeah, him."

"Was it him?"

"Dunno," Tate said. "Never saw his face. He had his back to me."

Normally it didn't take much for Hudson to want justice. He'd go after the punk who bumped into a kid at an ice cream store and force him to pay for the scoop that wound up on the floor. He was a pain in Conroy's behind, but he was a man you kept on your side because he came through when it counted. And that was the point.

"I'm really glad I'm not paying you for this."

Tate said, "What's that?"

Conroy sighed. "So you're following him?"

Tate gave him the location, headed out of town. Close to the library and the community gym. Time was ticking too fast.

Conroy pressed his foot to the floor. He didn't care who got woken up by his lights or the siren he had running. Mia's life was in danger. He couldn't lose another Tathers sister. "Stay with him."

"He clocks me, it's over," Tate said. "I'm keeping my distance."

"Don't lose her."

"I know what I'm doing."

"I know." Conroy gripped the wheel and listened to Tate sigh through the car's stereo speakers.

"I'm on it."

Conroy didn't point out that the man was supposed to have been "on it" this whole time. Enough she didn't get taken in the first place. Maybe he'd been retired for too long. Gone from whatever his former job had been. The man was past forty-five, so perhaps he just didn't have that edge anymore.

"I can hear your disapproval through the phone."

"Did I say anything?"

"Hey," Tate said. "I'm the one who told you she wanted to talk to her sister. Gave you an in, right?"

"Sure, then my car exploded and Mia got bitten by a dog. I've got a dead man in my morgue and Savannah has *another* open case. You gonna let Mia suffer through a kidnapping now?"

"Of course not." Tate pretty much shouted it through the phone line.

"Good."

"That was some pep talk."

Conroy said, "I just turned onto Francesca."

"He slowed. Cross street is Arrowhead."

"Copy that." Conroy was still two miles behind. It wouldn't

take him long to get there with the full weight of his position behind him.

If he ever *couldn't* leverage everything about who he was and what he did for a living to protect those he cared about? Conroy didn't even know how he'd deal with that. Tate was a whole lot more…renegade was the only way he could think to describe it. The guy was loose, played loose, but still cared. And it couldn't be denied he took the time to get answers no one else could. Conroy didn't work the same way, and never would, but respected Tate Hudson all the same.

"Hold up."

"What is it?" Conroy didn't lift the pressure of his foot pressing the gas pedal to the floor. He tore down the street past cars that had pulled over in a line because of the sirens. A semi up ahead. Had the guy seen him?

"Two cars. They were behind me, but now they're pressing ahead."

"Who?"

"No idea." Tate paused. "One of them sped around him. He hit his brakes."

Conroy felt sick. He wanted to take a moment and deposit his lunch on the passenger side floor mat. He didn't want to clean that up, though. He rolled the window down enough for the crisp night air to blow on his face and then sucked in a few, clean breaths.

Better.

"What's happening?"

"I had to slow," Tate said. "They forced him to slow down. One in front and one behind. They boxed him in to a stop. Three guys got out."

"Summers?"

"I didn't see him. If I don't get out of here, they're going to know I was following him. I'll have to—"

There was a shuffle, then someone said, "Get outta here."

"Sure, man." That was Tate. "Whatever." After a moment of quiet, Tate said, "He's gone."

"Recognize him?"

"No. I'm turning the car around. I'll double back on foot."

"Make it fast."

"You coming in hot?" Tate asked. "Might spook them."

As opposed to being low key, and allowing Mia to get taken from his house?

Conroy bit back what he actually wanted to say and asked Tate where he'd leave the car. When Tate told him, he said, "I'll meet you there in thirty seconds."

He took a couple of side streets and came at it from the opposite direction. He cut lights and sirens a ways away, so they wouldn't hear. Got out. Pocketed his keys. Pulled his gun.

Tate was at the end of the alley. He spotted Conroy and lifted his chin, his face lined with experience and a wild youth. "They're getting her out."

Conroy peered around him and saw Mia upright. Stumbling. She touched the side of her head.

"Easy." Tate tugged on his shoulder.

Conroy shoved back, pressed Tate against the wall and got in his face. "Easy? You let her get kidnapped. The only reason I'm not about to shoot you is she's not with the psycho right now."

"What psycho?"

Like there was time to explain that?

"I'm on point." Conroy moved out.

He used a car for cover while he figured out what on earth was going on now. Two men held guns on the driver of the car. The third hauled Mia by her arm, away from the psycho's vehicle and into their own.

"Police! Hands up!"

She wasn't getting in that car.

Two men spun. Both fired at him. Conroy dove for cover.

The driver, who he assumed was Anthony Stiles, though he couldn't see the man, never got out of his car. He hit the gas and sped away, sideswiped one of the cars, and fled up the street.

The men who had Mia kept firing. Tate grunted and landed on the ground beside him. Then he rolled away, came up, and fired twice. Conroy set his arms on the hood of the car and squeezed off two shots.

Mia was shoved into a vehicle. He heard her squeal, or scream, but it got muffled. All he knew was that she was farther away from him than he wanted, and the chance he would get her back from these guys grew slimmer with every second.

He tagged one of the guys with a bullet. Just a graze. The buddy dragged him up, and they stumbled into the car.

Conroy ran out from behind the vehicle he was using for cover and raced after it. License plate. He started from the last digit. Maybe Tate got the first few.

He pulled his phone and called in the kidnapping. But not kidnapped by the guy they were after, that was a different car. He had to explain it twice before the dispatcher got what he was saying.

Tate didn't come out.

"Hudson!"

"Yeah." His voice sounded strained.

Oh no.

Conroy found him behind the car on his back. "You okay?"

Tate unzipped his jacket, wincing. A vest covered his T-shirt. In the center was a bullet, embedded in the protective material. He pushed out a breath, then inhaled.

"Ouch."

"Yeah," Tate said around gritted teeth. "You should call Wilcox. I might need mouth-to-mouth."

"Call her yourself. It won't be good with you this far off your game."

Anyway, Conroy had a woman of his own to find.

# 16

M ia shifted on the hard, bare floor and stared at the blank wall across the room. She didn't want to see a correlation between this room and her life, but it stared her in the face anyway.

Her head still pounded from the gunshots, and it had been hours since she'd been hauled away. But she knew what she'd seen. Tate had been shot.

Mia saw him go down.

Conroy had been there, too. She wanted to pray that both of them were all right. No, she shouldn't just "want" to do it. Mia refused to be so stubborn she couldn't give them that one small bit of grace. Things might be bad right now. Really bad. But they could be a whole lot worse for Conroy and Tate.

*God, help them. They really need you right now.*

Even if they were fine, she still figured they needed His help to find her. Assuming they were looking. Maybe they weren't. They probably had no idea what was even happening. She'd had hours to figure it out and could still barely make sense of it. Anthony Stiles? Maybe. But she couldn't see who'd been driving the car because she'd been forced into the trunk. And if Stiles had been driving, would he have been so compliant to lose her to a second set of kidnappers? She didn't think so.

If there was one thing she was sure of, though, it hadn't been Stiles who took her from Conroy's house. It had been someone else. But that didn't mean he didn't have a guy there to do his dirty work for him. Could be this wasn't related to Anthony Stiles at all, but that theory was becoming less and less plausible as time went on.

Mia stared at the empty room and tried to figure out how she was going to get out of here. That might be an easier problem to solve.

They'd locked the door after unceremoniously shoving her in so hard she fell. Probably should have tied her up. Then again, her arm didn't feel good at all.

She held it against her front and stood, walking on shaky legs to look out the window.

Morning had risen, the sun muted behind gray clouds over the fresh layer of snow. She was in a neighborhood. The back yard of this one-story house was small. Overgrown dead grass, and pallets stacked to make a fire. A tree that probably needed cutting down.

Mia touched the heating vent on the floor. Stone cold.

She shivered, moving around the room for warmth. She stomped her feet to try and get her blood flowing. She needed to be warm. She also needed a pain pill. She'd probably missed two doses now and things were getting real. No more inducing sleep by disguising her pain with medicine.

Instead, she'd sat in the corner all night and stared at the dark while she wondered where Conroy was.

A door slammed across the house. Mia spun around but no one came in. She hissed out a breath and leaned back against the wall. Her legs wouldn't hold her up much longer, but she intended to meet this new threat standing up.

Voices on the other side of the door. A man, and then a woman.

The door was unlocked and she stepped inside.

"Meena."

Her sister wore expensive jeans and high-heeled boots. A blue chambray shirt that draped on her under a black leather jacket with silver zippers and buckles. Her hair was a huge mass of dark curls that hung over her shoulders. Her makeup was way too heavy, designed to make a statement.

She set her hand on her hip. "You're really back."

"This was all you?" Mia asked. "A delightful one-night stay in these five-star accommodations?"

Her sister's makeup seemed to sparkle, but in a way that hid the slight droop in the skin beneath her eyes. Too light, the corners that should be shadowed beside her nose. She didn't smile. Her face seemed to be set in a permanent scowl, giving her lines between her thick brows that she probably hated.

She looked older than Mia, despite the fact she was three years younger.

Meena rolled her eyes. That was something Mia remembered. The familiarity of it rushed back like the smell of store-bought muffins on Christmas morning. There had been a couple of years where the roll of eyes was almost constant. Which made Mia force herself not to do it at fifteen, even when she'd wanted to. Apparently, despite appearances, her sister hadn't changed all that much.

"I wanted to talk to you," Meena said. "And you should be thanking me, since I probably saved you from that guy everyone's looking for. Who is he, anyway?"

"Anthony Stiles? He wasn't there." Mia said it as a statement, hoping to get Meena to give up what she knew.

She shot Mia a look, like that statement was so dumb it was obvious. "Who is he?"

Mia tried to look like this was no big deal. Everything was fine. No pain. No fuss. "I killed his brother."

Meena's thick eyebrows rose. "Didn't know you had that in you. I'm almost proud of you."

Mia said nothing.

"Word on the street is he's asking about you. No one knows anything, since you don't live here. And they wouldn't give up anything about a townie anyway, even if they did." Meena's lips curled up. "Hiding at Conroy's was a nice touch."

Mia really didn't want to get dragged into a conversation about Conroy. She wanted to talk to Meena about what *Meena* was doing—the reason she'd asked Tate Hudson to find her in the first place.

"Guess it didn't keep that Stiles guy from finding you, though. Even with Conroy's security system." Meena shrugged one shoulder. "Wonder why it wasn't working?"

Mia bit the inside of her lip. She hadn't been hung out as bait just so Stiles would go after her again. She knew that, because it hadn't worked. If she'd been a key player in the trap to catch him, then that trap would have been sprung a whole lot earlier. Anthony Stiles would have been caught. Multiple cops, lights and sirens. Roadblocks. The whole deal.

He'd have been tossed and cuffed and thrown in jail.

Instead, it hadn't been him at all. And the driver had gotten away because Meena sent men to retrieve her from Anthony Stiles' clutches.

"Is Tate Hudson okay?"

Meena said, "How would I know?"

Because he'd been shot?

"Maybe you could answer a different question." Since she had her sister here, she might as well ask what she wanted to ask. She might not get another chance.

Meena shrugged.

"What are you doing with Ed Summers?"

"Wow, judgy much?" Meena made a nonchalant face Mia didn't all the way believe.

Mia shifted her weight, trying not to look like she was in as much pain as she actually was.

Meena seemed to be waiting for her to say something. After a minute of quiet, Meena said, "We have an arrangement."

Mia wasn't sure that was true. "He killed Mara."

Eye roll. "In a car accident."

"He was drunk." The result had been a tragedy that tore wide the rift that had already existed in their family.

"You're still hung up on that?"

Mia said, "I can't believe you'd associate with a man like him."

"Gotta make money somehow."

"So you'll sell your soul for a dollar to the man who killed your sister."

"You haven't been here," Meena argued. "You have no idea what it's like trying to make it in this town." She pulled out her phone and swore. "Speak of the devil." She typed at a furious pace with her thumbs. "Geez, he's pissed. Ed is on a rampage." She looked up at Mia. "Like I was gonna let that guy turn you over to Stiles so he could do whatever to you?"

Okay, so there was a lot there. "He was going to hand me over?"

"Uh...duh." She typed furiously with her thumbs. "Why do you think I saved you?"

Was Mia supposed to say, 'thank you'? She wasn't sure what Meena expected. "Great. You got me away from him. Now I'm leaving."

Mia crossed the room and pulled the door open. A huge guy in a denim shirt and heavy brown jacket stood there. He had no hair on his head, but two eyebrow piercings and what looked like a tattoo on his neck that disappeared below his collar. A spider web, if she wasn't mistaken.

Meena said, "Not so fast."

Mia turned back to her sister. "What?"

"You don't just leave. That's not how this works."

"No?"

Eye roll.

"There's no reason to keep me here. It's been long enough, but eventually you'll need to realize that I'm a federal agent. Kidnapping me and detaining me against my will isn't going to go well for you."

"There's the big sister I remember. Up in my face, thinking she knows everything."

"If you want to do federal time, that's up to you." Mia shrugged. Her sister wasn't the only one who could act nonchalant. Whatever game this was, there were two players here. Not counting the brute in the hall. The one who'd *shut the door* again, leaving Meena and Mia alone. Was he guarding the door?

"If you're such a hot commodity—" Meena waved at Mia and smirked. "—then where's the cavalry, huh? I don't see no team of ATF heroes here to save you."

"They're not going to get in the middle of a family squabble."

Meena's phone screen flashed, but she didn't look at it. Didn't want to be told off again? Perhaps things with Ed Summers weren't as "arranged" as she'd thought.

"Do you really want to be with Ed Summers?"

"Trying to rescue me?" Meena smirked. "I never needed saving, and I don't need it now. I run my life. I make my own choices. Not no one tells me what to do."

Mia wondered if that was true.

Meena looked at her phone and blanched. "He told Conroy where we are. Guess the cavalry is coming, after all." She strode to the door and pulled it open, so she could tell the big guy, "Head out. I'll catch up."

"Sure?" The one word was a rumble, so low it was almost not even audible.

Meena huffed, "Just go when I tell you to." She looked like she wanted to stomp her foot. Throw a tantrum like a recalcitrant child.

She threw the door shut again and turned back to Mia. "We

won't have much time. Conroy is going to stroll in here and try to get me to hand you over."

"You could go with your guy. I'll wait for Conroy."

Mia was beyond tired. She figured even if she had the strength to combat her sister, the woman likely wasn't averse to fighting dirty. Mia didn't want any more injuries.

"And miss seeing the lieutenant?" She waved off the suggestion. "I missed him at the house. I'm not missing the chance to see it for myself now."

"See what?"

One of Meena's eyebrows rose, like it had a life of its own. "What everyone in town is talking about. Obviously." When she realized Mia had no idea, she said, "The way he's looking at you. Letting everyone else cover for him while he drives you around, and then he personally parks you in his house so you can be safe." She smirked. "Not that it actually worked, of course—"

The door opened. Conroy stood there, a thunderous look on his face.

"That's it!" Meena laughed, but there didn't seem to be any humor in the sound. "It is true."

"Ed is outside."

Meena blanched. She swung around to Mia. "Nice to see ya." Then she squeezed between Conroy and the door frame.

"You okay?"

Mia tried to speak. No words came out. She just shook her head.

He lifted an arm and held his hand out to her. "Let's go."

She wanted to be mad. She should ask how Tate was, and accuse Conroy of orchestrating this. She wanted to cry over her sister, over the fact the first kidnapper thankfully hadn't taken her to Anthony Stiles so he could do whatever he'd been planning.

Mia walked to him. Right to him. She wound her arms

around his waist, over his shirt but inside his jacket. Her fingers glanced off his gun.

She felt him tense, but ignored it.

They weren't two cops right now. Just two people who were looking out for each other, whose lives intersected. It wasn't even about that attraction between them.

She stuck her face in the warm skin of his neck and held on while her body shuddered. Conroy's chest rumbled under her cheek. His arms wound around her and he held her close, but not too tight.

This had been her sister's intervention. Meena, figuring she was doing Mia a favor.

He had come for her.

The only one who had come to get her when she'd been taken by some guy, like an errand for Stiles.

No, she didn't trust Conroy.

But she also didn't have anyone else.

---

## 17

"That's all she said?" Wilcox asked the question, sitting on the edge of Mia's hospital bed while Conroy leaned against the wall.

He figured being silent and allowing his detective to take Mia's statement would give him the chance to calm down. He'd been steaming all night and most of the day. It wouldn't take much to set him off. Then he'd be in his car, headed to Summers's house where he would dearly enjoy tearing the man a new one. What that would even look like didn't matter, he just wanted to pummel somebody.

Mia looked at him. She had more pink in her cheeks than she'd had when he got to her at the house. Her sister had held her captive most of the night, and afterwards she'd slept all morning. The doctor had given her something that knocked her out. Apparently sleep and medicine had done her good.

"Just that," Mia said, "and she wondered why Conroy's apparently notable security system hadn't worked."

"It was active." Yet another thing he was mad about. "For some reason, it didn't notify me when the door was breached and left open. Someone had to have known."

He knew his tone was cold and hard. He was furious

someone had messed with it. That *had* to be what happened. Only, who could have done it? An obvious choice was that Anthony Stiles had gotten to someone in town. Paid them, forced them, or convinced them to allow the breach so he could get inside.

So he could get to Mia.

"It wasn't Stiles who took me, but it could've been one of his guys." She told them about another man. "They knew him. Meena's boys, they knew who he was."

Her sister had known she would be taken. Meena had intervened, faster than Conroy, which seemed to have been against Ed's wishes.

He gritted his teeth while Wilcox reassured her they would figure it out.

One of Meena's people had known what Anthony Stiles was planning. Or they'd been watching the house. Conroy and his detectives had a lot of people to question in order to get to the bottom of this. Someone had opened the proverbial door and allowed a dangerous man into Conroy's house.

And he was going to find out who that was.

Except, that wouldn't give him a location on Stiles himself. Unless the person had an ongoing relationship with him. A way to find him, or contact him. Conroy didn't want to pin everything on hope, but sometimes that was all he had to go on.

Without hard evidence, what else did he have?

Not much, except an investigation to run.

"Knock, knock." Tate pulled the curtain back, exposing them to the buzz of activity on the hospital's second floor. He saw Conroy and hesitated.

Conroy said nothing. He didn't move, just tried to tamp down the anger he felt that Mia had been taken and Tate had been slow to do anything to stop it.

"Hey." Mia lifted her hand. Tate came over and shook it. She said, "Heard you took a hit."

"Not even a scratch." He laughed it off, but wound up sounding nervous.

Conroy watched as Tate charmed her. Mia accepted Tate's attempt even though she'd been essentially glaring at Conroy since she woke up. And after that hug? Maybe she'd forgotten about it. Conroy figured he wouldn't forget for the rest of his life. She'd been scared. Exhausted, and in pain. Not to mention grieving over her sister and the choices Meena had made. Choices she was still making.

On the surface Meena seemed put together. Flashy clothes. A convertible she whipped around in. But underneath it all there was a much different story. When Conroy looked at Meena Tathers, he saw a scared girl in over her head.

She put on a good front, though.

Mia had likely seen through the façade as well. She'd been trained. She was a fed who worked cases involving all kinds of criminals and was accustomed to not getting the truth. He wondered if those instincts and skills extended to her sister.

Or if they would extend to Tate.

Conroy didn't want to believe the private investigator had sold him out. But who else knew where Mia had been, and how to get to her through his system?

Tate took a step back. "I'm outta here. They're letting me go."

"Is that true?"

Conroy nearly smiled. Maybe Mia saw through *everyone*.

Wilcox shot him a glance. Conroy motioned to the door. She hopped off the bed. "I should head out too. You need a ride home, Hudson?"

Conroy figured she referred to him by his surname to keep the distance between them. To try and convince herself that he was just a colleague.

Tate said, "I was gonna call a cab, but sure."

They trailed out, leaving him alone with Mia. She said, "They like each other, right?"

"I try not to get into that stuff with my subordinates. But, yeah. I think so."

"He's older than her?"

Conroy nodded, pushed off the wall and came to the end of the bed. "He's late forties. She's nearly ten years younger."

"But you're the boss?"

"She's new to town. And you know seniority isn't about age."

He hoped Wilcox could do her job, instead of getting distracted by whatever feelings she might have for Tate. Then maybe he would get an answer as to whether Tate Hudson let a person of interest in his house so that Mia could be taken.

Kidnapped.

Killed.

Better that Wilcox conduct that interview. If Conroy did it, he'd wind up having to explain why Tate looked like he'd had the snot beaten out of him.

Mia said, "A detective and a private investigator." She even smiled a little. "That sounds like it might be interesting."

"As interesting as a police lieutenant and an ATF Special Agent?"

Something crossed her face.

"What?"

She started to shake her head, but stopped herself. "I had a few hours to think, locked in that room. Waiting for Meena. Though I didn't know that at the time."

"Did she hurt you? Or did any of her guys?"

She shook her head.

Conroy had asked the question already. But it beat asking her how she felt yet again. If she was all right.

"Good." He settled on the edge of the bed, kind of like how Wilcox had. Non-threatening. Easy. He wondered if anything in her life had ever been easy. He knew nothing had been for him. "Tell me what you thought about."

The look on her face made him think she appreciated that he wanted to know. Good.

She said, "About my job, mostly. And my life."

"Come to any conclusions?"

"I don't know. More just musing on being here, in Last Chance County, versus being in Seattle. Or anywhere else, if I'm on the road working." She shrugged one shoulder. Her bandaged arm had a sling now. "My dad's house, versus my apartment, and which one feels more like home."

Then there was his house, which she'd been kidnapped from. He didn't figure she would want to go back there any more than she would want to go back to Rich's lake house where she'd encountered a middle-of-the-night intruder.

Maybe he should call the hotel. Get her a room no one knew about so she could be safe while he hit the streets. Find Anthony Stiles himself.

The possible sightings kept coming across the wires from his people, but no one had actually been able to nail down a location on Stiles.

Yet.

He was out there. Making plans. Waiting to strike.

Conroy much preferred criminals who moved too fast and made mistakes. The patient, crafty ones scared the everloving crap out of him.

"I was probably just overly tired. Having an identity crisis." Her eyes glinted and she said, "I probably need to take an extra month of vacation and 'find myself'."

"I'll give you a clue." Conroy leaned in like it was a secret. "You're right here."

Mia chuckled like she had a secret of her own.

Things were just about to get interesting when his phone decided to ring in his pocket. He looked at his smartwatch and saw the caller ID. "It's your dad."

Mia shook her head, eyes wide as though she had been caught doing something wrong.

"Don't want to talk to him?" He swiped the screen with a smile on his face. "Barnes."

"Wanna tell me why I'm standing in my living room and my daughter, who *you* said you'd found, *isn't* here?"

"You're at your house?"

Mia frowned. Conroy knew how she felt.

"Of course I'm at my house. She got kidnapped while she was on the phone with me. You think I wouldn't drive home after that? You said you had her."

Her eyebrows rose.

Conroy figured she could hear her dad yelling. His ear was getting blistered. "She was admitted for observation. I'm with her at the hospital."

"She okay?" His tone had calmed.

Conroy mouthed to her, asking if she wanted to talk to him. Mia took the phone. "Hi, Dad."

Conroy shifted to stand, but she touched his hand. He turned back.

She held on so he couldn't go anywhere.

"Meena." Mia frowned again and was quiet for a moment. He could hear Rich talking rapidly. "I know. It wasn't pretty." Pause. "I should be." She glanced at him. "Conroy's living room. Okay."

She handed back the phone. He looked at the screen and saw her dad had hung up. "What was that about my house?"

"He uh...asked where my duffel bag was."

Conroy nodded. Of course she wouldn't want to go back to his house. It was dumb to think she could possibly feel safe there after the way he'd let her down so hugely. He'd been so determined to prove to her that he could protect her. That he wouldn't let anything happen to her. He'd been wrong about that, too.

"As soon as they get you discharged, I'll get you back to your dad's house."

"He's actually headed here. He said you can bring my duffel over after he relieves you."

"He wants to take charge of your care?"

She shrugged. "I guess. He never has before."

"Could be he got shook up. He heard you scream. He called me right away." Conroy said, "Maybe he just needs to see for himself that you're all right."

"Probably."

"Then when you're back at his place, he'll be with you. You don't have to be alone."

She nodded, not meeting his gaze.

"And I'll be out finding this guy."

"Back to business as usual."

"Kind of." He wasn't sure what she'd meant by that, anyway. A guarded look had come over her face like a shutter pulled down. She was hiding behind it. Not letting him in. Conroy said, "That way you don't have to be in my house. It'll give you nightmares knowing he got to you there."

She nodded again, this time not looking like what he'd said made her feel any better.

"Mia—"

She waved a hand. "You're right. We don't know who that was."

"I'll get you a mugshot book. Think you could look at pictures?"

She nodded.

"So long as you're safe with your dad, I'm going to do everything in my power to get this guy. I want him found."

"Me too."

He turned his hand and held hers. "I don't like leaving you at all while he's still out there, even if you'll be with your dad."

"But your skills are better served on the job, finding that guy. And Stiles." She tipped her head to the side, some of the tension gone now. "I just wish there was a…safehouse or something like it."

Maybe she liked the idea of him leaving about as much as he liked the idea of leaving her. As in, not at all.

"Usually we just get a hotel room for the person. If it's a high-value target, there's a cabin. Last time didn't go well though. The people who own it are...particular about what happens there. There was a lot of damage. Smashed windows. Bullet holes in the drywall."

"For a safehouse, that doesn't sound very safe."

"Domestic issue." He didn't even know how to explain what it had been. "I wound up owing them big enough I better not need another favor for..." He looked at his watch even though it was unnecessary. "Another six years."

She chuckled, then winced.

"Okay?"

"I'm just ready to get out of here and get a full night's sleep. Then I'm going to persuade my dad to make his famous breakfast burritos."

Conroy nodded. "Those are good."

She frowned. "How would you know?"

"Men's breakfast at church. Your dad always makes them."

"My dad goes to church?"

"I didn't think it was a secret."

"You said he called you directly." She measured her words. "You guys really are friends?"

"Yes."

"He forgave you." She said those three words like it was an accusation.

"A few years ago. Yes."

Mia pulled her hand out from under his. She glanced around, disbelief warring with fear on her face. Why was she scared?

"Mia—"

"Go tell the doctor I want to leave. *Now.*"

## 18

Her dad held the door open. Mia was just glad the neighbor kid hadn't come over again. She didn't need to see those little faces, so distraught. Or the mom.

He closed it behind her. The place was still a mess. She'd left quickly and hadn't cleaned up after the intruder. The fingerprints. The kitchen—dishes on the counter instead of in the sink.

"I'll just tidy up."

"You'll do no such thing." He strode past her. "Go park it on the couch." He headed for the kitchen.

He wanted to clean up after her—first time in her life. That was fine by her.

Mia slumped onto the couch and toed off her sneakers. Wilcox had brought her duffel bag, and she'd opted for her slouchy clothes. Who cared that Conroy had seen her in these old leggings and ratty T-shirt? Certainly not her.

She curled her legs up on the seat and lay on her side. Licking her wounds. No, more like just being stubborn.

She'd flung the words at him like an accusation. And seen the hurt on his face after. Soon as her dad showed up, Conroy had excused himself. After waiting until she was covered—protected—he got out of there as fast as possible.

Mia didn't want to think of her sister, Mara. She didn't want to think of Conroy. Maybe she should just leave now. Go back to Seattle and hang out at the office until the call came in that Anthony Stiles had been caught. Problem solved. The danger would be over with no one in the line of fire. Then again, it also didn't prevent Stiles from hurting someone else. Here, she would be his focus.

The door to the dishwasher closed, and she heard it start to run. Her dad came over and sat in his chair. The same worn recliner he'd been sitting in for as long as she could remember. And the way she'd lain down—to take the weight off her arm—meant she could see him without moving.

"Don't look at me like that."

He lifted his hands, palms up. The guy was huge and always had been. She could barely remember what her mom looked like at this point, except for a vague memory of dark hair and a purple shirt with sparkles on the front that scratched her cheek. She'd gotten her height and build from her dad. They were both solid and stocky. It looked good on a man, not so much on her considering it had the effect of making her look like a heavy, Olympic volleyball player.

"Guess you found me out, huh."

She scrunched up her nose. As much of a shrug as she had the energy for. Mia didn't like being helpless, but this was where she was.

Maybe she'd always been powerless and just never realized it.

"You really forgave him?"

That would be the ultimate take back of her power. Offering forgiveness was what she was supposed to have done.

"Just like that?"

He shook his head, sighing. "It wasn't easy. Don't brush it off as no big deal, or some quick decision."

Well, that was something.

They sat in silence for a while.

"How was hunting?"

"That really what you want to ask me?"

She did the mouth thing again. "I don't know. I guess...how did you end up at Bible study, and forgiving Conroy?"

"Fridays, I get lunch at the diner."

She nodded since he'd been doing that for as long as she could remember.

"Pastor Daniels started to join me about a year ago." His low voice rumbled through the room. "At first we just chatted. Then it turned more serious. We talked about everything. Your mom, you girls. Religion. He told me what God did in his life, taking the pain and bitterness. Says He scoops it right out and replaces it with Him. He has to do that daily so the bitterness doesn't creep back in."

Mia nodded. Pastor Daniels was a good guy, and he'd led the youth back when she'd avoided going. The captain of the football team's dad dragged their family to church, so all the girls had gone a few times at least. Mia had goofed around the couple of times she did go. Some of it had stuck, though.

Enough that when she'd needed connection in Seattle, she'd sought out a local church.

"Took a few months, but eventually I decided to see for myself what God could do in my life. So I made a commitment to Him. That came with forgiving Conroy." Her dad sucked in a breath and pushed it out, long and slow. "Wasn't easy and didn't happen right away, like I said. But I had to let go of it. I couldn't let the anger and pain keep me chained up anymore."

"So now you're friends?"

He shrugged one shoulder. It probably looked a lot like when she did it. "We talk. But it's not like we go on BFF vacations."

Mia's lips spread into a smile. That would be a pretty funny scenario if it didn't birth in her mind images of her dad in shorts.

"Get some sleep, okay? I'll be here."

Mia wasn't so sure she wanted to go to sleep. It was early afternoon and she'd taken more than one nap already today. She would probably be awake all night at this rate.

"You need anything? Some tea or a sandwich?"

She shoved up so she could sit with her back against the cushion. "You're going to make me lunch?"

He shrugged one shoulder.

She nearly laughed. "You're really different than you used to be."

"In a good way, I hope."

Mia smiled. She loved that he was happy, maybe joyful even. For a lot of years her father had been bitter.

But faith hadn't changed her like that. She'd held on to things he'd let go of, choosing instead to keep her pain inside. So while she appreciated how he'd changed, it also made it all too obvious that she hadn't.

Maybe she'd been doing it wrong.

"What?"

She said, "Just thinking about some things." Mulling over her life, as she'd told Conroy she'd done while she waited in the empty room for Meena.

"Like that job of yours?"

"I always thought you just didn't like me being a cop."

"It's not just that," he said. "It suits you, I guess. But that ATF thing is not what you were put on this earth to do."

"So what was I put on this earth to do?"

He said, "Not for me to answer."

The doorbell rang.

He stood. "That *is* for me to answer. Because it's my front door."

"Hey, Rich. How are things?"

Mia sat up. That was… "Cassie Barnes." Conroy's sister was here?

"Cassie Edwards." She corrected as she strode in. She was as tall as Mia but with generous hips that swayed as she moved, in a way she was probably completely unconscious about. "Has been for a while now."

"Sorry." Mia pushed off the cushions and sat up straight.

"No worries." Cassie smiled. "I just came by to give you guys this." She lifted the dish in her hands, a covered, foil pan.

"Thank you, Cassie." Her dad took the offering. "I'll set this in the kitchen."

Cassie didn't wait for an invitation. Which Mia wouldn't have given her, anyway. She wandered into the living room and sat on the opposite end of the couch. "How are you? I heard about your rough week. And then being kidnapped." She winced. "And having to face your sister."

Mia didn't have time to say anything, let alone ask her if Conroy was in the habit of sharing police business with his sister.

"I saw her in the grocery store a few months ago. One of those days when I was tired, the kids were tired. My whole cart was full of frozen pizza and corn dogs. Cans of that cheese you squirt and a huge variety box of chips. I was eyeing brownies and cupcakes, trying to decide which to get, when your sister waltzes past with a bag of salad and a package of all-natural chicken sausage. She gives me this dirty look you would not believe." Cassie paused to take a breath, but only barely. "Brendan—he's my son—he asked me if her face was stuck like that all the time. She *heard*."

Mia felt her lips curl up, entirely involuntarily.

"I know, right?" Cassie glanced over Mia's shoulder, shot her dad a smile, and then said, "Anyway, Leora—that's my daughter—she's in the cart. She holds out her sucker and asks your sister if she wants a lick. I thought your sister was going to vomit right there on the spot. As if kids are the source of all germs, like little Petri dishes, happy to spread the love."

Mia just blinked.

"Your sister stormed off like she did that time when you said you wouldn't do her math homework for her."

Cassie went quiet. Like she was waiting for Mia to say something.

Mia broke the silence. "Uh...it's good to see you."

"Been a long time since high school English lit."

"Yes, it has." She wanted to smile, but this was kind of weird.

"And now you're a federal agent. That's really cool, Mia." Cassie smiled. "And you're here. Conroy is helping you out."

"Trying to catch a guy who kidnapped me." And the other guy who'd come after her.

"Yeah, but he's also seeing to your protection. *Personally.* Right?"

Mia frowned. "Cassie—"

Her dad sat on the arm of the couch behind her, so she couldn't twist far enough to look up at him. "He has been looking out for her. Even sat with her at the hospital so she could rest easy."

Well, when he put it like that it sounded—

Cassie beamed. "I always thought so."

Mia said, "You've always thought what?"

"He had you stay at his house, right?"

Mia shrugged.

"Protecting you." Cassie grinned. "In *all ways*. Which means he probably made you grilled chicken and a salad. It's what he does when someone isn't feeling well. He thinks healthy food *is* comfort food."

Mia didn't know where to start. "It doesn't matter because it didn't work. The guy he's looking for kidnapped me right out of Conroy's house." Mia sighed. "But I don't think that's what you meant. What did you 'always' think?"

"That Conroy would end up with you." Cassie shook her head like that was obvious. "You thought he hung the moon. I thought having my best friend be my sister one day would be the *best thing ever*. What he had with Mara, it was getting cold. If it wasn't for the accident, I think you two would have ended up pretty differently." Cassie shrugged. "Mara would've been mad, but she'd have gotten over it."

This was so far out of left field that Mia didn't even know what to say. "That's a pretty big 'If.'"

What was the point in dwelling on something that hadn't happened and probably never would?

"If Ed hadn't crashed the car, then Conroy would have been free to pursue you." Cassie smiled like that had been her greatest dream, and maybe still was.

"What do you mean?"

"Mara broke up with him. She was dating Ed Summers, and she'd been cheating on Conroy with Ed for like…a *month*. It all came out that night. They told him. Mara even said they were through, right to his face. Then she walked off with Ed. But they were both drunk, and Conroy wasn't. So he went after them to make sure they got home all right. Ed was in the driver's seat already and was about to take off, so Conroy jumped in the back. He was trying to convince them to stop the car when Ed crashed it."

Mia stared at her.

If Cassie was right and Mara *had* broken up with Conroy… Why would he still try to save their lives? Why not. Of course it made sense. Conroy wouldn't have done anything else. Even back then, he'd been all about protecting the people he cared about. Even people who had betrayed him.

"He tried to save their lives, even after they'd dealt him the worst blow he could have been dealt by the people he thought were his friends."

## 19

Conroy leaned back in his chair and blew out a breath. He'd read Anthony's file so many times he could practically recite the thing. Anthony's and his brother's.

He was still missing the connection to Ed Summers.

"Anything?" Wilcox strode across the bull pen and dumped her backpack beside her desk.

He shrugged. "Nothing that might tell us where Stiles is hiding out in town."

"Assuming he is," she said. "Unless, of course, he's in his car and parked somewhere no one can see him."

That wasn't what he wanted to hear. "What about Hudson?"

"I drove Tate home. He's in some discomfort, but other than that he's okay."

"That's it? He's 'okay'?"

"No, but it's a start." She sat. "He had nothing to do with the breach of your security system. He confirmed that, and I believe him. Did you hear back from the company?"

"They're getting me a full report by end of day." Heads were going to roll.

Wilcox nodded. "You look like you want to punch someone."

Conroy pressed his lips together.

She winced.

"I'm keeping a close eye on Tate." He didn't think the man was completely innocent.

Mia had kicked him out and gone with her dad. Pushing him away, trying to protect herself. Conroy couldn't force her to forgive him. She had to come to the decision on her own. To make the choice to let that hurt go. Maybe if she knew all the circumstances then she would soften some. She'd see the fact that it hadn't been his fault. He'd been trying to stop it.

Ed Summers would always be the one solely responsible for the death of Mara Tathers.

Conroy had spent years trying not to hate the guy for that, kind of like Mia hated him for his role in it. He figured he'd moved past it. Just that he had a pretty loose hold on that forgiveness. And it had nothing to do with the fact that, at any given moment of any given day, Lieutenant Conroy Barnes was actively looking for a way to shut down Ed Summers's operation and arrest the guy.

Conviction would be up to a judge.

Conroy would do everything he could. But that meant building a solid case with overwhelming evidence. Something he hadn't managed to do.

Yet.

He'd regret Meena Tathers being caught up in it, as she would likely be caught up in any sweep that brought in everyone connected to Summers's operation. But that was the choice she'd made. The life she lived, lining her pockets with the fruits of Summers's ill-gotten gains.

What he needed to do was prove to Mia that he could protect her. That it would be worth it for her to put her trust in him.

"How's the chief today?"

Conroy glanced toward the old man's office. "Jess came in early. He's not doing well."

Wilcox pushed out a breath through clenched teeth. "That's too bad."

"Yeah."

This had to be bringing up memories for her. She'd watched her own father suffer to the end through a cancer diagnosis. One of the few things he knew about her life before Last Chance County. "Savannah…"

She shook her head. "I'll talk to Jess. Make sure she's all right."

Conroy hadn't exactly been after that. But he was grateful anyway. "Thanks."

"Lieutenant!"

He spun around in his chair as Bill lumbered over. Conroy winced that he hadn't gotten to his feet and met the guy halfway. Probably Bill didn't want that, so he'd held off calling for Conroy until he was past that point.

Conroy took the paper the dispatcher handed him. The old man was a Vietnam veteran, the fastest typist he'd ever met, and the calmest, most competent dispatcher Last Chance County had ever had. He was built like an ox and never took sick days. In fact, he never even got sick. His sister covered for him when he was off.

"What is it?"

"Address for the place Anthony Stiles has been staying. Got a call from a neighbor who'd seen the local news and the photo we put out, and recognized him as coming and going next door." Bill paused. "She was a bit upset, but I talked her through it."

"Thanks." Conroy pulled his suit jacket off the back of his chair.

Savannah stood as well. "I'm coming with."

"You just wanna get out of doing paperwork."

She grinned. "Like you don't hate it."

"I don't hate it when you have to do it." He grabbed his wallet and pulled his weapon from his desk drawer, sliding it onto his belt.

Wilcox wasn't smiling now. She glanced at the chief's office and the old man in the bed on the other side of the glass.

"I'll keep you posted if there are any changes."

She said, "Thanks, Bill."

"Appreciate it." Conroy led the way outside and handed her the paper. She typed the address into his phone so it came up on the dash screen when his Bluetooth connected. The car directed them to the house, and he halved the estimated time to their destination.

"Doesn't look like much."

Conroy agreed. "I think it's one of those short-term rentals."

"If it is then there will be an agreement. A signed contract. He probably used a fake name, but it's still evidence."

They got out and made their way down the drive to the front door. "Kind of looks more abandoned than a vacation rental."

"Yeah." Wilcox let go of the two-handed grip she had on her weapon and pushed the front door open. "Inside looks the same."

They parted ways and swept the house.

"Clear."

He found her in the kitchen. "Clear."

Wilcox's nose wrinkled. "Of people, at least."

He knew what she meant. Dishes piled in the sink. Paper plates and pizza boxes overflowed the trash can. "See if you can find anything that will confirm it was Stiles living here."

"More like squatting."

Conroy made a noncommittal noise and wandered back to the bedroom.

"I don't know what you're expecting to find," Wilcox called out. "Maybe a picture of Mia with darts thrown at her face?"

"Keep an eye out for that," he called back.

The bathroom was in a worse state than the kitchen. He checked the cupboards and found a toothbrush, which he put in an evidence bag Wilcox brought him.

Not much else to find, though they checked everywhere. Even under the couch, finding a flip flop covered in dust and dog hair.

Wilcox swallowed, her nose crinkled.

"Suck it up, detective. You're starting to look like a girl."

She planted a hand high on her chest. "Moi?"

"Yeah, you."

"Newsflash, boss, I am a girl. And a detective. A woman who is a cop. Which means at any given time I can be both, or either."

"Is that supposed to make sense?"

Maybe that was why he couldn't get through to Mia. It was like they spoke a different language sometimes.

Wilcox grinned. "Definitely not."

"So what do you expect guys to even do? We literally have *no clue* what you girls are even talking about."

"I don't know." She shrugged. "But I know it's not me who has to figure that out."

Conroy shook his head.

"So this was a bust?"

He said, "Physical evidence can prove he was here, illegally occupying this house."

She looked at the screen of her phone. "Bill says it's been empty for months."

Conroy nodded slowly.

"So…squatting as a charge?"

"For starters. Maybe criminal harassment." He didn't like it any more than she did. But it was what it was. Like the way he'd been looking for an in that would get them an arrest warrant for Ed Summers for *years*. Basically since he'd been accepted to the police department.

They could only get what they could get. Which was what they could prove.

Another kind of cop might force a conviction, probably based on falsified evidence. But neither Conroy nor Wilcox were that type of cop. And it wasn't worth the risk.

If they were going to do this, they were going to do it right.

His phone rang.

"I'll meet you outside."

Conroy didn't know why he was the one who had to be inside where it smelled, but given the caller came up as Mia, he was grateful for the privacy.

"Hey."

"Uh…hey." She paused for a second. "You're not busy, are you?" Her breath came fast. She sounded scared. Or irritated.

"What's up?"

There were a few seconds of quiet, then she said, "Why didn't you tell me that Mara broke up with you the night she died? And that she was actually dating Ed Summers?"

Conroy squeezed the bridge of his nose. "Would it have made that much of a difference?"

Her sister would still be dead. It wouldn't change the fact he'd tried to stop the accident but hadn't managed to do so. He relived it nearly every time he got behind the wheel. The one time he'd been in a fender bender, on the job at the time, it hadn't gone well. The other driver had wound up calling emergency services and asking for an ambulance for him—the freaked out police officer they'd hit.

Talk about embarrassing.

He'd gone through meeting after meeting with the therapist in town before he'd been able to explain it all to the chief fully enough to get released back to active duty instead of being stuck at a desk.

But he'd closed four cases at that desk.

Mia sighed. "I can't believe you didn't say anything."

Maybe Mia was upset that he hadn't told her Mara had broken up with him, even after she had bared all about her failed relationship with a coworker, that night in his condo, right before she fell asleep. Was that what this was about? Maybe she was embarrassed. Didn't she get it that he hadn't wanted to tarnish Mara's reputation? Or maybe it was true that he'd felt discarded by Mara that night. She had chosen Ed over him, and he hadn't wanted to admit it.

"So I guess now you know," Conroy said. "She didn't want me."

"I know what that feels like. With my coworker. Not sure I'd still try to save his life, though."

"No?" She wouldn't have done that for the man she'd liked?

"His dog was the one with me when I took out Thompson Stiles. He just carried her away and didn't say anything. Didn't even check to make sure I was okay. I was lying there with Stiles on me, blood everywhere. I think they were all mad I'd killed him when he hurt the dog. They couldn't haul him in for questioning and read him his rights."

"Are you at your dad's house?"

"Yes—why?"

"I'm coming over." He shoved out the front door where Wilcox waited ready to hang police tape on the door. "We should talk."

It was that or drive to Seattle and punch his way through her team until he got to the right guy. Seriously? Surely there were some good people in the ATF. Probably more than a few, and this was just a case of one bad egg. But he couldn't believe she would want to keep working there.

"Don't. You don't need to come over. I'm fine," she lied. "My dad is here."

"Mia—"

"I don't wanna talk about it. I want to know why you didn't tell me Mara had just dumped you. Didn't you want me to know?"

He walked down the drive, far enough Wilcox wouldn't be

able to hear. "Not exactly something a guy wants to admit to the woman he's attracted to. Someone he likes and respects." And hoped to convince to move back to town and take up a job as a cop in his department.

"Have you found Stiles yet?" It almost sounded like an accusation.

"We found the place he's been staying."

"You…really?"

"I haven't been sitting around." Wallowing over her. Or brooding. Women liked guys who brooded, right? "I've been working."

He wanted to ask who told her that Mara had dumped him, but he was pretty sure his first guess would be right.

If his sister thought he was bringing rolls to Sunday dinner still, she was going to be disappointed.

"Of course." She cleared her throat. "Any sign of him?"

Conroy said, "No." But he glanced up and down the street as he did. Like Stiles would be sitting on the street in his car. Watching. "No sign of him here."

"Keep me posted." She hung up.

Conroy stowed his phone, about as frustrated with all this as she sounded. Summers's men had let the guy working for Stiles drive off, and they'd done nothing. No, not true. They'd shot Tate and taken Mia for themselves.

"What's next?"

He glanced at Wilcox. "Pull the tape down. We need to talk to the neighbor. I have an idea."

## 20

"Call him back. Let him explain."

Mia shook her head. She grabbed her keys and pulled on a jacket, moving to the front door. She turned back at the last second. "I'm going to get some air."

"With a guy after you?"

"Conroy is on it."

But just in case, she switched her jacket for her dad's and grabbed an orange beanie he'd worn hunting. It smelled. She took a ball cap instead, and the keys to his car.

Her dad made a face, the stubble on his jaw shifting as he worked his mouth.

"I have a gun."

He sighed.

"So do you," she said. "Keep it close."

She headed for her car. He was probably going to call Conroy the second the door shut behind her. Considering he'd been exactly right that there was a guy after her, she didn't mind overly much. Mia's pain meds had kicked in. She'd thought about taking a nap—that was the same thing as taking one, right? —and she'd eaten. Full belly meant fully-loaded energy stores.

Now she was ready to take this guy down.

Mia might have been knocked on her proverbial behind. That didn't mean she was down forever. Conroy thought he needed to take care of her. Guys liked that, having a woman they could rescue. One who made rescuing them worth it instead of a chore. She could handle that, but she couldn't handle having to sit back and do nothing while everyone on the police force in Last Chance County found Anthony Stiles.

Driving around town was like a trip down memory lane. Main Street. The bowling alley and the movie theater. The gym that used to be her dance studio as a kid, before she quit dance to spend more time on the phone with her friends. It was hard to see places she'd been with Mara. Bittersweet was probably the best way to describe it.

Those were the old days. Ones that made her wonder why she'd resisted coming back for so long. Because it was easier to hold onto her bitterness than it was to offer Conroy forgiveness? Pain was often more comforting than the fear that accompanied letting it go and waiting for what else might come. It was like a wound that was never allowed to heal. The alternative—forgiveness—was hoping that what came after would be something good. Not more pain that was different, and likely worse. Fresh, at least.

Her phone rang. She glanced at it, perched in the cup holder. *Conroy.*

She ignored it, too tired and uncomfortable to deal with more emotions, and continued her trip down memory lane. She just didn't allow her mind to go *all* the way back. Not when there was danger in the present.

Gun in the glove box. She was ready for Anthony Stiles this time. He wasn't going to catch her unaware again. Not him, or whoever he sent to get her.

The phone in the cup holder went dark. She headed for the highway, mostly so she didn't wind up going in circles. If the restaurant just fifteen minutes out of town was still open…well then, she'd just have to stop and get some pie.

All part of the job.

Car headlights flashed in her rearview. A tug on the control lever to literally flash their brights at her, or just a creation of reflection and angle? She looked down at the phone and then said to the silence of the car's interior, "Probably you, Conroy. Right?"

Maybe.

She turned with the bend in the highway and saw the car. Red, a small SUV. It was definitely not Conroy. Fear rolled through her like that old adage of someone stepping on your grave. She'd never believed that. There was nothing magical in the world. All the spiritual, and there was plenty unexplainable about that, was governed by God.

And behind her, this guy was just a man.

Men made mistakes, just like everyone did. You broke the law, you got caught. Eventually.

Mr. Red SUV revved his engine.

"Anthony Stiles, is that you?"

He pushed the car up close to her back bumper.

What was he trying to do, run her off the road? Kill her. Kidnap her again?

Mia's mind flooded with second thoughts. She swiped up the phone and thumbed through her contacts while she drove with one hand. Not exactly safe, but it was always better to put out a call for help rather than face the unknown alone.

Wilcox answered on the first ring. "He's looking for you."

She didn't know if Savannah meant Conroy or the bad guy.

Mia tapped the speaker button and dropped the phone back in the cup holder. "Anthony Stiles? He already found me." She told Savannah about the car, and gave her a location.

Savannah spoke, but it was muffled. "We're on our way. Keep him behind you." She was quiet for a second. Mia was about to say something when Savannah added, "Conroy said don't do anything. Just let him follow you."

"Not like I'm going to force the issue."

A roadblock was one thing. Reaching for her gun and either firing at the car behind her or turning the car around in a high-speed maneuver and firing at the car straight on? Those were entirely different.

She tapped her brakes. Just another driver on the road who thought the person behind them was too close.

He didn't back off.

From the cup holder she heard, "We're at least five minutes out."

"Okay."

Savannah said, "Still behind you?"

"Yep. I'm a couple of miles from Sunshine." That was the restaurant on the highway. Huge cedar beams, a tall, wooden bear someone had carved from an old log. A tree that fell down during a storm, painted like a black bear. Chicken fried steak. Waffles.

Best pie in the northwest.

"Pull in," Conroy demanded, his voice close to the phone's mic. Evidently he'd grabbed the device from Savannah.

"The parking lot?"

From what she remembered, it could be a good place to box Stiles in and force a confrontation.

Behind her, Stiles revved the engine and got closer to her.

He could hit her. Send her car into a spin.

She could slam into a tree and not walk away from the scene.

"I could use some pie." Levity. That was what she needed. "What's the special this week? Do you know?"

"Pie?"

Savannah came on. Sounded like they were on speaker now, too. "Blueberry cobbler," she said. "I have their web page set as the homepage on the browser on my phone. I check it every Monday morning."

Mia gripped the wheel and tried to force a smile on her face. "I think you might be my new best friend."

"You need to focus," Conroy ordered.

"I'm headed to the restaurant. I'm trying not to freak out," she said. "Cut me some slack, okay? I'll be there in a minute. Where will you be?"

"Right behind him." The words were short.

He had about as much patience as she remembered. When Mara told him she was throwing him out in favor of Ed Summers, he had to have lost it. Even back then, Summers had been into petty stuff. Why her sister ever wanted to trade Conroy out for Ed, Mia would never understand. Then again, Meena had done the same. She'd chosen Ed.

"He's still with me. It's going to be fine." She was half a mile out from the restaurant. "Maybe I should call ahead. Make a reservation."

For a suspect take down. Followed by three orders of pie and ice cream, assuming Conroy was going to have calmed down by then. At least enough he would sit and have dessert with them.

The highway turned again. Pine trees flanked either side, interspersed with a dusting of snow. Elevation was climbing. It was getting colder. She was starting to sweat though, so she eased off on the heater while she kept one eye on the road.

Savannah asked, "Where is he now?"

"Still right behind me." Like a dog, determined to sniff another dog's butt. Gross, but part of doggie life. This guy definitely had the front of his car up somewhere she didn't want it, and she'd rather he backed off.

Which only reminded her of Daisy, running at her full tilt. Just thinking about it made her arm throb and a whimper work its way up her throat.

"Mia."

She sniffed but gave herself a second to absorb Conroy's concern. He cared about her. She wasn't alone. "I'm okay."

Wilcox and Conroy were both coming. Mia could face one man on her own, especially with her gun in her hand this time. But just knowing they cared enough to drop what they were doing and come after her to help? The fact they were here made all the difference in the world.

She wasn't sure her own teammates would have done that unless it had been an order from their group supervisor.

"I see the restaurant."

"We're here," Savannah said.

Mia looked in the side mirror and saw their cop car right behind the red car Stiles was driving. Just the sight of it gave her a rush of adrenaline.

She held her breath. Doing anything else would cause her to broadcast what was about to happen.

At the last second, Mia tapped the brake and turned into the restaurant parking lot. Thankfully there were no pedestrians that she could see, but she still kept her eyes peeled for anyone walking. Or a little kid who might dart between two parked cars.

Stiles pulled in behind her. She hit the gas, tore down to the end of the row, and pulled up her handbrake. She twisted the wheel all the way to the right, two handed.

Stiles turned out of the way but not entirely. He clipped her back bumper and sped on. She saw the man's face. Her kidnapper. Not Stiles.

Conroy was so close behind that he bumped the back of the kidnapper's car.

She spun to a stop and watched Conroy and Savannah blow past her, after the red car, the female detective looking concerned as they peeled out of the parking lot at the far end.

"You okay?" Savannah asked, her voice displaying as much concern as her face had.

Mia got her car turned around and followed as quickly as she could.

"Mia!" Conroy yelled.

"I'm fine. Are you guys okay?"

"We're good," Savannah said.

She fought to catch up. They were moving fast. "Where is he going?"

"My guess?" Conroy said, "That would be Ed Summers' compound. It's the only thing on this road unless you're heading to the city, and that would take another three hours."

"I'll run out of gas before then."

"I guess we'll see if we're right. Or we'll turn back. It's coming up."

Mia got as close as she dared. Certainly not as close as Stiles's guy had been riding her back bumper. "You think—"

She didn't even get a chance to finish. Up ahead of Conroy's police department vehicle, the red SUV turned down a lane flanked by wood posts. Strung up high between the two posts was a huge sign. Weathered too badly for anyone to read.

Mia forgot whose place it was, but thought it might have been where Ed Summers and his mom had moved in with his stepdad. Too long ago for her to remember much about it. She'd hardly cared. Summers hadn't been on her radar back then.

Not the way Conroy had been.

Conroy pulled their car over. Mia parked right behind them, at an angle that would allow her back onto the road easily. They all got out and met in a huddle between their back bumper and her front. Guns out.

"You need a vest."

Conroy was right. "We're going in now?"

He nodded. "Got one in your trunk?"

"No."

He turned back to their SUV while Savannah gave her a look. "You good?"

"Why wouldn't I be? This guy tried to kidnap me and was about to hand me over to a crazy man. Then Meena and her people did it for real. Now they're harboring him?" She shook her head. "I don't think so."

Conroy handed her a vest, the edge of a smile on his lips. "That's my girl."

She was a woman, thank you. But she got his point. And saying she was "his girl" meant something entirely different.

But not unwelcome.

There was so much still to resolve between them, but working as a team in this meant putting their past aside for the moment and getting on with the take down.

Anthony Stiles—and the kidnapper, for that matter—needed to be in cuffs.

## 21

C onroy took point. They walked the drive down to the main house faster than necessary. All three of them itching to grab Stiles.

He could see it in the way Mia moved and the way Wilcox held her gun, loose but ready. Same for him. But this was a balancing act, like everything else.

"There's the car." Mia lifted her chin in the direction.

Conroy saw it. Sticking out around the side of the building, the back bumper had signs of damage. The white paint from his SUV was stark against the red of the paint.

He wandered to it. "No one inside."

"What if he's hiding in the trunk?" Wilcox said.

Conroy tried the door handle. "It's locked." He touched the hood, still warm from the engine's heat. "Doubt he crawled into the trunk to hide and then locked himself in."

Wilcox tipped her head to the side like she conceded the point. At least until they got a warrant to search the car and could check inside for themselves.

"Think he ditched it and went into the house?" Wilcox scanned the area.

Conroy had his eyes on the out buildings. There were a lot

of places to hide here. "Guess we'll find out."

And if the guy didn't give himself up willingly, Conroy was going to have more of a problem with Ed Summers than he already did.

Charges of harboring a fugitive for starters.

"Or he ditched it," Mia suggested, "and headed out into the surrounding area."

"Which means we'll need a team of officers and search dogs." Conroy glanced at Mia to see how she felt about that.

A tiny shiver was all she let through the defensive shield she had tucked around her.

He'd been there when she was bitten. Because of that, dogs wouldn't be his first choice, even though that incident and this one had nothing to do with each other.

But this was about pulling out all the stops to find Stiles.

They stopped in the front yard. The very empty front yard in front of the quiet ranch house, surrounded by at least six vehicles in different states of repair—or disrepair—depending upon how you looked at it. There were people here.

So where was everyone?

Conroy was just about to call out and announce their presence—like it wasn't obvious to anyone who cared to look out the window—when the front door opened.

Tate Hudson stepped out onto the front porch.

Wilcox actually flinched. "You cannot be serious."

"You wanna explain this?"

Before he could answer Conroy's question, Mia strode forward to confront Tate herself. "You're in there while he's harboring a fugitive? You're working with him, yet have no idea who this psycho is."

Hudson said nothing.

The door behind him stayed open, and Ed Summers strode out wearing jeans and a T-shirt. Running shoes. Beanie. A silver chain hung over the collar of his tee.

He took a drag from his cigarette. "Mia Tathers. That you, all grown up?"

Conroy held his breath. It was a test. Ed knew she was fully aware of his role in her sister's death. No one here was confused about that. What he really was asking, was what that made them now. Enemies? Nothing? Their connection could go several different ways, and Ed needed to get the lay of that land so he knew how much to reveal and where they stood with each other. Particularly considering the fact she was a federal agent now.

If she had an ax to grind and some determination to see it through, Mia could become a very painful thorn in Summers's side. One he'd be determined to rid himself of.

Summers's interference was the last thing Conroy needed when he was still working to persuade her to stay.

She said nothing about their connection. Just asked, "Which one of your guys showed up in that car?"

"What?" He half smiled, as though this was a joke.

She didn't even react. And she wasn't joking. "He drove here in that car—" She pointed at the red car, busted up bumper. "—and then disappeared. So either you're harboring a person of interest in a case we're hoping will involve attempted murder charges…or you're about to tell us where he ran off to. You get to decide. Talk, or this becomes a case with multiple defendants."

Still smiling. "Is any of this supposed to make sense to me?"

Conroy said, "Drop the act. We're not playing around, and you definitely don't want to be mixed up in this guy's business. He's got your boys running around doing his bidding. You're gonna let that stand?"

Tate shifted his weight. "Stiles is not inside any of these buildings."

Wilcox scoffed. "What are you, Summers's lawyer or just his lackey?"

Tate didn't even glance at her. He stood by Summers on the porch and kept his gaze on Conroy.

Did he really want to throw down with a known drug dealer? Or was he doing this to get in with Ed and gain the evidence Conroy needed to bring charges? Finally.

Conroy could have used a heads up, but he would roll with this.

Wilcox took a step closer, her grip on her weapon a whole lot more determined now. Still just ready. If she did want to shoot someone, it would likely be Tate Hudson.

And he didn't miss that. "Stand down, Wilcox."

Tate had his thumbs in his pockets, which had the added benefit of his hand being a little too close to his weapon.

Conroy would've said he trusted the private investigator. Before Mia had been taken from Conroy's house. Now with this? He wasn't even sure what the guy was about. There was that edge of uncertainty, knowing he wasn't under any of the rules that Conroy or his people with the police department lived and worked by. A loose cannon could be both good and bad.

Mia shifted. Conroy didn't like her being exposed. He'd rather be standing in front of her, but she was here as a federal agent doing her job.

She said, "Where did Stiles go?" sounding like every inch the cop she was.

"No one here saw Anthony Stiles."

Conroy wondered at Tate's statement. "So who got out of that red car?"

"One of my guys," Ed answered. "No one saw where he went."

"But he's not inside?"

"Nope."

Conroy gritted his teeth. "You want to give me his name?"

"Had a guy you were looking for. He turned up dead." Ed took another drag on his cigarette and spoke around a mouthful of smoke. "Why'm I gonna tell you about another one?"

"Who got out of the car, Ed?"

"Don't answer that." Tate didn't turn, but was clearly addressing Ed.

Wilcox said, "You really are his lawyer."

"Stay out of this."

"Yeah? Then get ready for a world of problems," she said.

"You gonna jam me up?"

"Guess we'll find out what sticks when you get swept up with the rest of them," Wilcox said.

Conroy was done listening to this. "Time for you to decide what side you're on, Hudson."

"By giving us Stiles, or whoever was driving that car." Mia used a "cop" voice he had to force himself to not get distracted by. This was a woman who could get the job done. One strong enough to weather a whole lot of stuff life threw at her. Especially if the past couple of weeks were anything to go by.

Tate turned his back to them and leaned in close to Ed Summers, in a way that prevented them from reading his lips. Tate could do things Conroy, as a police lieutenant, couldn't. He had access to people and places that Conroy would never have, as certain types clammed up when a cop came around.

What Tate thought he'd get from Ed, Conroy wasn't sure. Could be he was trying to prove himself after he'd screwed up with Mia being kidnapped. Conroy seriously hoped whatever Tate got from this would be enough for probable cause, so Conroy could persuade the judge to issue an arrest warrant for Summers.

Tate finished talking. Ed glanced at Mia. Then he lifted his chin to Tate, who had turned back around to face him. "The driver of the car ran to the northwest. There's a path out into the woods." He moved down the porch steps while Ed stayed where he was. "I'll show you."

As Tate got close to Wilcox, Conroy heard her hiss, "Because you know so much about this place?"

He shot her a frown. "You came here to get what you want. So let's get it."

"I don't think you understand, Hudson. This guy is a killer."

"Ed's guy, no. The guy y'all are after, maybe. Yeah." Tate shrugged.

Mia said, "Just show us where he went so we can get on with this and get out of here."

Tate shot Wilcox a look, as though Mia was the only reasonable one there. Conroy said, "Let's go, Detective."

Wilcox wound up behind them, bringing up the rear.

Conroy glanced over his shoulder. She might want as much distance from Tate as possible while still actively participating, but she was still alert and watching out for Mia. Protecting their backs.

She met his gaze and nodded. Unhappy with Tate, but all in on this case—and with Mia.

Conroy figured he'd ask Tate the questions Wilcox probably wanted the answers to. So he said, "Why are you here, mediating between us and Summers?"

Tate kept walking, glancing once over his shoulder. "Figured you could use a go-between. Help everyone keep their heads on straight."

"Thanks."

Wilcox said, "Don't expect gratitude from me. You're protecting him. Helping him skate out from under pressure."

"Your kind of pressure don't work on some people, Van," Tate argued.

"I told you not to call me that."

Mia, beside Conroy, said, "Did you see who got out of that car?"

"Yeah."

Wilcox said, "So you were already here?"

Tate sighed. "Yes, Savannah. It's a free country, and I can go where I please."

She said nothing.

Conroy wanted an idea how far the guy could have gotten considering the time they'd wasted talking to Summers. How able bodied was the guy, and how long was this path? "Can we have a name or get a photo? I'd like to know the guy when I see him."

Tate shot him a frown. "So none of you saw the driver's face? That isn't good."

Mia said, "I got only a quick glance at his face. It was the same car Stiles put me in before Meena and her boys took me out of there."

"But you can't ID him as chasing after you today? Means you have no reason to bother Summers and no reason to believe he's in league with Stiles."

"Don't over analyze this. The common denominator is Summers."

Tate's eyebrows rose. "You, Conroy Barnes, are going to play this one fast and loose?"

Mia shot him a glance out of the corner of her eye.

Conroy said, "We do this right. People's lives are at stake and that cannot be forgotten. This guy, Anthony Stiles, has proven he's not immune to concocting elaborate scenarios to scare the ever-loving—"

Savannah said, "Yeah." Covering for him, so he didn't say something he shouldn't.

"—out of people." He didn't want to be bringing it up but hadn't actually mentioned the dog incident to Tate. Or the explosion. Or the intruder.

Tate turned and stopped. "Are you sure you didn't get a concussion when your car exploded?"

Conroy kept walking. Maybe he'd read about it in the paper.

"Did you?" Mia asked as they moved past Tate.

"No." He almost wanted to laugh or hug her. The compassion on her face was so cute. Conroy glanced back to tell Wilcox to get a move on.

A gunshot rang out through the trees.

Conroy launched himself at Mia, who grabbed for him at

the same time. They fell together. Guns. Limbs. Everything got tangled and they rolled, coming to a stop side by side.

Conroy said, "Okay?"

"Yeah." Her voice was breathy, her face close to his.

He looked over at Wilcox. "Detective?"

She was under Tate, who had shielded her with his body. He'd dived on her to protect her. In the heat of the moment, choosing to risk himself to safeguard her.

"I'm good." She shoved Tate off. "Ugh. You're enormous. Get off."

Tate rolled to the side and sat up. "One shot."

"Job done?" Conroy held out a hand to help Mia to her feet. They clasped wrists and he hauled her up.

"Let's go find out."

Tate and Wilcox followed. They all fanned out, eyes open as they searched the area.

"Over here." Savannah had stopped. When they'd caught up, she said, "One shot."

Right between the eyes. Another person involved in all this was dead.

Conroy sighed. "Summers isn't going to like this at all."

Mia said, "He isn't the only one."

## 22

C onroy called it in. Tate did the same, though Mia didn't know who he called, and he walked too far away for her to listen in.

Wilcox wasn't happy.

"I guess you didn't need another open case." Mia stowed her weapon in its holster.

"Cases I don't mind. But I could use help." Savannah lifted her brows. "Looking for a detective's job? Cause I'm in the market for a new partner."

Mia didn't even want to think about working for the Last Chance County Police Department. Having Conroy be her boss. Might be good. Might also be a total disaster.

She moved to the body and crouched, looking at the face. It was always better when there was a face, even if the person *was* dead. She didn't do grizzly violent crimes. At least not without going home and not eating for two days.

There had only been that one shot. This guy was executed. Shot at close range by someone he knew, or at least well enough to let them get that near. "Scorched."

"What's that?" Savannah shifted close to her side.

"The burn mark around the wound. He was shot at really close range, meaning someone caught him off guard."

"How do you know it wasn't suicide?"

It sounded like a loaded question. Mia figured it was a test. Partly to figure out if she knew what she was doing, and partly to distract them all by processing the scene.

She said, "The angle is straight. I think. Can't tell for sure without the medical examiner, or coroner, saying for sure, but the scorch is a circle. Not a smudge. Center of the forehead, square on, shows that he didn't kill himself."

"So Anthony Stiles killed him because we got too close after the wild goose chase he took us on."

Mia straightened. "It's a theory."

"You got a better one?"

"No, but I'd like to know why he didn't just wait around and pick the rest of us off, too. Why kill this guy who probably doesn't mean a thing to him and then split?"

Savannah frowned. "Well."

Tate wandered back over. "She's got a point." His attention shifted, and she turned to see what had caught his gaze.

Two cops, a duffel bag and backpack between them, trudged down the path toward them. Conroy met them twenty feet away, and she could see in their stances the respect they had for their lieutenant.

"Is there a medical examiner in Last Chance?"

Wilcox said, "There's a doctor who'll take cases like this. He's solid."

Mia nodded. As soon as the officers headed their way, she said, "Gloves?"

One glanced at Conroy, who nodded. "This is Special Agent Tathers."

"Rich's daughter?" The cop evidently knew her. He was older, maybe pushing fifty, but still trim and strong in appearance. Older than Tate for sure, though she didn't think she knew him.

"Among other things," Mia said. "Yeah."

She'd never been satisfied getting pegged as one thing. Defined by someone else. She could barely tolerate the way feds were defined by the badge, much preferring to earn someone's respect because of the job she did going forward. Not because of the title she had earned in the past.

The other officer, younger and looking at her with respect, handed over a pair of rubber gloves.

Mia pulled them on and then dug into the victim's front pocket. The outline of his wallet on one side, a faded edge in the denim. This side was clearly his cell phone. Men and their deep pockets—able to carry their belongings on them without needing a purse because a cell phone would actually fit in their pants pocket. *Lucky.*

Tate said, "Passcode?"

Mia realized that the two cops, along with Conroy, Wilcox and Tate, were standing around her. "No." She reached over and swiped the home button with the victim's thumb. "And, there we go."

She handed it over to Conroy.

"Don't want to look at it?"

She shrugged. "You know some of the players. Might make more sense to you."

He actually looked impressed.

"I want to know if you find anything about Stiles, though."

"Okay."

Mia pulled off the gloves and wandered around while she surveyed the area. Just wilderness. Overgrown land peppered with old trees. Most had fallen down. Dry and dead. Winter had come, leaving the damaged and struggling trees with no resources to fight the onslaught of cold.

She felt like that.

Brittle. Frozen from the inside, without the strength to fight the season that had come.

Why did it have to be so hard?

"No!"

Mia recognized the voice before she even turned.

"No, no, no!" Meena ran right for the body. Leggings and a shirt short enough to reveal a sliver of her midriff. No jacket. Big earrings, wild hair, and a pair of black boots. She stumbled and kept screaming.

Mia jogged to meet her halfway. Conroy did the same, but he let Mia wind an arm around her sister and haul her back. The two of them crowded her. Mia let go.

Her sister screamed and launched herself toward the body. Mia caught her around the waist again. "Don't." She clutched her sister's arms, even though it hurt, and held them by her sides so she could stare into her face. "There's nothing you can do for him. Not anymore."

Meena's legs gave out. Mia didn't have time to catch her. She crouched, wincing. "It's cold."

Conroy handed over his jacket, and she tugged it around her sister's shoulders.

"You knew him?"

Her sister shot her a teary glare.

"I have no idea who this guy is," Mia said. "So why don't you tell me who he was to you."

It wasn't the same guy who'd been in the hallway at the house. Likely it was the man who'd been driving the red car, though she couldn't be sure when she'd only gotten a split-second look.

Meena sniffed. "We were…" She didn't finish.

"Involved?"

Meena nodded. A tiny movement. She'd cared about him.

And Mia unashamedly intended to use that care and intimacy as leverage to get her sister to tell her everything about her lover's involvement with Anthony Stiles. As much as she knew. And even more, considering there were likely things she could point to that would help them find this guy.

Last time they'd talked was after Meena had held her captive for hours. That put her in the position of power, and Mia in the vulnerable spot. Now the tables were well and truly turned. Mia held all the authority here. She could make or break her sister's life over this.

Which was why she was a cop.

Because justice meant more than what she wanted.

It occurred to her then that was why she'd left Last Chance County in the first place. She'd known being a cop was what she wanted to do. She'd gone seeking justice elsewhere. In her own way.

Conroy said, "He was talking to Stiles?"

Meena made a face, while Mia figured he'd asked it because she'd just been silently standing there not doing anything or saying a word.

Conroy said, "Probably when we look at his phone, we'll know. Am I right?"

Meena said nothing. Another look ghosted across her eyes.

Mia knew that look. She grabbed her sister's elbow and pulled her to her feet. Meena was so surprised by Mia's actions, she reacted by straightening her legs under her. Given the heels on her boots, that put her slightly taller than Mia.

"You're coming to the police department. Voluntarily." She tugged on her sister's elbow. "I want to know everything you know about Anthony Stiles and your boyfriend's association with him."

"Boyfriend?" Summers stormed over. "What are they talking about?"

"Get out of the way." Mia moved past him.

Her stomach could hardly stand the sight of him. She wanted to hurl on the ground, but she might end up puking on key evidence that could nail Anthony Stiles.

Summers turned to the body, then followed them. "Garrett? Really Meena?"

She spun back, twisting in Mia's hold just above her elbow. "Yes, Garrett!" Meena screamed the words at him.

"Easy." She tugged on her sister's arm.

Meena shoved Mia away, a two-handed push at her shoulders that sent her stumbling back. "Leave me alone! I'm not going anywhere with you!"

"You're out."

Both of them spun around to Summers. Meena said, "What?!"

"You're done, woman." He leaned close to her face. "Not worth the trouble I always have to haul you out of."

Meena actually looked scared. "Don't—"

She stopped herself. As though she'd suddenly decided not to argue with Ed. Then Meena said, "He…"

"Yeah." Ed nodded, knowing and amused by whatever it was that he knew. "Done."

She screamed in his face. "I hate you!"

"Newsflash, Meens. I wasn't in it for this." He waved at her, up and down. "And now our arrangement is over."

Because he was angry she'd been involved with someone who worked for him. Mia had thought her sister had power in whatever operation Summers had going on. Now, it was clear she didn't. But apparently there was someone in charge. Someone *else*.

She screamed again in his face.

"Let's go." Mia tugged on her arm.

Meena went with her, but it was obviously under protest. "Like you're trying to help me out."

"Maybe I am."

Meena let out a pfft noise.

"So don't believe me." Mia shrugged. "Your guy is still dead, and there's another guy trying to kill me. Since we have the same build and similar enough hair, I'd think you might have a vested interest in helping me find him. Otherwise you could get picked off by mistake."

"Like Garrett?"

"This wasn't a mistake," Mia said. "Don't let your death be one."

"Like you care."

"You're my sister."

"You and I haven't been sisters in a long time. No point pretending otherwise when you all abandoned me."

"Mara is dead. I left. Dad's still here, right? At least, he was when I left the house."

"Nice for you. Getting to stop by for a visit." Meena said, "He told me to never come back."

"When?"

"I haven't seen him in years."

Mia said nothing. They walked down the path, toward the house. *Years* since she'd seen their father? At least Mia and her dad sent each other the occasional email.

She looked at the trail in front of them and something occurred to her. "You've been on one path for a long time. Probably longer than I even realized." Mia didn't give her sister the chance to argue. She just said, "It's time to get off that path. Find a new one that doesn't put you in a place like this."

The house was in view now.

Mia motioned to it. "Drug dealers. Thugs. And you're what? I don't even want to know. But it's time to be done."

"Give them all up to save your life?" Meena's painted-on eyebrows rose. "No matter that mine is worth *nothing*." She leaned in, talking low right in Mia's face. "Not without the pull I got being here. And you'll never persuade me to trade that in."

"Ed already did. Our sister's killer has tossed you out."

Talk about having nothing. It was like a bad breakup and the dissolution of a business partnership all in one swoop.

"Anthony Stiles is out there. He shot that guy, Garrett, between his eyes. Executed him." Mia paused. "And for what?"

Meena pressed her lips together. "Fine. I'll tell you what I know."

## 23

C onroy turned back to Wilcox. "What was that?"
She'd said something, but he'd been watching Mia
and her sister so hadn't caught it.

"Go." She waved towards the two women. "I got this."

He glanced between Summers and the two officers. She was
right. "I'll get the phone to the office."

Wilcox nodded. "I'll call if we get anything here."

He realized what didn't fit. "Where is Tate?"

"Gone."

She turned away before he could read on her face how she
felt about that. Conroy approached Summers on his way to
follow Mia. "Stay back. Let them work."

Summers said nothing, but his face was plenty loud.

"Don't get in this." Conroy said, "Unless, of course, there's
something you want to share with me about Anthony Stiles?"

"Who?"

Conroy wanted to sigh. Loudly. Instead, he pulled out his
phone and showed Summers a picture. "Seen this guy around?"

"That the guy who did this?" Ed motioned at the man.

"Was Garrett really sleeping with Meena, cheating on you?"

Ed shrugged. Summers didn't seem too bothered by the fact

his "girlfriend," or whatever Meena was to him, hadn't been faithful. He said, "It's not that kind of thing. She and I." He said nothing else.

"I'm leaving." He tossed his keys over to Wilcox, who caught them one-handed out of the air.

"Later, Lieutenant."

Conroy walked away, wondering why that sounded like an insult. Or a threat. Ed Summers might have stolen Conroy's girlfriend, but that was years ago. It had no bearing on what was going on now.

He would get Summers eventually. Probably when he figured out what Ed knew about Anthony Stiles. What Tate was working on. Most of that would come when Ed decided it was in his own best interest to tell Conroy—which would be when Ed had a mess he figured Conroy should clean up.

He'd do it to bring a criminal to justice and keep people safe. But that didn't mean he'd try and pin any old charges on Ed Summers.

Conroy picked up his pace to a loose jog and caught up with Mia. She stood close to her sister. Low conversation, body language pretty tense.

Meena spotted him and said something to her sister he couldn't hear. Mia broke off. They both turned to him.

"You're taking her back to the police department, right?"

It wasn't really a question. He needed to get whatever Meena had to say to her sister on record. Officially.

"To do the interview I'm already conducting?"

Mia said it, but Meena was the one who smiled. Conroy said, "I want this all done above board."

He didn't mistake her look. "This is my case."

"That may be so," Conroy said. "But you're also the victim. That can't be forgotten."

Meena twisted back to her sister. From the look on her face, it seemed she hadn't realized that, even though it was, in part, because of her.

Conroy shot her a look. "You want to help us, then this needs to be an official conversation."

They needed a lead to follow, something admissible in court. But there was no way she would consent to a conversation on the record.

"You think this Anthony Stiles guy has anything to do with me?"

"I think he killed your boyfriend." Conroy folded his arms. "Which means you have motivation to help me bring him in."

Meena scrunched up her nose. "Not sure that's what I got outta that." She motioned up the path. "That guy's gonna pay, though. You can count on it."

"You wanna go off on a vendetta?" He had a serious problem with people who took the law into their own hands. Conroy was the police. He had people that were trained—and the shields to prove it—to help him bring about justice. Meena wasn't the one who would be doing that. Nor would Ed. Not if he could help it.

Mia turned to her sister. "A vendetta is what started all this. Don't let it spiral out of control so that even more people get hurt. It won't end well."

Two men were already dead, one of them someone Meena cared about. But Conroy *still* didn't think appealing to her sister's emotions was going to get them anywhere. Except perhaps on the sidelines while Meena tried to take out Anthony Stiles herself. An act to avenge her boyfriend's death.

Mia motioned toward the car. "Let's go. I'm sure Conroy has work to do. He can…catch up, or something."

"I'm coming with you." She had to realize that. If he was to ever prove she could trust him—and if she was ever to put aside her grief over her sister's death in order to forgive his part in it —then they would have to be around each other to work on things.

"Besides," he said. "I left Wilcox the car, so I need a ride."

She spun back to him, not in the least bit fooled. "I don't

need your help. I'm a federal agent, remember? I know how to interview a witness. And if you want that done officially, then fine. Your jurisdiction—"

"Good you know that."

"—but I don't need a babysitter. This is my case, and I'm investigating it."

"Victim."

He said that one word, low and close to her face. He'd rather be talking softly this close to her face for an entirely different reason. But apparently he wasn't going to have the chance to do that anytime soon.

Guess that meant it was just work between them.

For now.

She wanted to play it that way? Fine by him. Not that he thought this was a game to her. But he did think she was still pushing him away, using her job right now as an excuse to protect herself from all the ways Conroy made her feel vulnerable.

"Why are you smiling?"

"No reason." He let his lips part, thoroughly amused now. She was off-kilter. He threw her, challenged her, probably infuriated her, and definitely attracted her.

"Whatever. I'm taking my sister." She set off. "See you later."

Conroy just stood there smiling. "I don't imagine you'll get very far."

"Don't doubt me. I'm good at what I do."

"Mmm."

She glanced back at him, serious irritation on her face.

Conroy said, "I need a ride back to the police department. That's you." He rocked forward, then back, on his heels. She knew this. Now the ball was in her court for what happened next.

"I should just leave you here. Or make you walk to town."

"But you wouldn't do that. Because you're a professional."

If he wanted to play dirty, he could. Conroy had the ability to make things difficult for her if he said anything to the ATF. Mia was technically supposed to have reported to them what was happening. She hadn't called in even once, for whatever personal reasons she had.

That made him all the more determined to see this through with her. Make sure Stiles was caught, and she wasn't hurt. At least, not more than she had already been.

"Fine."

The ride into town was as frosty as her tone. Meena smirking. Mia not saying anything, determined to do what she'd set her mind already to do.

They walked into the police department with Conroy feeling pretty pleased with himself. "Kaylee, if you could find us a room, I'd be grateful."

"Lieutenant." She hit the buzzer and admitted them to the bull pen. "Room two is open."

He led the way, and Mia walked her sister into room two after him. "Have a seat please, Meena. Coffee?"

He took their orders—both women looking at him like he'd grown an additional head—and turned on the surveillance camera on the way out, so they'd have it on file if Meena said anything while he was out of the room. Conroy found their tech in his office, a room no bigger than a storage closet, and asked to have access to everything he could get downloaded from the phone.

The sisters broke off their conversation again the second he re-entered the room holding three mugs with two hands.

He set them on the table.

Meena tugged hers over and took a sip.

Conroy set his phone on the table between them so she could see the photo of Stiles. "Tell me what you know about this guy."

"I've seen him around." She shrugged one shoulder. She was more slender than her sister, but only in a way that told a story about who she was and the substances she'd allowed into her body.

"With Garrett?"

"Yeah...maybe."

"You either did, or you didn't." Mia leaned against the table, her coffee untouched. "Either you know this guy and you can help us, or you can't and this was a waste of time."

Meena glanced up at her sister. "This guy really the one who killed Garrett?"

"And poisoned a dog that bit me."

"Yeah, but...he killed Garrett?"

"That's what we think," Conroy said. "We just don't know why. Can you tell me who was driving that red car, the one that pulled in right before we got to Summers's place?"

"Garrett came back to the house in that. But I have no idea where he got it from." Meena spread her fingers on the table. "Never even seen it before."

"Then he ran off into the woods."

"No idea about that either, until I saw you guys walk in. Tried to call him, but he didn't answer."

That would be easy enough for Conroy to confirm, since they had the dead man's phone in their possession.

"How did you meet Stiles?"

"Ed. They were in his office. I went in to ask him something, saw them talking."

Mia barked. "About what?"

Conroy kept his composure. She didn't know how to conduct an interview with a partner, where two officers of the law played off each other in order to tease the information out of the person. Seemed like, in her world, the person across the table either gave up what they knew, or they didn't.

Conroy said, "It seem amicable? A fight, or a bargain?"

"Like an arrangement." Meena nodded. "Like that."

"Did you see him after that?"

Meena shook her head. "Not at the house."

"How about Ed, after his first man was killed?"

"He didn't care about Tyler. The guy was completely expendable. No muss, no fuss." Meena shrugged. Didn't mean anything to her, either. "Garrett..." Her voice broke. "He was good with computers, you know? Probably hacked your house, or something."

There it was, an answer. Of sorts.

"I'm sorry about your friend." He knew what it felt like to have a friend pass. But the friend Conroy had lost was Mara. Even if she had just dumped him right before she was killed.

Now he needed to look more closely into Tyler Lane, Stiles's first victim—and accomplice—in town. Had Garrett or Tyler been the one to wire the explosive device in Conroy's car and set up the Bluetooth speakers in Mia's house?

Mia said, "What would Garrett have been doing with Anthony Stiles?"

"Helping him, probably." Her sister shrugged. "Loaned out by Ed to do whatever Stiles wanted."

Whatever their agreement had been.

The new guy in town paid a visit to the established bad guy, who considered Last Chance County his turf. Struck a bargain. Respect, and cooperation.

Mia said, "Why would Stiles kill him if it was an arrangement?"

A business agreement gone wrong, maybe.

When Meena said nothing, Conroy offered up an idea. "Betrayal. Either on Garrett's part or on Stiles's. Which means recompense will need to be brought. Because one side was wronged and gave payback, the other is going to want retaliation."

"That's the last thing we need." Mia paced the interview room. "More blood."

"Hang here for a bit, okay? Finish your coffee."

Meena shrugged.

Conroy ushered Mia into the hall with him. "Look, we're

going to do what we can to prevent more blood being shed. Okay?"

"And if it's Ed who goes after Stiles?"

"What if it is?"

Mia said, "Surely you aren't going to look away because it serves your purpose? Wait until the smoke clears and then move in?"

"Not when they'll have no consideration for collateral damage. No." He touched her elbow. "I'm going to head out and see Summers. I want you to stay here and see what we get from the phone."

She would be where she was protected. Added bonus, he'd hear her take on whatever they got from the phone as soon as they got it.

"I know what you're doing."

"Yeah," he said, getting close again. Making sure she was getting used to him being near, enough to become more comfortable with it. "But are you going to let me?"

Her face softened in a way he liked a whole lot. Once she got past her need to be stubbornly independent and her refusal to forgive him, Conroy figured the promise was there. This could be good.

Sure, it might be weird after dating her sister. Some people might talk even though that was years ago. Conroy still wanted to see if it would be worth all that. Because he was pretty sure he already knew the answer.

Before she could say anything, her phone rang. She dug it out. "My dad." Swiped the screen. "Hey, what are——"

Her face paled.

Her voice tremored. "Dad?"

## 24

She felt Conroy shift closer to her. The strength and warmth of his hands on her shoulders. Too bad she couldn't enjoy it.

"Dad? Can you hear me?"

The line went dead. Mia lowered the phone.

Conroy's hands slid to her elbows. "Tell me."

"All I heard was a gurgle. Nothing more."

"Your dad?"

"Lieutenant!" An older man turned the corner, breathing heavy.

Mia blinked. The guy had no hair, a bright red beard, green tattoos on his old-man arms below shirt sleeves that had been rolled back. "Shots fired." He glanced at her. "I'm Bill, the dispatcher."

She nodded. "Mia Tathers."

"Nice to meet you, Special Agent."

"Shots fired?"

He swallowed. Glanced at Conroy. "Rich's house."

Mia ran for the door. Kaylee moved a hand to the door controls. Mia just ran to the counter, planted her hands on top and swung her legs over. She landed, overbalanced, wobbled to gain it back, then hit the bar on the door and ran outside.

Car.

Home.

Conroy pulled open the door on the passenger side and got in. Mia didn't have time to figure out why or say anything, so she just drove.

Conroy put his phone to his ear. "Tell me." He listened while she drove. He said, "Stay there. Walk through but don't touch anything." Pause. "Five minutes."

He hung up.

"Responding officers?" Mia could barely choke the words out.

If Anthony Stiles had done something to her father, she was going to lose it even more than she already had.

"They're going to sit on the house until we get there."

"And?"

"They need to walk through first, confirm whether your dad is there or not." He sounded like he was barely containing himself. Kind of like the way she was barely containing herself. He said, "But the front door is open, and they said first glance that the place is a mess."

She prayed he was there. Right then, driving to her dad's house, Mia pleaded with God that if He'd ever loved her...

No, that wasn't fair. God wasn't some overlord to be bargained with. Regardless of what could happen, she would trust Him.

God loved her. He also loved her dad, and her dad had apparently found Him. That meant Rich Tathers was likely praying right now as well.

That realization of the solidarity between her and her father gave her a warm feeling. Not exactly hope. More like community. Fellowship that came with shared faith, even if he might be hurt, and she didn't know where he was.

He could be dead.

She didn't even want to think about that. Just get to the house first and find out for sure.

*Shots fired.*

She wanted to pull over and pray long enough that composure would come. Instead, she drove. Her brain filtered through with random pieces of information as it processed what had happened.

Tate had been with Ed. Had he gone over to the dark side as well? Now her father was gone.

"I didn't say bye to him."

Conroy looked up from his phone. "What?"

"I walked out, mad at you. I didn't say bye."

"When you called me?"

"Right after. He told me to trust you. Said to let you explain, and all I told him was to keep his gun close."

"I guess he could've used it. There were shots fired."

"Your officers would have reported in if they'd found him. If he had fought back, then he would be there now, hunkered down."

Conroy said, "You don't know that. He might have done damage but been overpowered."

"Or Anthony Stiles already killed him, and my dad is dead as Garrett."

He reached over, hesitant. Squeezed her knee. "You don't know that."

"I didn't tell Meena. She's back there, finishing her coffee, with absolutely no idea why we ran out."

"If she even saw. I'll ask Kaylee to brief her, since they'll need to cut her loose anyway."

Mia tapped the wheel with one finger. "I don't like keeping her in the dark."

"Looping her in might help. She'll be with you, supporting you."

He really thought that? "Or she'll split, round up all her

'boys' and go out hunting Stiles like she's the leader of some Wild West posse."

She took the road for the lake too fast and prayed no person or animal stepped out into the road while she raced to her dad's house.

The black and white patrol car sat at the curb. Right in the spot where Conroy's car had exploded.

It almost seemed like weeks ago she'd leaned over him, trying to get him to wake up.

An officer rounded the house. One she'd seen at the park, handling the murder scene of Tyler Lane. His dead body flashed in her mind. He saw Conroy, and shook his head, mouthing the words, *Not here.*

Her dad was gone.

Conroy stalled her before she could get out of the car. "We're going to find him."

Probably he didn't want the officers here to see him showing affection to someone he hoped they would respect for her position, and because she'd grown up here. She appreciated that.

"Thank you for being here with me." Mia squeezed his hand over her knee. "But let's go."

He nodded. They climbed out and met the officer. Since Conroy wanted this to be professional, she stood so the cop wouldn't miss the badge on her belt.

She'd run out of the police department before either of them could grab their coats. It was freezing outside.

The officer spoke as they rounded the house to the front door.

She saw the neighbors on their porch. Mom and the two kids, anyway. She wondered how Daisy was doing, and if they were the ones who'd called in the shots fired. "Anyone talk to the neighbors?"

"My next stop," the officer said.

She remembered his name. "Officer Basuto, right?"

He straightened his shoulders. "That's right." They rounded

the front corner, and she saw the door was open. "Nothing's been moved or touched, and we completed the walkthrough. Checked everywhere. He isn't here."

Basuto stopped outside the door, his dark brows pulling together.

She said, "What?"

"Blood on the living room carpet."

"What about a weapon? He has a twenty-two and a shotgun."

"My guess? It was the twenty-two. He fired." Basuto stepped in, but faced the wall by the front door. "Hunkered down in the living room where the blood is. I think he hit the frame over here. See the slug?"

It was embedded in the wood.

She nodded. "So he returned fire. Where's the blood from Stiles....or whoever?" There wasn't any right here, in the hall. Whoever he fired at by the front door wasn't hit.

"Only over there." Basuto waved to the living room.

Her dad had been hit. He was the only one who'd been hit. Mia nearly tripped over the coffee table trying to get there.

"Easy." Conroy didn't come over. He started up a low conversation with the officer while she looked.

Mia gasped. She took a half step back and had to throw her hand out to steady herself.

That was a lot of blood. "Wherever he is," she told Conroy, interrupting his conversation but not caring one bit about that, "my dad needs medical attention."

"Can Stiles keep him from bleeding out?"

Basuto said, "Stiles is the guy that did this?"

"It's our theory."

"This guy is running rampage all over town." Basuto shook his head. "My partner and I should get back out on the street. See if we can find him."

"Find out from the neighbor if they saw a car after they heard the shots fired."

"Yes, Lieutenant."

The two officers headed out the front door.

"We should go, too." She didn't want to stay here. There was nothing worse in the world than standing around doing nothing while someone she cared about was in danger.

Probably why it hurt so much when her teammates had done nothing to help her when she'd needed them. Essentially. Sure, after the one walked off, another had hauled Thompson Stiles's body off her. Asked if she was okay. But no one helped her up.

Her shoulder had been screaming, but she'd neglected to tell any of them that. They didn't get the satisfaction of knowing he'd hurt her. Of understanding that she had feared for her life right before she took the life of Stiles's brother. Anthony understood what it was like to grieve a sibling.

So did she.

He knew what it was like to want the responsible party to pay.

But if she still held the grudge she'd always held against Conroy over his head, even now, it didn't make her any better than Anthony Stiles. And here she was supposed to be the good guy.

So why didn't she feel like it?

At least she should believe it. Try to live like one.

Conroy touched her cheeks with his warm hands. "You holding on?"

She grasped his wrists, needing to feel the strength there when she didn't feel strong at all. *God.* She barely even knew what to say. "He's bleeding. He could be dead already."

Conroy pressed a kiss to her forehead. "So let's go."

He stepped back. She'd figured he would head for the front door, but he didn't. "Walk through the house. I want the perspective of someone who lives here. You might see something the officers missed."

She nodded. Walking through the house was a good way to

get out from under the feeling of being so powerless. The warm press of Conroy's lips against the skin of her forehead filled her mind instead.

She'd never been a source of attraction to anyone before, at least not that she knew of. Mia was too tall, too stocky. Men didn't see her as anything other than "one of the boys." Especially her coworkers. She figured this was, for the most part, because of Mara. Conroy cared for her because she was Mara's sister.

Yes, he'd kissed her for real before. But he hadn't done it since.

Probably, he'd changed his mind. Realized it was a mistake.

Now he was just a nice guy, so he was here. He cared about her father and was willing to help when someone in his town was shot and kidnapped.

Fear rolled through her. She bent double and nearly threw up.

Conroy touched her back, his warm palm between her shoulder blades. She stood. "I'm fine."

"It's okay to not be."

She pulled open the door to the hall closet. "He's not wearing his coat. It's still here."

It was forty-five degrees outside. Her dad was used to cooler temps, but with the loss of blood, he'd be feeling that right now, and she didn't think Stiles was the kind of kidnapper who would crank the heat in his car.

She pulled out the coat and slipped it on herself, over her jacket, smelling her dad even as his coat warmed her. "We need the car make and model."

"Soon as we know anything, I'll put it out. Get everyone looking." Conroy said, "Your dad is well liked in this town, and there are some people who live here now who have special skills. I'll burn a favor, but that's one thing I'm happy to do to get your dad back."

"Because he's your friend?"

"That's part of it."

She went back to the living room but ignored the blood. "Where is his phone?"

"I figure he dropped it before Stiles took him." He pointed at the blood on the door frame to the hall. A smear she hadn't seen before.

She looked away from it, crouched, and searched under the coffee table for her dad's phone. Conroy lifted the couch and she looked under it. "No."

He felt between all the cushions. "It's not here."

"Does he have it with him?" That one question sparked a rush of hope that made her press her hand to her stomach. Her injured arm throbbed, but she mostly ignored it.

Her dad was bleeding.

Conroy shot a look of hope in her direction and held his phone to his ear. "Kaylee, get someone to my house. I want a GPS location for Rich Tathers's phone, ASAP."

His command center.

"That's right," Conroy said. "It's on my computer." Pause. "Copy that." He ended the call. "We're the closest available personnel."

"Then let's go." She hit the front door, nearly colliding with that little girl from next door. Whatever the kid's name was. "Sorry." She ran. "Gotta go."

## 25

"This is it?"

Conroy slammed his car door. "This is where my computer says your dad's phone is."

Mia looked around. Conroy knew what she saw—nothing. They were three miles from her dad's house in a secluded area nearly at the outskirts of town. "If he went this way and just tossed the phone out of the window, then he was going north. But what's out there?"

"Has to be a place he's holed up. Otherwise, it doesn't make sense. He has your dad, not you. Unless he contacts you and arranges a trade, then he didn't get what he wanted."

"And he threw away the phone. So this is likely all misdirection."

He looked around. Saw blood in a matted spot of grass. "He didn't toss the phone out the window."

She came over, touched his shoulder, and leaned against him for support while she looked closer.

The whole move made him wonder if she realized what she was doing. Probably not. He'd been trying to encourage her to lean on him. All the while, Mia was busy proving she was an

188 | LISA PHILLIPS

independent woman who didn't need anyone. Least of all a man who had played a part in killing her sister.

Conroy walked around the area. The grass was long. Logs covered with snow that had collected in the shady spots.

"You did well with Ed." He tossed it out like a random comment, instead of something he desperately wanted to talk to her about. "When you saw him."

"Because I didn't pull out my weapon and shoot him?"

"Did that cross your mind?" He glanced at her and saw her face. "Because I've thought about it a time or two."

"He was your friend."

"Yeah," Conroy said. "Emphasis on the 'was' part of that."

She nodded. They searched the area, the two of them falling naturally into a spiral pattern as they scanned the area around them. "Please tell me we're going to get Stiles and Ed Summers. I'd dearly love to get enough to bring them both down over this."

"Especially if Summers's guys are working for Stiles."

"You think he…what? Loaned them out? Like Meena said. Stiles showed up, gave Ed a little respect, and got something in the bargain."

"Maybe." He kept walking, eyes on the grass.

"I think if he did that, then it's not money Ed is after." She paused. "I think it's something else. Like a way to get at you."

"Through you?" Conroy straightened. If she thought that, then she was finally willing to acknowledge there was something between them. And it had weight to it. Not inconsequential.

Something he wanted to explore.

"We'll have to figure it out later." She bent. "I found my dad's phone."

Mia straightened, using a winter glove from her dad's pocket to hold his cell out so Conroy could see it.

Conroy pulled an evidence bag from his pocket, and she slipped the thing in. Bloody fingers had left smudges over the glass front. "Let's get this back to the office."

It seemed like they'd been driving back and forth all over town. As he got back in the driver's seat yet again, Mia said, "You think Meena is still there?"

Conroy shrugged his shoulder that was closest to her in the passenger seat. "Probably not. I figure she got bored and Kaylee let her walk out."

"Would Kaylee have told her what happened to my dad?"

"We'll find out." He squeezed her hand, as he'd done a few times today. Both of them knew he meant more to the squeeze than just concern over what Meena knew.

He meant they were going to find her father, and he was determined to do that. Conroy didn't want to think about the fact Rich could die. Or even that he could already be dead. He figured he'd covered it well enough that Mia didn't know, but he was seriously scared they wouldn't get her dad back.

Fear was like a sour feeling in his gut. Like the worst food poisoning.

If Rich was dead, then he would never get to see Mia forgive Conroy, as he himself had done. Conroy knew seeing that miracle happen with his daughter was his friend's greatest wish.

"What?"

He glanced over.

"You had a look on your face."

"I think your dad purposely went hunting right before you got here."

"To kill a deer?"

"No." Conroy shook his head. "I think he was hoping you and I would run into each other."

"We did."

"Because you took down my suspect outside the grocery store?"

"I was trying to avoid you. You're the one whose life collided with mine."

Conroy smiled to the road, holding the wheel as he meandered through town. "That it did. I think Rich had hoped that you would…come around." See that it wasn't worth holding onto bitterness over Mara's death.

"You'd rather I blamed Ed Summers instead?"

"He was the one who was driving drunk. But that's not what I mean."

"I didn't know she'd broken up with you," Mia said quietly. "And you still got in the car to try to convince him to pull over."

"Yes." Among other things, like how he'd begged for an actual reason from Mara—*why* she'd dumped him for Ed. His fragile self-esteem hadn't been able to handle that blow. He'd even pleaded with her. And then vowed never to allow himself to be that vulnerable again.

Until he met Jesus, who saw to the heart of who he was and still loved him anyway. Something he and Rich had talked about many times.

Conroy said, "When I realized he was going to just keep driving, and she was truly done with me, I asked them to let me out."

He pulled into his space outside the police department and shut the car off but didn't get out. "Told them to pull over. That I would be gone from them. Ed said, 'good' and angled to the side of the road. He didn't see the vehicle that came out of the sidestreet opposite until it was too late. He didn't stop before the intersection as he should have, and they plowed right into us. Right into the passenger door."

Conroy didn't look at her. "His dad had argued with the judge. First offense, that they knew of. Kids being kids, and all that. Like he should just be let go. The driver in the other car had some bruises. Ed's dad paid for all the damage and it was done. Ed would have had his license revoked, but he'd get it back eventually."

"But Mara…"

"You know she passed away in the hospital a day or two

later. Injuries sustained. The judge changed his ruling, and Ed went to juvenile detention."

"And that judge now?"

"He's as committed to bringing down Ed Summers's empire as I am. Considering everyone Ed works with now, except your sister, were people he met in juvie. The judge thinks it's all on him for sending Ed there."

"That's crazy. You can't stop the choices a person is going to make."

Conroy's phone buzzed in his pocket. He pulled it out and looked at the text. "The tech wants to know where I am. He can see from my phone's location that we're here, and he has something to tell us."

"Ready to go inside?"

He liked it that she'd asked. Conroy nodded. "I'm okay."

He'd basically admitted the worst thing about himself. That he'd been so caught up in his own hurt feelings that his actions had indirectly caused Mara's death. Ed had been charged and convicted but at an age where it was all about sealed records.

He said, "Thank you for listening."

"And if I decide to join the club that consists of you and this judge?"

He couldn't help a smile. "Membership is currently open. Though you should know, your dad is one of the founders."

"Secret society. Love it."

She shoved the car door open, and he kept smiling at her as she shut it and strode to the sidewalk. He'd been all about trying to distract her and hadn't even done it well. In the end, she'd managed to distract him.

A secret society? He shook his head at the idea. The most organized group he was a part of was the Bible study he and Rich both attended.

Conroy followed her in and saw the tech standing with Mia, waiting for him. Ted was nothing like the typical nerd type he remembered from high school. He wore skinny jeans, Converse shoes, and a rock band T-shirt that was faded. He had a Bluetooth earbud headset around his neck. His watch was the smart kind. Conroy had the same brand, mostly because Ted had told Conroy all about it enough that he'd finally buckled and bought one for himself.

Anything that meant he didn't have to pick up his phone as often was a good choice in his estimation.

Ted was also Dean's kid brother. Dean being the Navy SEAL who'd shown up right after Conroy's car had exploded, initially treating his injuries.

Conroy said, "What is it?"

"I dumped the victim's phone and went through it."

*The victim.* Garrett. Not Rich. "Already?"

Ted was about to answer when he saw the bagged phone in Conroy's hand. "Another one?"

"That's my dad's," Mia said.

"Oh." Ted glanced between them. "Oh."

"What did you get from Garrett's?"

"From the look of his latest text thread, Stiles arranged to meet him. Garrett wanted the money he was owed for the job Stiles hired him to do." Ted shrugged. "They were supposed to meet on the far side of Summers's property. Seems like Garrett was the one who poisoned the dog, and took you from the Lieutenant's house, but I don't think he set the explosives that blew your gas tank."

Mia shifted to face him. "So, was the first dead guy—Tyler Lane—also someone who was doing jobs for Stiles? Because that really is a serious coincidence."

Conroy nodded, his brain still spinning over it all.

"And if it's true," Mia continued, "then it could be there's another one out there still, working with him. Right? Maybe another one of Ed Summers's guys took my dad out of his house. They could be planning to meet up so he can hand my dad off to Anthony Stiles."

"It's a theory." But without evidence, that was all it was.

Conroy wondered about going over to Ed's place, rousting out all his guys and making Ed do a headcount to find out if anyone else was missing. Not exactly above board, but it would make him feel better even if it got them nothing as far as results.

He asked Ted, "Can you get me a location on the phone that communicated with Garrett's?"

Ted shook his head. "Already tried, since it's implicated by association. The phone is either off or it's dead. No GPS, and no cell towers can see it."

Conroy nodded. If Ted couldn't find it, then there was nothing to find.

The chief's door opened. Officer Ridgeman stepped out. Ted shifted in a way that broadcast a whole lot more than even he was probably aware.

The corners of Jessica Ridgeman's lips curled up. "I'm just getting some tea."

"Help her out, will you Ted? The machine was acting up yesterday."

They wandered off. Conroy smiled as they started a quiet conversation.

Mia said, "Uh...what was that?"

"What?" Conroy shrugged. "Wilcox fixed the tea machine this morning but that's not the point, is it?"

"You're a romantic."

He had no time to answer.

The front door to the police station burst open. Men in black masks with handguns, some with rifles, poured in the door.

Kaylee screamed. One of them fired and an officer across the bull pen screamed. The man fell, blood spraying behind him.

Conroy hit the ground. Mia right beside him.

He twisted to see Ted and Jess in the break room, through the glass. He waved them off and pulled his gun.

A shotgun ratcheted.

"Any of you guys decide to play hero, things are going to get real ugly real fast."

## 26

M ia's senses crystalized. She shifted up against whoever's
desk drawers these were, enough to peek over the top. A
split second was all she needed.

Down. She twisted to Conroy and help up four fingers.
Then two, which she motioned left with. The other two she
motioned right.

He nodded.

Mia turned back. Looked again. Her mind debated procedure versus the potential loss of life. Rules were meant to mini-
mize casualties, but bad guys didn't often do as they were
supposed to. Logic went out the window when a person was
running on adrenaline. Desperate.

A fifth man.

She saw the guy by the door, over the reception counter. It
was his eyes that broadcast what he was about to do. She'd seen
it before; the intention to take someone's life.

Kaylee.

The man lowered his gun to angle down, over the counter.
He could see her even though Kaylee was desperately trying to
hide. Mia saw him close one eye and shift his finger to the
trigger.

She planted her elbows on the desk and fired.

The man fell back. Dead, in the waiting area.

She ducked back down, Conroy grabbing her as she moved. Motion erupted in the room. Gunshots went off.

Three planted themselves in the desk above her head. Someone cried out, and then whimpered. Scared, not in pain.

*Sorry.*

She needed to make sure the person who'd been shot when they first came in was all right. She didn't like not being able to help them.

Conroy still had a handful of her shirt sleeve in his grip. She turned to him and mouthed, *Kaylee.*

Conroy shifted forward and pressed a quick, hard kiss on her lips. "You go that way," he whispered, pointing back over his shoulder. "I'll go that way." He pointed ahead of himself.

That meant they had to shift around each other. It also meant he'd be the one more greatly exposed as he headed for the two gunmen on the left, while she went for the other two in an area with plenty of cover.

Mia was about to argue when he pressed another kiss to her lips. "Copy?"

She nodded. He had switched back to business mode now. She saw it in his eyes. Save his people, take these guys out. Don't lose anyone. Else.

She scrambled across the floor, rounded the desk, and at the front corner, peeked around. Her two guys stood with their guns aimed.

Waiting for someone to pop up from behind a desk—like that carnival game—so they could pick them off.

She studied her two. Grunts. Not the boss, the one with the shotgun Conroy insisted on taking care of personally. She understood that. This was his house, and these people were under his protection.

Jeans. One had cargo pants. Heavy coat. Leather jacket… that coat. She felt a tiny niggle of familiarity. They had wool masks over their faces here, but the bigger one? Mia had seen that spider web neck tattoo before. Though she could only see a tiny portion of it now, she was pretty sure that it was the same one.

Had she been with Meena when she'd seen this guy once before? She honestly didn't remember.

"Get the phone!"

Someone moved. Fast.

The two on her side stayed put. Covering the room.

Mia could hear Kaylee's short, sharp breaths but couldn't get to her from where she was to ask if she was all right. Whoever had been hit initially was whimpering again.

The partner with spider web guy seemed to find that distress amusing. His eyes were the eyes of a killer. Crazy. Someone who got a rush out of putting fear in people. Watching fright play out across their faces while he hurt them. Spider web guy didn't appear to be anything but cold to it all.

What was Conroy doing? She figured he had a plan, but maybe he was just watching and waiting like she was. Would he pop up all of a sudden? If he did that, then they could both open fire. Take these guys out.

She realized crazy guy had disappeared. Mia shifted to get a look and heard a voice.

"Well, well, well."

She froze.

A gun barrel pressed against her spine. "Stand up."

Crazy guy had a gun pointed right at her. No chance he'd miss. He could end her life with one squeeze of his trigger.

Mia forced her legs to hold her weight as she rose, locking her knees as she straightened.

"Now hand over that gun."

The one in her hand? No way. No cop would willingly hand over their weapon. "I'm putting it away."

"I said, 'hand it over.'" He shoved at her with the barrel.

She winced. "I'm not giving it to you."

The phrase, "over my dead body" entered her mind, but she figured if she said it aloud, he just might take her up on the offer.

Given the fact Conroy had just kissed her, for real again, Mia didn't want to chance dying here. For the first time in her life, she thought she just might have something to live for.

And that changed everything.

Mia holstered the gun. The guy behind her grabbed for it. She snatched up his wrist and spun, figuring at least she could plant a hand on his chest and shove. Before she got shot.

He pressed the gun to her chest.

Mia held her breath.

Spider web guy said, "Stop screwing around, bruh."

Crazy-eyed guy laughed like this whole thing was hilarious to him.

"There's a person hurt back there." She pointed to the corner of the room. "I need to go check on them."

"What I want," he said, "is something entirely different."

He moved to grab her, but she stepped back. Her thigh slammed into the corner of the desk and she winced. No way would she whimper. A guy like this wasn't going to get that from her.

She gritted her teeth together.

"Seriously, bruh." Spider web guy grabbed her elbow and pulled her away from crazy guy.

Her gun was holstered, but the snap was still open. She could pull it out at any time. Squeeze the trigger and blow these guys away.

Crazy guy would go down in a hail of fire. This guy with the spider web tattoo would find a different ending. Or so he seemed intent on doing so. Smarter, somehow.

"I wanna use a cop gun." Crazy guy was whining now.

Spider web guy shook his head. "Give it up. And keep watch like we're supposed to do."

"I could just off all these cops. We get the phone and get out. Boom. Done."

Mia scanned the room for Conroy, trying to figure out where he'd gone. To get the phone before these two hoodlums could?

"Too much heat," spider guy said. "Not a good idea."

Across the room she could see the tech—Ted, she thought his name was—and the officer whose grandfather was the chief. Ridgeman. Both very young, probably inexperienced with real hostage situations. They huddled together in the break room.

She decided to engage the gunmen. Keep them somewhat distracted. "What phone?" she asked. "Why do you guys need a phone?"

"Kill that guy who killed our friend," crazy guy said. "Sneak up behind him…"

She felt a gun press against her back again.

"…bang, he's dead."

He laughed and stepped away. He went to another officer, an older man, and kicked him in the ribs. Mia wondered whether Basuto and his partner, or Wilcox, knew what was happening.

*Conroy.*

He hadn't left her alone. That wasn't what was going on here, and she couldn't let her fear convince her that he'd kissed her and then abandoned her. If he had gone somewhere else to do some*thing* else, then it was all about respect. He trusted her to take care of herself.

Only, she'd always thought that if you cared about someone, then you fought to protect them instead of letting them take care of themselves. Just because they could take care of themselves didn't mean they should be left unprotected. Regardless of how capable someone was, you looked out for the people in your life.

The way Conroy had done even after Mara dumped him.

It hadn't saved her life. But it had been the right thing to do.

Even if he'd given up in the end. Even if he believed that he'd caused the accident.

Spider web guy tugged her toward the door. She took two steps.

A gunshot rang out from the back hallway.

Mia stumbled. Her whole body tensed, and she yanked her arm out of spider web guy's grip. She gasped. "Conroy."

Two men came out of the hall. Conroy was not one of them. The front guy held up a phone in his hand.

"Great." Spider web guy said, "Let's go."

"Good idea." Mia stepped behind him, away from crazy guy. "You got what you wanted. Now it's time to leave." She saw the look on crazy guy's face. "Before something is done that cannot be undone."

Assuming they hadn't already killed more than one person.

*Conroy.* She wanted to whimper.

Crazy guy got close. "Sure you don't wanna go for a ride?"

"You get that I'm a federal agent, right?" When he said nothing, she said, "I'm also Meena Tathers' sister. Which means there's nothing you have that I want. Less than nothing, actually." She wanted to fold her arms, to further make her point, but that put her hand too far from her holstered gun.

"Hold up."

One of the men grabbed the phone from the man holding it. He looked at the phone. Her dad's phone.

"This isn't the one."

The man who'd held the phone walked right up to her. He grabbed her throat with one meaty hand. "You tryin' to play us?"

She couldn't even breathe to reply. Just shook her head the tiny bit she was able to move it. Someone took the gun from her holster, and she heard crazy guy snicker.

This wasn't good.

The man holding her throat yanked on it. Hard. He hauled

her past the desk, where she stumbled and landed on her hands and knees on the thin carpet.

He kicked her side.

Mia rolled over, teeth gritted. Better to do that than bite her tongue. Or cry out. They weren't going to get that out of her.

"Get me that phone."

She used the desk to aid her in standing. "Garrett's phone?"

He said nothing.

"So you can find Stiles and kill him?" She waited, then said, "Sure. Why would I stop you? Save us all some time."

Plus it was the fastest route to getting these gunmen out of the police department. Before the officers probably collecting outside even now could bust in and start another gunfight. Enough blood had already been shed here.

She led them to the side hall. The tech's office was past the bathroom. As soon as she walked into the room and saw the phone on Ted's desk, a rush of relief washed over her and she leaned over to scoop it up.

"Let's go. You're coming with us."

She spun around, the phone in her hand. Where *on earth* was Conroy? "I'm not going with you."

She held out the phone.

Everyone else was in the hallway, except the guy who seemed to be in charge; he was with her in the tech's office.

She said, "Take it."

"Yeah, no." He grabbed her wrist and dragged her back into the hall, forcing her to brush past crazy guy on the way out.

She pressed her lips together, feeling his hands places they should not be.

The group moved to the exit door.

She said, "You don't need me."

"Not what I heard," he said. "Which is that you're the trade he'll accept. We find him. This guy gets you. He leaves town."

"Or so he thinks." Crazy guy grinned.

"Then probably one of *your* people shouldn't have kidnapped my father."

The leader guy said, "Rich is there? Nice guy, your dad. Shame he probably won't make it."

She whipped around, about to speak, when he said, "This guy gets you, he doesn't need your dad anymore, does he now?"

Stiles was going to kill her.

And her father.

Conroy rounded the corner at the end of the hall, gun up. Sweat. Blood. "Let her go!"

"You wanted Ed, right?" he said to her. The guy spoke loud enough for Conroy to hear but otherwise ignored him. "So then move."

## 27

C onroy ran to the door, gun first.
Shots exploded like fireworks. One sang past his ear. He took cover against the wall, pinned down and unable to look outside.

They'd taken her.

*You wanted Ed.*

Car doors slammed. Another shot hit the wall by the door, outside.

"Lieutenant!" Officer Ridgeman stood at the far end of the hall, face flushed. Gun ready.

"Stay there." He waved her back.

After a few seconds of no shots, he looked out. Engines revved on two vehicles, an old, small SUV and a car.

Through the window, one of the men made a gesture directed at Conroy.

He really wanted to shoot at the fleeing car, but not doing so was safer for innocent bystanders. And it was a good rule, even if he didn't want to follow policy right now.

"Lieutenant!" Dean Cartwright, the medic and former SEAL—and Ted's brother—raced around the building.

Conroy waved him over and went back inside.

Jessica Ridgeman stood at the end of the hall. "Mia?"

"They took her." He reached her side. "How's the chief?"

"I need to go check. The nurse was with him."

He nodded. "Go." She'd shown loyalty to the whole department by protecting the house and everyone in it first. Not just her grandfather. The lines of blood family and family in blue probably blurred for her.

Dean pounded down the hallway.

Conroy turned in time to see him frown at Jess's back as he slowed. "What?"

He turned that frown to Conroy. "Nothing. Anyone hurt?"

"Yes. In the bull pen. And tell Kaylee I want a headcount."

"Copy that." Dean headed through the same door Jess had gone through.

Conroy hadn't managed to take any of them out, though not for lack of trying. He'd had to dive out of the way to avoid being seen. But he'd heard a shot right before those men emerged with Rich's phone. Who had they shot at?

Conroy checked Ted's office. No one. The bathroom?

He pushed open the men's room door, then the ladies. "Hey!"

On the floor. He raced to the far end, where a leg stuck out of a stall. Thankfully the person was dressed. Probably hiding.

He tugged the shoulder over, and her blonde hair fell back. "Wilcox? When did you get here?"

She didn't answer. She was unconscious; a bullet embedded in the vest she was wearing.

"Did you hit your head on a toilet?" He gathered her in his arms and stood. "What am I going to do with you?"

She'd probably entered from that same side door where they'd taken Mia, trying to take down the intruders herself. He shook his head and turned sideways to get through to the bull pen. A one-woman powerhouse. Until they'd clocked her and put a bullet in her vest.

Kaylee gasped. "Is she okay?"

Conroy said, "Chair."

She held one steady so it didn't roll while he set Wilcox in it, then crouched and patted her cheek. "Wake-y, wake-y, Savannah. Rise and shine."

She didn't rouse.

"Dean?" He called the guy's name across the bull pen.

The former SEAL lifted his head up. "This one has one to the shoulder, through and through."

"Officer Allen?"

"I'm good, Lieutenant." His call out was full of pain.

"Get it taken care of." He turned back to Savannah and watched her grumble something too low for him to hear. "Rise and shine, detective." Then he turned to Kaylee. "You made the calls?"

She nodded. "Bill is running point on that. Everyone's asking if they can help. Ambulances are on their way."

"Both of them?"

When she nodded, he said, "I want to know if Tate calls in."

"Copy that." Kaylee turned back to her desk. Probably to call Tate himself and ask why he wasn't calling in when the Lieutenant expected him to. Like he should just know to do that.

Ted stepped out of the chief's office.

"How is he?"

"Slept through the whole thing, thankfully. The nurse is ready to throw a freak-out fit to end all freak-out fits, though. Jess is talking to her."

Conroy nodded.

Ted said, "Where's Mia?"

Dean stood up, Officer Allen's good arm draped over his shoulder. He was so big that Dean's bulk lifted the guy off his feet. "Ambulance?"

Kaylee said, "On its way."

Dean started walking. "Tell them I'm headed straight there in my truck. We don't need to wait."

She glanced at Conroy, who nodded.

Dean said something to his brother as he passed. Ted frowned, even after Dean hauled Officer Allen to the front door.

"What was that?"

Ted didn't seem so inclined to tell Conroy the answer to that.

Savannah moaned. He crouched in front of her. "Okay?"

She hissed out a breath. "Did I really get shot in a bathroom?"

"You're still alive."

"If I die that way, you've gotta tell my mom it was clean. Okay? She'll be mad."

He squeezed her shoulder. "Sure thing. Give yourself a minute. Get checked out by these EMTs." They walked through the door, so he waved them over. "When you're ready, and not a minute before then, there's work for you to do."

"Copy." She didn't sound happy about it. "Hey, where's Mia?"

He got out of the way of the EMTs.

"Conroy."

He glanced at her.

"Respectfully? Answer the question, Lieutenant."

"They took her."

She grasped the chair handles, ready to launch herself up. He held up a hand, palm out to her. "Not until you're ready."

He walked to the hall again, looked at the door they'd taken her out of. It had been a coordinated attack, but more about brute force than any kind of finesse.

His mind flashed back to the events leading to Mia being kidnapped. Again. He'd made his way to the store room, diving to keep from being seen in the process. He'd gotten a vest, hearing the shot that hit Wilcox as he fastened the straps. The shotgun had been his next grab.

To the hall. But not in time to save her from being taken.

Second time something happened to her on his watch. Though he couldn't help thinking of the man's words.

*You wanted Ed.*

She'd gone with them, instead of fighting. Some people would have done that same thing. Others would fight to their last breath even if it meant losing their life, just for the sake of not being taken.

Mia had training. She knew the odds of survival after the victim was put in the car, but probably didn't consider herself a victim, even now. She would fight.

They had her gun.

Stiles had her father.

She would hedge her bets, account for Conroy and his department, and consider the risk to her own life worth it.

*Lord, help me get them both back. Mia and her father. Help me bring justice to Anthony Stiles.*

Was this his ticket to getting Ed Summers as well?

That could not be the focus right now. Not when Mia might be in Stiles's clutches already; fighting for her life against a known psychopath.

Ted strode past Conroy to his office. "You okay, boss?"

"No."

"Come in."

Conroy leaned against the door frame. Mia had grabbed the phone right before she'd been taken. "Now we'll never get that location. And they have Rich's phone as well, so we have no leads."

Ted frowned. He tapped two keys on his keyboard, a shortcut to something Conroy didn't know how to do. When the login window showed up, Ted tapped a mind-numbing series of letters and numbers.

"Please tell me you have something."

"Not that I want to burst this bubble of misery you've got going on, but…" He clicked a few keys and a folder popped up. "This is everything we got from the dead man's phone…Garrett whoever. It's currently running a program on Tyler Lane's phone that will look for correlations, or anything else that's notable."

"You have everything?"

Ted nodded. "If they were trying to handicap us, they should've worked a whole lot harder than this. No one is dead, and we've lost nothing."

"Except Mia."

"Is that really a loss?"

Before Conroy could bite his head off, Ted held up one hand.

"Hear me out. What I mean is that it could be an 'in.' Maybe the one we've been looking for all this time."

Conroy folded his arms. "I'm not in the mood for a 'Ted' talk." The kid was always going on about having a growth mindset.

"Just trying to think positively."

Conroy shot him a look.

"It helps. Sometimes." Ted turned back to his computer. "I'll send you the location for where Garrett was going to get his money from Anthony Stiles."

"Thanks." He walked to the door. "Do you need anything?"

Ted glanced over. "Not something you can help me with."

"If you're sure?"

"Yeah." Ted nodded. "Thanks anyway."

Conroy left him to it and went back to the bull pen. There were more officers here now. Helping. Cleaning up to get the place to rights. Two uniforms who worked nights, dressed in plain clothes, stood in the chief's office talking with Jess and the nurse.

The second Wilcox saw him, she stood. "I'm good, boss."

The EMT didn't seem to agree, and his associate just seemed to find the whole thing hilarious.

Kaylee wandered over. "Tate said he'll call you. I think he might have something."

"Thanks."

Wilcox made a face. "What do we need his help for?"

Kaylee held up both hands, flashing the warm, dark color of her palms. "*Girl.*" She dragged the word out. "If you need me to explain it to you..."

Conroy felt his lips curl up. Humor was good, even in the middle of a crisis.

Wilcox said, "I didn't mean *that*. He was all buddy-buddy with Ed, and don't even get me started on him being there when Mia was taken from the Lieutenant's house. We should haul him in for questioning. Try to get an accessory charge to stick."

Before she could make a plan, Conroy said, "I'll get my keys. We're out of here."

Kaylee nodded. Conroy crafted a quick update email he sent to everyone in the department, so they'd know to get assignments from Kaylee. She wrote down what he wanted them to do. Increased patrols for tonight. Photos out for everyone they knew to be involved, as well as notes to look for Mia and Rich. Stiles was top priority.

He needed officers to go through the security footage for the department building. See if they could ID any of the men who'd broken in.

Repairs.

Cleaning.

Conroy stood by his desk and gave himself a second before his head could explode. He squeezed the bridge of his nose and prayed again. For safety and protection, for both Rich and Mia. That he'd find them. Get them back. That neither would be hurt beyond what they were able to heal from.

Ted's email came through.

Conroy dismissed the notification and scrolled through his contacts and hit Meena's name.

She didn't pick up.

When the message system beeped, he said, "When you get this, you call me." No exceptions, no arguments. It was time for Mia's sister to do the right thing.

Wilcox followed him out to the car. He turned the engine on, and as soon as the vehicle connected to his phone, Conroy called Tate.

"Hey."

"What've you got?" He stepped on the gas and pulled out as he asked the question, ready to find Mia already.

All the while his mind screamed that it was some kind of double cross. That she hadn't called her ATF people because she'd been working with Ed Summers all this time. Just like Tate —in cahoots with Conroy's enemies. The way she'd talked in low whispers with her sister. Leaving with those men.

No. He'd seen that look of fear and pain on her face. He couldn't let his mind believe what it insisted he should. He had to remember who she was and the look on her face, right after he'd kissed her.

Wonder.

There was no mistaking a look like that. Conroy wanted to see it again, maybe when he rescued her from Ed Summers. Or Anthony Stiles. Either way, he was going to get her back.

Tate said, "I was trying to follow Stiles, but I got a call from an associate. Ed has Mia."

"What?!" Wilcox's yell filled the whole inside of the car.

Conroy winced. "Just give us the address."

Wilcox said, "He probably got it from playing kissy face with Ed."

"Savannah." Conroy kept his voice low, but the fact he was chiding her came through loud and clear.

She folded her arms, mushing her lips together like every teen girl he'd ever met who'd been denied a trip to the mall. Except that was sexist, and she didn't just look mad. She regretted what she'd just said.

Tate said, "What's your problem?"

"I'm sure it doesn't have to do with the fact I was shot half an hour ago."

Conroy wanted to shut his eyes and sigh, but he was driving. "Just send me the address."

Wilcox abruptly ended the call right as Tate started to roar. "Oops."

Conroy said, "Super professional."

"Sorry. I'm just scared. I get weird when I'm scared." She rubbed her hands on her pant legs. "He gave me the address. We need to get to Mia."

"Yes," Conroy said. "We do."

## 28

Crazy guy shoved her into an empty bedroom at Ed Summers's house. Her sister sat in the corner, leaning against the wall. Face turned away.

Mia said, "This seems familiar."

How could she not see the correlation between the two times she'd had some one-on-one time with her sister these last few days? Trapped within four barren walls. The fact her sister had something to do with her previous abduction.

This time, however, they'd taken her badge and gun. And this was Summers's house. And she was being held in one of the upstairs rooms. She glanced out the window. Not the place where Meena took her.

Her sister didn't move.

"Meena." She strode over, crouched, and shook her sister's shoulder.

The only answer she got was a low moan. Then she turned her head and the swatch of dark hair over her face fell to the side as she looked up at Mia."

"Oh, baby." She crumpled to sit beside her sister on the floor. "What did they do to you?"

Meena's body shook. Mia started to gather her sister to her

so she could hold her. That was when she realized her little sister was laughing.

"Nothing about this is funny," Mia said. "They beat you."

"You think I care? Not the first time. Won't be the last."

Apparently she thought Mia was a total sap. Still, she'd like to know what made Meena so sure it would happen again. And why it'd happened this time. "Why?"

Meena sucked in a breath that appeared to be painful. "Talking to you and Conroy."

The official conversation. "So you talked, and you still wanted back in. But this is the cost?"

"It's my life." Meena shifted away from her but didn't get far.

"Well it doesn't make any sense to me."

Meena pushed a breath out between her lips.

Mia said, "They took me—and for what? I'm not a bargaining chip in this. It makes no sense for Ed Summers to drag me into his thing. Not after what he did to us."

"You mean Mara?"

"He drove drunk and she *died*." Did Mia really have to explain that to her sister?

"Ancient history. People around here barely even remember." Meena lifted a finger and touched the cut at the corner of her lip. Someone wearing a ring had punched her repeatedly in the face. What wounds did Meena have that couldn't be seen—ones her sister could hide from everyone?

Kind of like the wounds Mia carried around. Self-inflicted, since her refusal to forgive Conroy for his part in Mara's death had really only succeeded in hurting one person. Mia.

"I remember," she told her sister. "I'll never forget what happened to our sister."

Meena said nothing.

Mia was working on forgiving Conroy. Did that mean she would have to forgive Ed Summers as well? After all, Conroy hadn't done all he could to prevent it, but it also hadn't been his fault. And maybe it wasn't so fair to presume he even could have saved her life.

Not quite so difficult to let that go and forgive him. On the other hand, Ed Summers had been convicted of his actions, serving time for Mara's death. He'd been the responsible party. Responsible for her safety and, when he made the poor choice to drive drunk, responsible for her death.

He was culpable. Mia knew he would be much more difficult to forgive.

Meena looked around. "What's going on here?"

Mia said, "I don't know. I was hoping you would tell me." She held her breath. Would her sister finally come around? Would she finally see Ed for who he really was? "This man killed our sister. Yes, it was in the past, but he took something important from us. And now, by the look of your bruised body, he also took something from you."

What could she say to convince her sister that working against Ed was the right thing? She had no idea how long her sister had been living this life. What she'd come to believe about herself, and the way the world saw her.

Maybe she had no hope.

"Women like us," Mia said. "We have to fight to prove that we're worth it. Otherwise we start to believe we're not. Because no one sees us the way we think we should be seen."

Meena shifted to meet Mia's gaze.

"You're just as beautiful as you always were. Just as smart, and street savvy. That's been twisted, and they've probably made you do things you never thought you would. Right?"

Meena glanced away.

"You can have a clean slate." She squeezed her sister's hand. "I know. I've seen it happen. I've seen people who didn't believe it was possible to start again do exactly that."

"Not people like me."

"You don't know some of the people I've met."

"Criminals rolling over on their bosses to get into witness protection?"

"Some of them," Mia said. "Others were good people who just made some bad choices. One day, they woke up and realized they were so far in over their heads they were drowning." She touched her own throat, where that guy had held her. She could still feel the squeeze of his fingers. "Feel like you can't breathe?"

Her sister shifted again.

She couldn't tell if she'd said anything right. Couldn't tell if her sister had even heard a word she'd said, let alone been persuaded to leave behind her allegiance to Ed Summers. To make a new life for herself.

"You probably feel like that, too," Meena said. "What with this guy after you."

"Ed's guys have been working for Anthony Stiles. Doing favors for him. And then Stiles kills them instead of paying up?" Mia said, "I guess Garrett didn't know what happened to the first man. He didn't know to be cautious."

Mia realized they were talking about Meena's boyfriend now and added, "I really am sorry for your loss. I didn't mean for my problems to cause all this."

Meena's eyes were dry. "You brought this guy here?"

"I think he's recreating the events that led to his brother's death. But he got stalled out at the death part. He tried to take me once, and *you* saved me from that."

A muscle twitched in Meena's jaw.

"Now he's killing others instead of me. Now he's got dad." She swallowed the lump in her throat. "He's still trying to get to me, or so I believe."

"Watching you. Waiting for the chance." Meena's voice was hollow.

Mia nodded. "Yes. I feel like he's been watching me since I got to town. Like any moment now he's going to close in, and I'll have a hand around my throat again."

"Who is he?"

Mia looked at her hands. They were dirty. She wrung her fingers together, aware of feeling slightly naked without her gun and her badge. "The man I killed. Anthony Stiles is his brother."

"What does he want, money?"

"No. He's a psycho, and he wants revenge." Mia looked at her sister and saw something different in her eyes. "He wants to kill me because I killed his brother. Maybe I'm wrong. But I don't think I am. What else could he want?"

The man was a psycho. He tormented people, particularly women. She'd seen it on Conroy's computer. How many ways would Stiles make her suffer for killing his brother?

Meena shifted and stood. She walked to the door and pulled it open. "He just wants to kill her. Nothing else."

Ed Summers stood beyond the door, waiting. His eyebrows rose. "Well, then. Problem solved."

"We just give her to him."

Ed said, "You don't want your dad back?"

Meena shrugged one shoulder, the sharp angle of her shoulder blade visible under her shirt. "He got shot of me a long time ago, just kicked me out. Why do I care if he buys it, too?" She shrugged. "He'll be dead."

Mia tried to stand. Her legs gave out, and she collapsed to the floor.

It took a few tries to get back up, while Meena turned and stared down at her with a sneer on her face. Eventually Mia got to her feet. "What did you do?"

Meena laughed.

"They beat you up!"

"Yeah," her sister said. "Because I told them to." Meena set one hand on her hip and cocked her foot out. "Now we know what we need to know, and I'm back in. Conroy doesn't have jack. He'll never find you or dad. Or Stiles. We do our deal.

Stiles is done here, and he walks away. We don't lose any more of our men and the chips fall...wherever they may."

"With dad and me buried in a shallow grave." Mia swept her arm out, encompassing the wooded hills to the west of town.

Everyone said they were haunted. She'd never believed it before. Not until now, when the possibility that she might end up buried in them seemed more and more certain.

Meena walked out. "I'll make the call."

Ed stepped in, closing the door behind him so they were alone. Her whole body shivered.

He grinned. "That's what I'm thinking, too. But there's no bed in here, and I'm not a fan of hard floors." His knowing eyes glinted as he shook his head.

Mia pressed her lips together, swallowing the bile back down.

"We'll have some time before Stiles makes the meet to get you."

"And what do you get in return?"

Ed shrugged. "That man out of my county. Then maybe my men will quit dying."

"But you don't care enough to kill him? You just want him to get what he wants so that he leaves." She didn't get that. Not when two men were dead.

"You think Conroy won't pin it on me if I kill him? Regardless, whether I'm the one who pulls the trigger or not, he'll find a way to make it stick. The man's had it out for me since..." His words trailed off, and he waved a hand.

"Since you killed Mara."

He rubbed a spot on his chest. "Only person I ever killed. Sorry about that. She was fun."

"Fun?"

"It was high school and she put out." He tipped his head to the side. "At least, she did once I persuaded her to dump Conroy and that Jesus-loving thing he had going on and get with me so we could have some *actual* fun. Been turning all the good girls since."

"Like Meena?"

"Your sister was never good. Not one single day in her life." He said, "What we have is an arrangement."

Mia didn't want to think of her sister like that. She didn't want to believe anything Ed Summers said. After all he'd taken from her? She wanted to launch herself at him. Scream. Maybe claw his eyes out with her fingernails that needed to have been filed like a week ago. It'd come in handy now.

"You look like you're plotting my death."

Mia said nothing.

Ed Summers laughed.

"I don't forgive you for what you did to my family."

He kept laughing.

She leaned forward and screamed, "I hate you!"

He grabbed her arm and dragged her from the room. Practically shoved her down the hall to where her sister waited in the entryway.

Meena said, "Done already?"

Ed shoved Mia forward. "Like it would even be worth it. I'd get frostbite."

Meena laughed. "Ain't that the truth?"

Two men, one with the spider web tattoo, dragged her out to a car. They opened the trunk and shoved her in.

"Hey. Wait—"

"Shut up. Just shut up." Spider web guy slammed the trunk shut, closing her in darkness. Why did he look irritated? That was just bizarre.

Then she realized she was alone. They were taking her to Anthony Stiles.

Mia kicked and hit the trunk, screaming her head off. She tried to kick out the tail lights by aiming at the corners of the interior. Nothing happened.

She screamed in frustration.

"Shut up!" The voice was muffled, from farther away. Inside the car.

She didn't care.

Mia screamed again.

Music blasted through the car. She clapped her hands over her ears and whimpered, but couldn't hear the sound of her own distress.

They drove. She cried, great sobs rolled through her and she just let it flow. Why not? She was going to die just as soon as they handed her over to Anthony Stiles.

The car stopped.

Doors slammed.

Her dad was there. She had to believe that, otherwise she had no interest in what was about to happen.

There was nothing for so long that she thought they might have forgotten about her. Then a door slammed again and the car began moving. She had no idea how long it was before the car stopped again. The trunk opened, and there he was.

Stiles reached over with something in his hand. She gasped as electricity rolled through the stun gun and into her body.

With dried tears on her face, Mia's world descended into black.

## 29

Conroy strode up to the house, hand itching for his gun. He was ready to reach in and pull it out. Only when his fingers glanced over his badge did he remember himself. Who he was. He'd never considered soul searching to be a thing until he found himself doing it now. Conroy was a lieutenant. He was a follower of Jesus.

Not just a man who wanted to know the whereabouts of the woman he cared for. Though that last one stoked the fire in him like nothing else had in his life.

Ed Summers emerged from the house just as Conroy started up the porch steps. Conroy grabbed the man's T-shirt with two hands and shoved Ed against the siding beside his front door. "Where is she?"

Two other men stepped out and moved to stand by Conroy's elbows. Close enough they could stab him, and he'd never be able to defend himself. He didn't look at them.

"Tell me."

It had been a couple of hours since she was taken from the police department. There was no sign of Mia, Tate kept calling —if the buzz in his pocket was anything to go by—and everyone here seemed—something. His guys were on edge. Summers was definitely hiding something.

In fact, as Ed's gaze roamed over his face, Conroy saw an answer there. He just couldn't discern what that answer was.

Then his expression shifted and all Conroy saw was that cocky know-it-all he'd once called his friend. That was a long time ago. Conroy hated that look.

"*Tell me,*" he roared in Ed's face.

"Or what?" Ed lifted his hands as though he was the injured party here. "You'll shoot me? Arrest me?"

He shoved at Conroy, who let go and took a step back. The guys on either side of him stepped back as well, and they formed a loose group of four.

Conroy fisted his hand and punched Ed in the face. Knuckles to the man's cheekbone. Ed slammed back against his house with the force of it and clutched his cheek.

Two sets of hands hauled Conroy back, shoving him against the porch rail. He ignored the way his hip bone glanced off the splintered wood.

"No." Ed held out a hand to his men and stared down Conroy. "You get one freebie. For old times' sake."

"How nice of you." Conroy wanted to do that again. Only his hand hurt now. A lot.

He wanted to tell Ed that wasn't the way things worked. But Conroy was the law in Last Chance County. He wasn't an Old West, win-at-all-costs kind of lawman. He had to run things by the book. Toe the line in the way that justice would stick, and he'd still be able to look himself in the mirror. See something he was proud of, something his father always told him was the most important thing for a man.

Honor.

Truth.

"You took Mia from my house. Where is she?" Tate had told him this was where she was.

"Not here." Ed lifted his chin.

Conroy's phone started up again, vibrating in his pocket. "You had her. If she's not here, then you won't mind me looking around your house. Just to be sure."

"Not without a warrant." That was one of the men beside Conroy, to his right. The guy had a spider web tattoo on his neck. "We know our rights."

"Like your right to storm a police station, shoot two officers, and kidnap a woman—alongside stealing evidence?" Conroy said. "Rights like that?"

Spider web guy folded his arms across the expanse of his chest in a way that made Conroy feel like a little kid surrounded by bullies. He shoved off the feeling. Or, tried to.

Conroy said, "I'm happy to come back with a warrant. Then your life will be wide open to police search."

Which of course meant they would scramble as soon as he left. Destroy any evidence, and then clean up the whole place so there was not even a gram of something illegal left lying around.

"We've all gotta do what we gotta do."

Conroy didn't disagree. He turned to Ed. "I will find her."

Ed said nothing.

"Where's Meena?"

"Salon, probably. She had a manicure appointment."

Conroy didn't like how quickly Ed came up with that answer. He took half a step back. "You're going to let Mia die, too? Haven't you done enough damage to that family?"

"You're still stuck on that? Seems to be going around." Ed sniffed. "Whole lot of people in this town all about the past. Rest of us are trying to move on with our lives."

Conroy's phone quit vibrating with the incoming call.

And then an additional single vibration. He lifted his watch and pulled back the sleeve of his coat. A text from Tate. It beeped in succession; several texts in a row.

"Guess you should be going now." Ed pushed off the siding.

"I'll be back."

"Wouldn't miss it."

Conroy pulled out his phone as he walked. Before he could return Tate's call, the man called him again. He swiped his thumb across the screen, feeling the three men—maybe more— staring at his back. Though it was tempting to glance over his shoulder, he didn't.

"Barne—"

Tate cut him off before he could even finish. "I thought you were gonna kill that guy."

"Didn't." Not until he got her back. And her dad, too.

Probably not even then, if he was honest. He might want to. But that didn't mean "want" had a right to override good sense. It would destroy his career, his life. Every relationship he had *and* his standing in the community.

"You know…" Tate was quiet for a second. "If you did want something like that, I might have this friend of a friend. If you know what I mean. You wouldn't have to…uh…get your hands dirty."

Wilcox's voice rang out in the background of the call. "You did *not* just say what I think you just said."

Conroy agreed with her. "You're not going to have him killed."

"Just saying."

Whether Tate was talking to him, or Wilcox—who was apparently with him—Conroy didn't know. He said, "There are things about the private investigator life that you might want to keep to yourself. An association with hit men is one of them."

"What did he…" Wilcox's voice faded off. "Give me the phone."

Tate said, "Back off, Savannah." Like her name was an insult.

Conroy didn't have time for their bickering. "Where are you guys?"

Up ahead he saw them both move around the car and into view. Conroy hung up and jogged over so he could get to the point quicker. "Whether she was there or not, she isn't now."

"You're sure about that?" Wilcox looked as worried for Mia as Conroy was. He knew they'd become friends in the short time they'd known each other. Savannah didn't have many women in her life who she trusted to have her back. But when they got Mia home, he knew with certainty that she'd be the kind of woman Savannah could rely on.

Something that was in short supply in both of their lives.

Conroy turned to Tate. "What have you got?"

"Now you wanna know?" Tate asked. "Or are there more people you want to shake down first and take your frustrations out on."

Conroy took half a step toward the private investigator. Savannah slapped a hand on his chest. "Don't."

He gritted his teeth. "Want me to sweep you up along with all of Summers's people? Obstruction of justice charges." Conroy folded his arms. "For starters."

Tate shrugged. "It'll get me closer to my contact in Ed's organization. So...maybe."

Wilcox spun to him. "What contact?"

"Guess what, Sweetheart," Tate said. "You don't know about everything I've got going on."

She strode away. Tate glanced at her back and the muscle in his jaw twitched. Conroy had no intention of getting in the middle of it. Except for the fact it seemed Wilcox was more hurt than anything else over the antagonism she was getting from Tate.

Conroy said, "Easy."

Tate got the message. He looked back and forth between them and that muscle twitched again.

"Do you know where Mia is?"

Tate said, "I know where *Stiles* was. At one point."

"I know. We were at the rental house."

Tate shook his head. "This is a campground."

Conroy moved to the car. "Let's roll. And I'll forget how you could have told me that three minutes ago when I first ran up to you. We could have been halfway there already."

He pulled open his car door.

Tate said, "Wilcox, you riding with me or the boss?"

She got in Conroy's car.

He said, "Lead the way."

Tate nodded and climbed in without another word. He drove onto the highway, and Conroy pulled out behind him.

He glanced at Wilcox. "How'd Tate even find us?"

"Those secret private investigator ways, I guess." She had her attention on her phone in a way that didn't invite him to ask her what the deal was. "As long as he gets us to Mia, I don't care."

Conroy nodded. "Exactly."

It still sounded like Wilcox planned on having nothing to do with the man after her friend was found. Maybe that was for the best, since Tate clearly had his own agenda. But given Conroy had recently received the gift of a possible future with someone special, he wasn't so sure that shutting things down was in her best interest.

Admittedly, there could be a host of things neither of them knew about him. Context to what seemed like foolhardy decisions.

Right now they needed to find Mia and Rich, and Tate's information was the best lead they had.

He decided to go for it. "Sometimes working to put aside your differences can be the best thing. It could even be the key to something great."

"Did you just—yeah, did. You just got all sentimental."

Conroy shrugged.

"Me and Tate?" She shook her head. "No way."

Conroy said nothing, even though it was tempting to point out that she might be protesting a little too much.

His phone rang. He tapped the screen to answer Tate's call. "Where are we headed?"

"The campground at Makewitch."

Conroy followed him all the way there, until Tate pulled over into a small parking area. They were two miles west of the lake, in an area where one of four state-run campgrounds were. This one was the most accessible, with cabins that could be rented as well as hook ups for water and power, and spots that had no utilities. This was also the only campground that had WiFi, plus a building with bathrooms and even shower stalls.

It was popular with all kinds of people for all kinds of reasons. And the subject of frequent drive-bys for the on-duty patrol officers during the on-season. Which this was not.

"Cabin four."

"And you know this," Wilcox said, "because how?"

Tate's lips curled up, and he leaned his hip against the hood of his car. "Need to know."

Conroy figured that was because of his contact. "Let's go." He led the way, and they circled to the cabin, staying away from the front path and the drive. "Wilcox, take the back door."

"Copy." She wandered left, headed for the back.

Conroy lifted up and looked in a window. "Two rooms?"

"Technically three, since there's a living room within the kitchen area. Bathroom. Bedroom." Tate leaned against the wall beside him. Gun out. "He in there?"

Conroy said, "Can't see much." The windows were dirty, smudged. The whole area smelled like someone had a fire blazing in their fireplace. Wood stove in one of the cabins, maybe. "Did your intel say she was here? Or Rich, or just Stiles?"

"Stiles had this pegged as an alternate location. And since you blew his primary, I'm guessing he's already here, or will be."

"I was going to sit on that rental house and wait for him to show up, but then Garrett started following her and we left to respond."

Did Stiles have somewhere else picked out to kill Mia?

Like a desolate spot in the woods where he could leave her,

barely covered by dirt, for animals to find. Before a hiker eventually stumbled upon her body.

"You with me?"

He ignored Tate's question and headed for the front door. "Let's go." It was unlocked. Conroy stepped in. "Cold in here."

"Any sign of him?"

He didn't get the chance to answer Tate's question before Wilcox joined them. "Clear."

Conroy nodded. Then he spotted a flash of headlights outside. "Down."

They all crouched. The car slowed. Conroy watched out the windows.

"Is it him?" Wilcox asked.

"Not sure." He stared, trying to make his eyes work beyond their ability. Surely if he kept looking, he would be able to make out the driver's features.

Tate said, "Front door is open."

They'd left it like that.

Conroy moved to it and looked out. He could see from there, enough to know the driver's identity.

"Anthony Stiles."

He stepped outside, gun first. Stiles hit the gas, spraying gravel as he drove away. Conroy took off running after him.

A dark-haired woman sat up in the backseat.

She put a hand to the back windshield.

"Mia."

# 30

The engine revved.

"Conroy!" Mia screamed his name.

Anthony Stiles swung the car around a corner, headed for the exit. Laughing. Mia's body flung to the left and she hit the door, crying out.

That was why he'd gotten her out of the trunk. To begin the torment.

"Conroy." She whimpered his name.

Where was her dad? How was Conroy going to find either of them? She'd looked for the rear license plate when he'd hauled her from the trunk. This car didn't have one.

It hadn't made sense when he shoved her in the backseat. Then he'd sliced the side of her leg. A deep cut that seeped blood all over her pants and the seat underneath her. Now it was clear he wanted her close so he could start messing with her.

Bile rose in Mia's throat. She swallowed it back but couldn't help the sob that escaped.

She reared up and grabbed for Stiles's shoulder as he drove.

Anthony twisted in his seat. The car swerved. He uttered some choice words and shoved her grip from his jacket. His fingers bit into hers, and she cried out.

Mia pulled her hand back. Shifting on the seat only aggravated the wound on her leg, and she couldn't hold back a cry.

Stiles just laughed.

Drove.

She looked back. No one was behind them. Conroy hadn't followed, and he wasn't coming.

He would never find her now.

Meena and Ed had taken her gun and her badge. Stiles had taken her will.

And next, he was going to take her life.

"Where is my father?"

He just laughed some more.

Mia collapsed against the seat, tempted to lose hope.

*No.* Things were bad, but she wasn't going down without a fight. She wanted to see her father. She wanted to tell Conroy that holding a grudge for what he hadn't been able to prevent was stupid. For years, she'd been nothing but a bitter, stupid girl. Blaming him for something that wasn't his fault.

Now she was a woman who needed to set those feelings aside. She needed to trust God and His justice. Trust His plan— the one that had brought her back to Conroy so she could see how she'd been wrong. So that she could find, in Conroy, something else.

Affection.

Care.

Maybe even love.

Those childish feelings, the crush she'd had years ago, had been warped with bitterness and grief. Suddenly it was growing and distilling into something more. She needed Conroy. Not just because she thought she might not be able to get out of this without his help. No, it was more than that.

He was the first person in her life—besides her dad, or God —who had looked at her and seen something of value. He'd chased the car until Stiles got too far away. He'd come after her. Determined to fight for her.

She had to put the hate aside. All the pain over her sister's death. "I know what it feels like."

Stiles said nothing. He just kept driving.

"Ed Summers killed my sister."

Mia looked at the car's back doors. The one closest to her was unlocked. She waited until he slowed for a corner and reached for the handle. Tugged on it.

Nothing happened.

He'd flipped the child lock. She had to get into the front seat if she was going to get out.

She continued the conversation as though nothing happened. "I wanted to kill him because of what he did to me."

Stiles spoke then. "You should have killed him while you had the chance. After today, you'll never have another shot at doing anything."

The words that had been in her mind and on the tip of her tongue suddenly evaporated.

He was going to kill her.

Knowing didn't make it any better. She would rather have not known, considering that meant she wouldn't have to be processing it right now. "I want to see my dad."

"And I should give you what you want?"

"Everyone gets a last request, right?" She tried to sound brave, but he already knew she was scared out of her mind.

She'd been wrong thinking Thompson Stiles was the evil one. His brother, Anthony? The look she had seen in his eyes had been pure evil. There was not one good thing in him. Only the will to kill. This time as recompense for her killing his brother. But after this, would he even need a reason? He would know that he could truly do whatever he wanted. No consequences.

Once he killed her, it would mean the death of his soul.

Mia would be a sorry tale in the history of a murderer who killed without conscience. Nothing but a footnote, given how few people actually cared about her.

She sucked in a breath and screamed. "I want to see my dad!"

He laughed. "Where do you think we're going?"

Stiles pulled the car over. Mia looked out at the deserted street; only a few houses. No one around this late at night except a cop car she spotted, parked down the street. He grabbed something from the front seat and got out, slamming the door. Mia started. She watched him move nonchalantly down the street, making his way to the police vehicle.

She moved then. Gritted her teeth and scrambled over the center console. Her foot got stuck, but she ignored it in favor of grabbing for the door handle. The unlocked door.

Her fingertips touched the handle.

The door lock clicked down.

Headlights flashed, and the car horn sounded a short beep. She pulled at the handle anyway, even though she knew what had just happened. He'd locked the car. Down the street, Stiles pocketed the keys.

She was locked in.

Mia tried to flip the lock, and pulled the handle, but nothing happened.

He approached a police car. She didn't know what the cop was doing on this street, just sitting parked on a regular residential neighborhood. Used to be a place families lived. In the eighth grade her friend lived in the blue house behind her, and they'd hang out there after school. Suddenly those lazy afternoons felt like a lifetime ago.

The officer opened the door.

Stiles closed in before the cop could even get out.

"No. Don't—"

She saw the flash of a gunshot in the car's interior. Stiles shut the door and headed back to her while she sat, frozen.

He pulled the door open and saw her straddling the center console. Teeth glinted in the dark. A smile?

She pushed off the seats and slumped into the back.

"Want some of that, or you want to see your dad?"

"Where is he?"

Stiles climbed in. He turned the car on and pulled into the driveway of the house the cop had been parked in front of.

"You killed him."

He yanked her out, leaving the car in the drive. Plain view was good. Someone would see. Conroy would come.

"You brought me to a place the police know about." She dragged her feet. "Someone will come." The officer had to check in, right? He'd miss the call and another cop would come looking.

"My guess?" he said. "We have about six hours until shift change and even more time before the questions start. Plenty of time."

Fear swelled in her. "*Where* is my dad?"

He shoved her against the side of the car and moved to the trunk, clicking a button on the key fob. The trunk popped up.

Her dad.

He'd been back there the whole time. Shoved there after she was moved to the back seat? She had to have been unconscious at the time, or she'd have seen him.

Mia launched herself at Stiles, stumbling as she put weight on her injured leg.

He pulled his gun. She stopped short. He said, "Get him inside."

Her dad was awake. He could walk, but not without leaning a considerable amount of weight on her. She helped him inside.

Stiles should just kill them right now, but there was no way she would be the one to point out that the longer he waited, the more likely his elaborate plan would fail. And surely not when that meant she and her father would be murdered any second now. If she kept playing along, she might be able to fight him. Get out of here. Or Conroy could find her—one of his people would come looking for his officer and realize where she was.

Hope rose in her again, and she thanked God for that gift. Even in the middle of all this, there was still hope of a way out. God *always* made a way out.

"Put him in the bedroom."

She walked her dad in that direction, teeth gritted against the pain in her leg, and found the bedroom. Her arm across her dad's back was damp from his shirt. Stiles came up behind them and flipped the light on. Her dad grunted. She helped him sit on the bed.

Stiles kicked at the back of her knee. She crumpled to the floor, crying out. He slammed the door shut and she could hear him chuckling as he walked down the hallway. Mia rolled to her back and sat up. She scrambled to her dad and winced. He'd been beaten, badly. She sat beside him, and they hugged loosely.

He sucked in a sharp breath.

She pulled back. "Sorry."

"Not your fault." His voice was gravel shifting against more gravel.

"What did he do?"

Her dad grunted. "Doesn't matter."

"Of course it does. We have to turn on him, together. As soon as he comes back."

"Tried." He shifted. The pale color of his face worried her. Then he lifted the side of his shirt, and she saw the blood on his back. That wet which had been against her arm.

She gasped. "Dad!"

"He cut me." His eyes crinkled, and he winced at the pain. "Like that." He motioned to her leg.

"Don't worry about it."

"Slow leak. You'll run out. Eventually."

She didn't really understand but got the gist of what he was saying. They didn't have a whole lot of time.

He needed rest. She helped him lie down. Teaming up to fight off Stiles wasn't going to happen. No matter how much rest her dad got, he wasn't going to be able to rally. He would only fade away.

Mia shook a pillow out of its case, balled the material up and pushed it on the wound. "Hold that there. I'll take care of Stiles, and then we'll get out of here."

Mia got up. She moved to stand behind the door. As soon as he came in, she could fight him. Do something. She had to, because the alternative was as good as lying down and waiting for death to come. That would only occur when she had no strength left.

"Conroy will come."

She shook her head. "I can't wait for that. Not when Stiles plans to kill us."

"Slowly."

"What?"

"He said he was going to kill me and make you watch. Then he was going to torture you until you begged him to kill you, too."

"He thinks I'll beg?"

She thought that was entirely possible. If he pushed her far enough, and the pain was great enough, Mia thought she just might scream for death.

But she was never going to let her father know that. If it came to it, he wouldn't be here to witness it anyway.

"No." She shook her head. "Not happening."

She huddled against the wall. Waiting.

Stiles came in. She held her breath, then lifted her good leg and kicked at the door with as much strength and all the frustration she could pull together. A scream escaped.

Stiles got trapped between the door and the frame, grunting in surprise. She shoved at the door again. He shoved back.

It nearly hit her in the face.

Mia stumbled backward. Her leg gave out, and she hit the wall.

Stiles set a camera on a tripod in the corner. "Good. I like a little fight. It'll make the video of me torturing you that much more interesting when I watch it later."

He lifted the gun in his other hand and squared his aim.

Then he pulled the trigger.

Mia screamed.

## 31

C onroy gripped his keys. "How did you get the intel about this house?"

They were still there, at the campground, despite the fact Anthony Stiles had driven off with Mia in the back seat almost half an hour ago. He'd called in the description immediately. Nearly every one of his officers on the street tonight was looking for that car, which had allowed them to stay at the campground to go through the house. Thoroughly. They couldn't risk missing something that could lead them to where Stiles was going.

Where he had taken Mia.

Where, presumably, he was keeping Rich now. If the man wasn't already dead.

Conroy gritted his teeth, still waiting for Tate to answer the question.

"Anonymous tip."

Wilcox looked about as impressed as Conroy.

"That's it?"

Tate lifted both hands. "Chill, okay?"

"You want me to chill?"

"You don't think I'm as worried for her as you are?"

"No," Conroy said. "I don't think that."

"Well, I am."

Conroy just stared. "I'm not going to debate feelings with you. We just need to find Mia, and that's all I care about."

"And Rich." Wilcox folded her arms, a severe frown directed at Tate. She didn't think much of him? The man had been decently helpful. To a point. Along with a whole lot of self-serving Conroy intended to unpack later, to see if any of it warranted persuading the district attorney to bring about charges.

"We're done here." Conroy shifted his keys in his hand. "Unless you'd care to share more about this 'anonymous tip'." Most of the time he figured those were a setup. The suspect, jerking the chain of whoever was looking at him. Trying to throw off the cops. Make their jobs more difficult.

Tate said, "It came from a private number, and I don't have the resources to trace a call like that."

That was the trade-off for not having to get a warrant every time he wanted to breathe, the way Conroy felt like he had to do sometimes. Tate had different procedures. Conroy would never trade his shield for the life of a private investigator, though. Not ever.

"Your tech could take a look, right?" Tate asked.

Conroy said, "Not enough time to get a result and then trace a location. If the phone is even on." The last one they'd had a number for that might have belonged to Stiles had been turned off.

"So we hit the streets," Wilcox suggested. "Look for that car."

"Yes, but..." Conroy pulled out his phone and headed for his vehicle so he could get moving. Standing here, doing nothing, was beginning to eat at him in a way that brought all those old feelings back to the surface.

Ones he didn't like.

That guilt. The shame. Powerless to stop what he saw coming. It made him want to prove he could make everything perfect again, even though it would never be that way, and it hadn't been in the first place.

Conroy turned away. *They were right, but.*

"What does that mean? Yes, but..."

He ignored Tate's question.

Wilcox said, "It means we close this house up for Conroy and further instructions will be forthcoming."

"Make it fast!" Tate called after him.

Conroy slammed the car door and got out of there. He gripped the wheel and hit the gas. Tried to keep his head straight when everything roiled in him. Fear. Doubt. Distrust. He needed hope, and faith.

He needed a miracle.

This guy Stiles had been motivated. But he'd also been seriously patient. He'd waited until the worst possible moment to make one final deal with Summers. A deal Meena had simply allowed to happen. They'd essentially given Stiles what he wanted just to get him to leave their people alone.

Conroy couldn't go after them when he needed to find Stiles.

This bad guy had caught them all off guard. Conroy prayed like he'd never prayed before that God would come through on this. That He wouldn't leave Conroy alone to figure out how to get Mia and her dad back by himself.

His phone buzzed. He tapped the screen in the car. "Barnes."

"It's Kaylee. The warrant to haul Meena Tathers in for another round of questioning, this time related to Mia, just came back."

"Okay." He tapped the steering wheel. "Call in Officer Frees. He goes and gets her, and he leans on her until she tells him *everything*. If she even thinks she knows where her dad or Mia might be, then he finds out."

"No holds barred?"

"By any means necessary."

"Copy that," Kaylee said. "Anything else?"

"The BOLO is still out on that car?"

"Yes, but half the department is at the hospital. The others are on their way there, or just left to get dinner after standing vigil for hours. We're spread thin on people actually looking."

"Is Allen okay?"

"I called his parents. They're flying in first thing tomorrow." Kaylee sighed. "He's in surgery, but they're saying he should be all right."

Allen was a good cop. If he couldn't remain a cop, it would be a bummer for both him and for Conroy. For the whole department. They didn't need to lose capable guys like him who did the job right and with a sense of purpose.

"I want roll call."

"Right now?"

"Yes. I want everyone who is available out on the streets looking for that car."

"You don't think he'd have parked it somewhere, out of sight?"

Conroy said, "We have BOLOs for a reason. Because we count on eyes being open, and our cops coming up with results."

"They shouldn't be at the hospital?"

"Not unless they need to be treated. I don't mind visits. But I need as many people as possible out there looking for the missing federal agent and her father—residents of this town who trust us with their safety."

In the face of a man intent on killing them.

"Copy that." She hung up.

Conroy drove the town in a circuit, from the center, spreading out. Plenty of places to hide a car. He dismissed the campground cabin. Whether Stiles had ever rented that place or not, Conroy would find out later. He didn't factor it in right now.

Stiles had been in the woods behind Summers's place. That was where he was supposed to have met Garrett after the guy ran through the woods. It was worth going over there. He searched the grounds. Cabin trails for hikers and bikers, and other tracks he'd always thought Summers used to get drugs in and out of town in a way that was off radar.

No blue car.

He checked the motel. The parking lots for stores and the car dealership. More than once he saw his officers out looking as well, and he slowed. Windows rolled down, Conroy chatted with them. He needed his people to know he appreciated them looking for Rich and Mia.

And not just because she was a fed.

Not just because she was the woman he'd fallen for. Or the fact he considered himself the interim chief, though he would never say that while the old man still lived.

Conroy pulled over and put the car in park. He rubbed shaky hands down his face. What would the old man do? He needed advice. He had to figure out a way to find someone when there were no leads. No idea where to look.

*I really do need a miracle, Lord.*

Not that God should step in simply because Conroy had no clue what to do. He always did what he could to take care of his own problems, and God showed up in His ways. Conroy didn't think he could just ask and get some miraculous answer. God had never done that for him before.

But this was serious.

Mia could be dying. Rich maybe already dead.

He pinched the bridge of his nose and dropped his elbow to his knee.

They were out there, and he had nothing. Powerless to save them. *You have to help them.* He sucked in a breath that shuddered through him. His vision blurred. Conroy slammed his hand on the steering wheel. "Why won't You help them?"

His voice echoed. He winced and wiped at his eyes. Crying wasn't going to solve anything. After all, he'd cried when he'd prayed for Mara to wake up. To survive her injuries and be okay again.

To not die because of him.

But his tears hadn't helped. Mara had died. God hadn't shown up. That was the last time Conroy had asked Him for help. Instead, he'd spent years getting the results he needed in his own strength. Distaste rose in his mouth now. He was asking for help, but God wasn't going to do anything. Conroy would have to solve this himself when he had no idea how to do that. Mara had been dead for years now. Was he supposed to live through the deaths of her father and her sister, too?

*Don't make me do this.*

Because, deep down, Conroy did want God to show up. He did want a miracle. There was no way she would be alive without one.

She needed to live.

The pastor always said that it was when a person had nothing left that God was able to work.

Conroy had nothing right now. The only other time he'd had absolutely nothing left, Mara had died. God had let him down. Would he be let down again?

He shoved the car into drive again and kept searching. Looking for the car. Waiting for the phone to—

Ringing filled the speakers. He tapped the screen. "Yes, Kaylee. What is it?"

"Everyone present and accounted for—well, almost everyone—and they're all out on the streets."

"I know," he said. "I keep seeing them. Wait, what?"

"One hasn't checked in."

Conroy tapped the brake. "Who?"

"The officer posted outside the rental where Stiles was staying."

"The house Wilcox and I went to? There was nothing there but a toothbrush and some dirty dishes."

"He didn't call back, and I can't reach him on the radio."

Conroy flipped the switch for his lights and hit the gas. "I'll be there in five. I want backup."

"Copy that."

He hung up and turned on his siren, peeling through town to the house as fast as he dared go. *Is this You, God?* He didn't like the idea that bargaining had caused God to show up. That wasn't supposed to be how it worked.

He'd asked for roll call before he even prayed. God knew, and He'd already set the answer in motion before Conroy even asked.

*Thank You.*

Conroy didn't understand more than to just be grateful.

Two streets from the house, he shut off lights and sirens. No point announcing his arrival to Anthony Stiles.

He pulled up behind his officer's car, watching the house for movement. He sent Kaylee a text that he was on scene, and then he got out. He already had on a vest, so he got his gun from its holster and went to the driver's door. The officer—an older man with years on the job—hadn't moved at all.

Conroy approached slowly.

He tugged on the door handle. As soon as he started to open it, the officer inside began a slow slide. Conroy caught him and laid the guy on the ground. He holstered his gun and called in an officer down. He asked Bill to send extra backup and to get the medical examiner on standby for when this was over and it was safe to come.

The scene was not secure.

A black and white police car pulled up, almost nose to nose with the dead officer's vehicle.

"Which house?"

Conroy pointed. "That one. And we need to move fast, or he'll kill them before we get in there."

Or this could quickly become be a hostage situation.

The worst option that flitted through his mind? A double murder/suicide.

None of those scenarios were what he wanted to see.

"Let's go."

He turned into the driveway. One of the officers followed, and the other stayed with the dead man.

Conroy saw the car in the driveway then, pulled far enough forward that he'd never have seen it if he hadn't looked directly at it driving past.

Police tape still hung over the front door. Back entrance, or side?

"Find the back."

"Copy that." The officer trailed past him, head low as he crossed underneath the kitchen window. *Be careful.* Too late to call out to him now. Conroy prayed for the man's safety.

He put his shoulder to the wall beside the side door where the car had been parked. Couple of long breaths. He turned and kicked at the door. It splintered in from the force.

A single gunshot rang out.

The blast hit him, square in the vest. Conroy fell back. His gun skittered across the drive, and his head hit the side of the car.

He dropped to the ground, out cold.

## 32

M ia blinked. The world was a blur, interspersed with white spots. She tried to move. Limbs sluggish, she realized she was slumped against the wall. Pain thundered through her head. It centered on her left ear in a sharp pain.

She touched her fingers to her ear. They came away bloody.

She gasped. Or, at least, was pretty sure she did. Her hearing was *gone*. Her auditory senses? Nothing at all.

Mia touched her face and then covered her ears for a second.

Anthony Stiles had fired the gun right beside her head, so the deafening blast made her head want to explode from the pain.

*Dad.*

She had to get to her dad. Moving hurt, especially with all the wounds she had. Bumps and bruises, the dog bite. Her shoulder. Now her head felt like it was full of glass shards rubbing together.

Mia gritted her teeth and tried to get her legs underneath her. She was pretty sure she'd groaned aloud, but couldn't hear anything. Not even the rush of her own breath through her nose.

She blew the breath out and fought the sensation of needing to hurl. There was no time for that. Her arm—wet with a red stain on the bandage where she'd been stitched up. There should have been more to that thought, but she couldn't think enough to finish it.

"Dad." Even though the word was little more than a moan from her lips, she still couldn't hear it.

The world swam again. Maybe it was just her head. She stayed leaning against the wall and breathed some more.

*You have to get up.*

She tried to stand. Everything spun, her equilibrium totally off, sending the world into a tailspin around her.

Dad. Was he okay? Maybe Anthony Stiles had killed him already.

Tears rolled down her face as she turned.

Eyes closed. He was so pale.

She crossed to him, off balance, and stumbled to a sitting position on the bed. Mia felt more tears roll down her cheeks as she pressed two fingers to his neck.

A slow, awkward beat answered back. She nearly sagged with sheer relief onto the bed beside her father. He was still alive.

Mia looked at the door.

If Anthony came back, she wouldn't be able to hear his footsteps. All the warning she'd have that he was coming back in would be the turn of that door handle.

She looked back at her father. *I don't want to leave you.*

Would that be the right move, or not? If she left right now, she could be killed trying to escape. And then her father would die before help came. She had no idea if she was even making sense. Maybe she was so out of it she couldn't tell what was happening or what she should do.

All she did know for sure was that it would be up to her to get them out of this. To go get help and subdue Stiles. Even though she hadn't been able to make that happen last time.

Silence continued to ring in her head.

Deafening, isolating silence.

What would it be like to live in solitude like this all the time?

*Quit feeling sorry for yourself and move.*

So far she'd managed to stay upright, but how long would that last? She pushed off the bed and stood, rising to her feet as she faced the door. Video camera. The bed. Her father.

Her head swam, and she groaned.

She had to go. She had to get help.

Mia stumbled forward. She wanted to stay with her father. He didn't look good at all, but she couldn't allow that to stall her. She had to focus on what was possible, not what she couldn't do.

Secure the scene. Locate the suspect. Take him down. Call for EMS.

The door swung open.

Stiles saw her. She froze. He spun to look back out into the hall, gun in one hand. She could see tension in the line of his body, but not fear. He lifted the weapon.

Someone was out there.

He would kill them.

Mia grabbed the tripod. Stiles didn't move. Or at least didn't consider her a threat. He had his back to her, his attention to the right. His finger shifted to the trigger.

She swung the tripod and hit Stiles on the back with the camera. His body arced. The gun lowered but went off.

Mia heard a blast, muffled as though it were miles away. She froze. Someone out there had a gun? They'd missed Stiles, whoever it was.

Mia hit Stiles again. Then she kicked him into the hallway, so that the armed person out there could deal with him. Stiles shifted to fight back. Before he could rally, she kicked out at the gun in his hand. The movement hurt as her entire body jolted, and yet more pain rolled through her head.

Then she waited.

A police officer shifted into view, his gun held on Stiles. Younger man, maybe Jess Ridgeman's age. He looked tired.

She saw him mouth something, but she heard nothing.

Mia turned her head and lifted her hair so he could see what she figured her ear must look like. Bleeding.

He blanched.

Mia pointed to her ear and then shook her head. *Ouch.* That was a bad idea. She lifted both wrists and motioned as though she was wearing cuffs.

He got the idea and pulled them from his back belt, still holding his gun on Stiles.

She rolled Stiles to his front and put her knee in his back. He fought her, but she got his arms pinned back and secured.

She didn't lift him to his feet. When he was secure, she patted him down one-handed. A phone was all she found, nothing else. Not even car keys or ChapStick.

She looked at the officer's name badge. *Donaldson.* Where was his backup?

Mia said the word "Lieutenant," but since she couldn't know if she even made an intelligible sound, she used her hands to make an "L" and then a "T." Was he even going to understand?

She could read his lips, *Outside.* Then Donaldson shrugged and lifted his palms, like he didn't know specifically where Conroy was. Maybe Donaldson had last seen him outside.

She motioned to Stiles, then him, and back again.

Donaldson nodded. *Go.*

She glanced down at Stiles. Teeth gritted. He looked about ready to rush up and tackle the officer. Mia wanted to kick him.

She gave Stiles a wide berth and walked down the hall, glancing back to make sure Donaldson was all right. When she turned back, a man had appeared at the end of the hall. She gasped, but quickly realized he wore a uniform. Not Conroy, but another officer. He said something to her. She looked back and saw Donaldson's lips moving. Probably explaining she couldn't hear anything. Mia didn't stick around until they were done. She needed to know where Conroy was.

But she did indicate her father to the other officer. Then she tapped the radio on his shoulder.

He nodded, suddenly energized. Good. Her father needed help, and it needed to happen ASAP.

She felt her strength waning. It wouldn't be long before she couldn't continue. Her body would shut down. Shock and pain, along with trauma. But she intended to be sitting with her dad in an ambulance—with Stiles in the back of a police car—when it all caught up with her.

She had to pace herself.

Mia took a long breath and pushed it out slowly, but not so slowly she got lightheaded. Hallway. Living area. Kitchen and the door they'd come through.

It was open.

Beyond it, the car was still parked there.

On the ground...

She stumbled outside and nearly landed on her knees. Was he dead? Mia had to plant a hand on the ground to catch herself. She cried out as pain shot through her injured shoulder and she almost landed on Conroy.

Like when he'd saved her life.

He sat up, suddenly. Mia must've whimpered. He twisted to her, and she could see his chest heaving with every breath. She studied his face. What had happened?

Conroy pulled open his coat so she could see...

"You've been shot." She said it but still could hear nothing. She reached out and touched the smashed bullet, dead center in his chest. If not for the vest, he would be dead right now.

She glanced up.

Conroy stared at her. He said something. Waited, then frowned down at her.

Mia covered her ears with her hands. When she drew them

away, he shifted the hair on her shoulder. Mia couldn't help the flinch. What was he seeing?

It might not be good, but it was her father who needed help right now.

Conroy's attention shifted, past her and into the house. When he looked back at her, his mouth formed the words, "Come on."

He shifted, moving to get up. To help her up. She just slumped farther into him, unable to move.

Conroy tucked her against him and held her. His arms around her. One hand rubbed across her back, side to side. How was it that he could be so reassuring without words?

She blew out a long breath that broke more than once. Don't cry. "Dad." There was still too much to do.

He patted her back twice. It had the same soothing feel to it, but it was his signal to get moving. She felt him shift against her, but his cheek didn't move from the top of her head.

When they finally stood, she saw him pull out his phone and speak into it.

When he was done, he turned to her and mouthed again, "Come on."

He guided her like a sleepy kid that didn't want to go to bed. Gentle but firm, like there were no other options than to just go. Conroy helped her inside. Her head hurt, and her leg, along with everything else. But there was no way to do this in a way that it wouldn't.

He shifted her over and bent down to touch the wound on her leg. She sucked in a breath and moved out of reach. That stung, but she didn't want to spend time on it. Not when her father was unconscious and one of his officers dead.

He tugged her good arm around his shoulder. They walked to the door. Laborious steps that shot tremors of pain through her head and shoulder. He had his gun out and held it by his side with his free hand. Because there was still danger?

Mia couldn't fight. Not when she was in serious pain. Even though it seemed like this might not be over, she'd never felt safer in her life than she did right now. He'd come here to save her.

Mia opened her mouth, then realized she couldn't have a conversation with him. Lights across the living room window flashed red, blue, red, blue against the curtains. Help was here. A tear rolled down her face.

He deposited her on a stool at the bar and moved to open the front door. An officer appeared at the mouth of the hall, the second one to show up. Whatever he had to say to Conroy, it wasn't good news.

EMTs stepped into the house. The first one came straight to her. She shook her head and was about to motion to the hall when she decided to just go there. Mia made a beeline for her father, shoving away the hands that tried to stop her.

She needed to see her dad.

Donaldson still held his gun on Stiles, who stood facing the wall. She moved into the bedroom where her father was still unconscious. Mia sagged onto the bed beside her father. She touched his face with the back of her hand. Clammy skin. The bed covers were damp under his side, blood from the wound on his back. She bent her head and prayed, which was how the EMTs found her when they caught up to her.

She kissed his forehead and went to leave, turning to the side so the EMTs could see him. When they entered, she motioned to him.

Conroy came in last, pausing for a brief conversation with Donaldson. They didn't speak long.

Donaldson said, "Okay," if she read his lips right. Conroy nodded and clapped him on the shoulder.

She watched as he leaned into Stiles, speaking low into the man's ear. Mia moved to them. She wished she could hear what he said.

His whole demeanor was tense, almost lethal. This man had

cost him. One officer dead, one shot. Two of Summers's men were dead as well. Her father…

People would grieve over the lives Stiles had taken.

She started towards Conroy. One of the EMTs got in her way. A nice looking guy she'd never met before. He shifted her hair the way Conroy had done, but this time she flinched.

Conroy touched her elbow. She grabbed his bicep and held on, their forearms against each other. He said something to the EMT.

She felt him touch her ear.

Mia gritted her teeth and let him do what he had to do. As soon as he lowered his hand, she turned to face him, her side close to Conroy's body.

The EMT glanced at Conroy and said something.

Conroy frowned. He motioned to her father and spoke. It was an order.

That was good enough for her, regardless of what the EMT thought of what he'd said. Whoever he was. She moved to Conroy, ready to do that thing again. The one where she sagged into his arms. Pure relief. Maybe a hug. Maybe one of his soft lip touches.

Donaldson's movement caught her eye.

Mia wanted to watch him walk Stiles out. She wanted to see the moment the cop did that top-of-the-head touch as he lowered Stiles into the car. Cuffs securing his arms behind his back.

They stood on the grass of the front yard while it happened. It was as satisfying as she'd hoped it'd be.

She glanced at Conroy.

He slid an arm around her waist, taking the weight of her arm off her shoulder. Wow, that felt better. She leaned into him.

A tiny smile curved the corners of his lips. He leaned in, and they hugged. It was more than that, it was a shared moment. Closeness. Intimacy. She'd been taken. He had come to get her.

Now they were all safe. Her father would go to the hospital, and Stiles was no doubt headed for jail.

When he pulled back, it was to take a towel one of the fire-fighters gave him. He leaned in and kissed her cheek, then pressed the towel to her ear. She probably moaned. He kissed her forehead.

She winced. *Ouch.* After she got seen at the hospital and made sure her father was all right, she needed to take a nap.

His lips curled up, and she felt them against the skin of her neck. At this rate he'd wind up enticing her to do more than just think about sticking around. She might even make a list of what she'd have to do to make that happen.

Quit her job, for one.

Move back to town.

Not failure, just a fresh start. A return home that would begin a new chapter in her life. One that she hoped would involve Conroy.

Mia touched her hands to his cheeks. She lifted up onto her toes and pressed her lips to his. It wasn't long or deep. Just a moment. A promise.

His eyes flared.

She'd surprised him, and he liked it. Until something else took his attention. Conroy moved half a step back.

She wanted to cling to him but forced herself to still so she didn't jar her body. She turned to see what it was.

The EMTs rushed out, wheeling her father on a stretcher. One was astride him, pumping her father's chest.

Conroy reached for her.

Mia scrambled out of his hold and raced for her dad.

## 33

"I've got a pulse. Let's go."

Conroy watched as they loaded Rich into the ambulance. Mia climbed in with them. She turned back to him.

He nodded.

She had to be free to go. Not only did she need to be with her father, but she'd been injured, too. If she hoped to make a full recovery, the hospital was the best place for her to be. The hearing loss could be worse than even she or anyone else realized. Long-term damage? *Oh, please, Lord.* He hoped not.

He'd wanted to get her an application for his police department, but now everything had changed. He needed to ask her doctors if she was still fit to continue her duties as a cop.

The ambulance doors shut and it sped away, lights and sirens going. Out front of the rental house where Stiles had held Rich and Mia prisoner, people now swarmed. Emergency services. Onlookers being held back by his cops.

Conroy pushed off the exhaustion and got to work. He had a dead cop on scene, visits to make. A hospital he'd eventually end up at to check on his officer who'd been hurt and, of course, Rich and Mia. But first, there was plenty to do here.

"Donaldson!" He trotted to the officer, about to leave.

The kid lifted his brows. "Lieutenant?"

"I'm headed to the office as soon as I'm done here. I wanna talk to you."

"Yes, Lieutenant."

"Good." He clapped the kid on the shoulder. Both of them knew he meant "good" more than just this conversation—they'd also done a good job here.

Conroy made sure everyone knew what their orders were. He wanted the deceased officer taken care of properly, with respect. It was a murder scene. But the deceased was also one of his people—a friend and brother to those watching.

He got into his car and drove to the officer's house. It was an hour before he made it to the police department, having first paid a visit to the officer's elderly mother to inform her that her son was deceased and making arrangements for her sister to come and stay with her.

Conroy was seriously running out of steam by the time he walked into the office.

Kaylee looked from her computer monitor to him, her phone handset tucked between her ear and shoulder. "Uh...you okay, boss?"

"No." He didn't elaborate. Just headed for the door to the bull pen. He hauled it open and walked through. "Where's Wilcox?"

Kaylee hung up. "I'll find out." She immediately picked up the phone again and got dialing.

Conroy poured himself a cup of coffee and found Donaldson. "Get Stiles in the interview room for me and then get some sleep. Yeah?"

Donaldson nodded, relief washing over his face. "Copy that, Lieutenant."

Conroy got the file he'd had Kaylee put together for Wilcox when they first learned someone was targeting Mia. Now, given all he'd done, Conroy figured he wasn't going to get a whole lot of cooperation. There was no deal to be made with Stiles—or anyone who thought they could show up in his town and tear through it, leaving destruction in their wake.

Anyone who would leave an elderly woman distraught like that...

"Hey." Wilcox shook his shoulder.

Conroy blinked. "Hey."

"What's up? Kaylee said you were looking for me."

"Where were you?"

Wilcox frowned. "I'm going to factor in how wrecked you look right now and ignore that tone. Considering I was with Tate Hudson this whole time, trying to ascertain exactly his involvement with Stiles and Ed Summers."

Conroy nodded. "Okay. Good." He ran his hands down his face.

"I'm glad you approve."

He updated her about what had happened with the officer, and how he'd finally found Mia, along with her father. Just in time.

"Oh." Savannah blinked. "No wonder."

"No wonder what?" He hadn't even told her about wanting to offer Mia a job, or what her hearing loss could mean. Stiles had to have discharged his weapon right by her ear. Would she fully recover?

Wilcox shook her head. "What's next?"

"We need to talk to Stiles."

She grinned. "Should I bring a phonebook?"

"Do they even make those anymore?"

"Okay, you're good." She stood and grabbed the file from him. "I was worried you weren't firing on all cylinders. But I'm still taking lead on this."

"Fine by me." He'd been shot and knocked unconscious again. Didn't take a doctor to tell him he really wasn't "firing on all cylinders," even if Wilcox thought he was all right. Even if the same thing happened to her earlier.

"What do we want from him? We already know what he did."

"Ed Summers."

She looked up from the file. "You want him to roll over on Summers? In exchange for what?"

"The knowledge that he did the right thing for once."

Her expression changed.

"I know. I figure he won't care at all. I still want to see what he says."

"We aren't giving him a break on any of this, right?"

Conroy nodded. "He tells us whatever he has, and we decide to use it or not. No deal."

They headed into the interview room, and Donaldson left them with Stiles. Wilcox pulled out a chair and sat. Conroy did the same but didn't pull his chair up to the table the way she had.

He leaned back. Arms folded.

Stiles just sat there. The only indication Conroy had that the man felt anything was the look of utter disdain in his eyes. Not just for him, or Wilcox. More like for cops in general.

"Protective vest?"

Conroy said, "What's that?"

"When I shot you."

Ah. "Yes."

Skin around the man's eyes flexed.

Too bad, so sad. It was juvenile to gloat, but Conroy was just exhausted enough to not care what anyone thought. What would count was how satisfying it'd be to rub the man's face in it. *Better luck next time.*

Wilcox flipped the file open. "Three murders. Two counts of kidnapping and attempted murder."

"Guess you caught me," Stiles said. "Time to lock me up and throw away the key."

She didn't react. "We'll get on that. First thing."

"Assuming Rich Tathers makes it." Conroy shrugged one

shoulder. "Because if he doesn't, it'll be *four* counts of murder."

Judging by Stiles' demeanor, Conroy didn't think the man cared overly much about whether he spent the rest of his life in prison or not. How a man could exchange his freedom simply for the right to do whatever he wanted, Conroy didn't understand. He'd been taught to deny his flesh, the human part of his will that was selfish and didn't want to listen to godly wisdom. He had to shed that every day, every minute, and look to God for direction.

And yet, for so long he'd still done whatever he thought was best. Sure, he at least attempted to make the more righteous choice, but he fought every battle on his own, instead of looking to God for supernatural strength. Instead of trusting Him.

Conroy blew out a long breath while Wilcox asked the introductory questions and got Stiles talking.

"So you show up and you pay Ed Summers a visit. You hear about him before you got here?"

Stiles frowned at the shift in conversation.

"Or you just need resources," Wilcox said. "So you hit up the big local baddie and borrow some of his guys? At least long enough for them to do a job for you, and then you don't need them anymore."

"Tell us about Ed." Conroy sniffed. "How'd that work?"

"Asked around." Stiles shrugged. "I needed...expendable."

"But when it came down to it, you're the one who did the real work." Like shooting Conroy, firing his weapon right by Mia's ear. Possibly killing Rich. "Am I right?"

Stiles shrugged. "Local yokels. Figured they didn't get out much, so I paid them to have a little fun."

"This guy?" Wilcox laid a photo of the first man he'd killed on the table, Tyler Lane. "And this guy?" She laid the second man's picture beside it. Garrett Hanson.

"How'd you know his woman didn't kill them?"

Conroy said, "Because they were both done the same as your brother."

A tendon in his cheek flexed.

"You figured you'd cause Special Agent Tathers distress by freaking her out, and then you killed Tyler and Garrett the same way she ended your brother." He leaned forward. "Which was completely justified, by the way. That ruling came down a few days ago. She's been cleared. She walks away free, no repercussions. You spend the rest of your life in jail."

Stiles lifted up. The cuffs that held him to the table clinked as the tether snapped tight. His face seemed to split with rage as he screamed at them. "She murdered him in cold blood! He was fighting for his life, run down like a dog. Then she shot him. Thompson is dead because of her! She had to *pay*!"

His rage was a visceral thing. It seemed like he might have actually watched it all go down somehow. Angry that he'd been powerless to stop it. Bitterness had poisoned him much like the way guilt and shame had directed Conroy's actions. The way Mia had held on to her anger towards Conroy that he'd not been able to stop her sister's death.

They had all carried pain. But in their own ways they'd dealt with it and tried to heal. Stiles hadn't wanted to move past it.

Recently Mia seemed to have been working to let those feelings go. Maybe even enough she might have fallen for him the way he had fallen for her. Mia was everything he wanted. He just had to persuade her that it was the right thing.

*And I shouldn't do that in my own strength. Should I? Maybe You could do that work, Lord. I trust You. Mia is what I want, and I trust You with that.*

The decision to take leave during the investigation of her conduct that led to Thompson Stiles's death was not made lightly by Mia. The reality of having to see Conroy again and process her feelings toward him had caused her some anxiety. On top of that, each time Anthony Stiles had come after her, things had gotten more and more serious. Using others first in his plan, and then getting up close and personal with Mia in his final attempt.

All she had been through had to have been hard for her to deal with. Not to mention confusing. Especially when Conroy sprung on her his idea that she could move back and work as one of his detectives. All while she was just sure she had lost her father. Forever.

"You didn't kill her," Conroy helpfully pointed out. "So I guess that means you failed."

"Sit down." Wilcox said, "It's over for you. Instead of just doing what you came to do—kill Mia, you miscalculated. You got greedy. Wanted to draw it out and make her suffer." She motioned between herself and Conroy with a flick of her fingers. "We don't allow that here."

She didn't even know the half of it—the part about the video camera Stiles had set up. He had likely been planning on killing Rich slowly, making Mia watch. Then he'd have killed her. Probably even slower.

Conroy said, "I don't care about you. I want Summers."

If that involved charges being brought against Meena, then so be it.

"And if I tell you what I know," Stiles said, "I get a deal, right?"

"No." Wilcox closed the file. "You get nothing. Except the satisfaction that someone like you is off the street. A man who killed a sibling and destroyed a family."

Conroy waited, but Stiles said nothing. Conroy stood. "Enjoy prison. You'll have plenty of time to work through your anger issues."

Donaldson stepped in even before Conroy could open the door. "Lieutenant?"

Wilcox said, "Who died now?" Then she stood. "Oh."

Conroy's heart sank. "Where's Jess?"

"In there." Donaldson swallowed. "The chief…"

Conroy squeezed his shoulder. "Get Stiles back down to holding. I got this."

## 34

"Can you hear me?"

Mia said, "My ears are still ringing. When I have any hearing at all."

The doctor nodded. "Surprisingly, that's a good thing. It means your hearing is coming back. It'll take as long as it takes, I'm afraid."

They'd admitted her overnight, giving her fluids she was still tethered to. Medicine that eased her aches and made her shoulder feel like cotton wool. "And my dad?"

"Your father is stable," the doctor said. "But we're not out of the woods yet."

On any other day, at any other time, Mia would have considered the doctor and swooned. He was seriously attractive, blonde like a movie star, and totally out of her league.

Then again, she seemed somehow to have managed to catch Conroy's attention. Probably she should peruse herself in the mirror more. Try and figure out what he saw.

"Thank you, doctor." She tried not to smile too much. That would be creepy.

"You good here?"

Aww, he cared about her.

The doctor's lips twitched. Perhaps she wasn't keeping her thoughts to herself as much as she'd thought. "Good stuff, huh?"

"Huh?" Mia shifted. Oh, that was what he was talking about. The cotton wool, drugs that were currently making her feel very mellow. And amused at every little thing.

Just not this irritating ringing in her ears that kept coming and going.

"Never mind." The doctor shook his head, out and out smiling now. "There's someone here to see you. She says she's your sister."

Mia frowned.

"You don't want to see her?"

"She's the one who kidnapped me."

His head jerked. "I'll have security—"

Mia said, "She didn't shoot my eardrum out." How was she even supposed to explain all that had happened? Stiles was in jail. That was what counted. "It's complicated. She gave me to the guy who did this." Mia motioned to her ear.

"There are plenty of cops in the hospital. You want me to get someone?"

"If they can wait outside. I would like to talk to her."

"I know you're this big shot federal agent, but—"

"It's okay, doc." She tried to look like she wasn't so mellow but in full control of her faculties. "If you could have an officer, or a security guard, wait in the hall."

"I'll make sure." He stepped back and opened the door to the room they'd parked her in to get her to sleep. Like that ever happened in the hospital. She didn't even want to think about all the poking and prodding they'd done.

He said, "I'll also have a nurse let you know if there's any change with Rich—your father."

She could already see her sister behind him, ready to step in. Like there was someone after her. Or, she was just really nervous.

"Thank you."

He nodded and stepped out. Meena passed him. Interested. At any other time she'd have taken a second and got her flirt on. The doctor just looked confused.

Meena shut the door.

"I'd rather you left that open."

Her little sister rolled her eyes. Her movements were too edgy, twitchy even. What had she taken? Something she thought she "needed" because of an addiction Mia figured she'd never admit to. Or was it just the courage she'd needed to come here? Something to take the edge off her nerves.

Meena sniffed and rubbed her nose with her index finger.

Mia sighed. They should have left her with some cuffs.

"You're thinking about arresting me, aren't you?"

"You took my badge and my gun."

Meena said, "You're still one of them, though. Right?"

"You'd be right that it doesn't make me any less of a federal agent not having my badge, or my gun." Given the ringing in her ears, Mia had to pray she didn't miss anything her sister was about to say.

Mia said, "But if you're trying to justify it as 'not that big of a deal,' I'm not playing that game."

Because it did kind of feel as though she wasn't a real fed right now. Without the badge and gun, she was...what? Just Mia. Banged up, with ringing ears. Not a feeling she appreciated, having been a federal agent behind a badge for years now. One with firepower on her hip.

She needed to get her badge and gun back.

Her sister said nothing. Mia said, "They had better not get used in the commission of a crime."

Yet another reason for her teammates and her group supervisor to complain about her uselessness. For a long time she'd thought she had done something to warrant their behavior towards her. Then she learned there had been a woman on their team before. That woman had been killed by a suspect they'd been chasing.

Now they considered anyone—especially a female—who couldn't bust doors in, take down a suspect single-handedly, and generally protect her own back as not worth their time or the cost associated with it.

Mia had never even had a chance of measuring up to that impossible standard.

It had taken time, but she realized that now. Not just from seeing Conroy and how he interacted with his officers, like Wilcox and Ridgeman. He trusted them to do their jobs.

It was a far cry from how her team acted towards her. Not their fault, given what they'd been through, but it was something they needed to right.

Her sister made a face and leaned against the end of the bed. She never stilled, and she was nowhere near relaxed. "I didn't come here to talk about your stuff."

"What did you come to talk about? Dad is stable. Stiles is in custody."

"So all's well that ends well?"

"Not exactly."

"I'm not going to jail." Meena's eyes widened. "It was all Ed. Not me."

"You think that defense will hold up?"

"It's worth a try," she whined.

"Meens, you can't live like this."

"I'm not going to," Meena said. "I'm leaving town. Forever. I'm sick of being in the middle of Conroy and Ed Summers. Then you show up, and all of it goes in the crapper. Dad is hurt. You're…" She waved at Mia. "All here and whatever. So I'm done. It's over."

"And when Conroy catches up to you, with an arrest warrant?"

"It wasn't me. It was like I said. It was all Ed."

Like that made it better. Mia said, "None of you? Just Ed?"

Meena pressed her lips together.

"You should argue the finer points of your defense with your lawyer."

Her little sister let out a frustrated sound. "I knew Conroy wasn't going to back down. He's relentless. Just because Ed killed Mara. Whatever. That was ages ago."

She'd taken the exact opposite stance than Mia had. Dismissing the whole thing, maybe because she'd been young enough she hadn't spent much time with Mara anyway. And she'd never looked up to either of them the way Mia had looked up to the oldest Tathers daughter.

Though, now she wondered if that hadn't been because Mara had been dating Conroy. That was the epitome of a good, happy life according to teenage Mia. How could things be any better?

Then she'd lost everything.

And in a way, Conroy had as well. Mia needed to remember that. He'd been there. It was a wonder he didn't have some kind of PTSD. Maybe he did and he'd just never told her.

Mia said, "If you had something that could help Conroy, it would certainly aid in getting him out of your life."

"Conroy, or Ed?"

"Yes." Mia lifted her good hand and spread her fingers. "Doing the right thing is the only thing that will give you the clean slate you're looking for. Otherwise, when you leave here, you take everything from Last Chance County with you."

Just as Mia had done.

The day she'd left, she'd thought crossing the county line, the state line, or any other boundary would give her a separation. Her life would be back there, and she'd be free to start over. Away from where Conroy visited when he wasn't in school, so eager to get home.

Mia had thought things would be different somewhere else. Instead, she was still her and the memories she carried—the hurts and feelings—were all still inside her. In fact, they'd stuck around until she came back to Last Chance County. Until she saw Conroy and realized the kind of man he was. Someone with a sense of honor and duty that put her bitterness to shame.

*Father, I'm sorry.* She'd thought she was the victim. The injured party. She'd never even thought about her dad, or Conroy. *Help me show him that I do forgive him.*

She wanted to say the same about Ed Summers but that was a different story, and she might need some time to wrestle with God over it.

"Meena." When her sister looked up, Mia said, "I forgive you."

"If I turn on Ed and give Conroy everything on him?"

"No, regardless of whether you do that or not. You're my sister, and you'll always be the only one I have left in this world. I can't believe you'd play me like that, and it doesn't mean I trust you, especially because of how you got me to open up to you just so you could give Ed information about Stiles. But...it's done."

"I'm still leaving."

"I won't stop you." It wouldn't be easier to live free of the chains of unforgiveness if her sister wasn't here. Mia had to face the fact that not seeing her wouldn't help her forget what had happened. Or put it behind her.

She had to move on.

With Conroy?

She wanted to. Enough to consider seriously giving up her job, one she'd thought of as honest, honorable work with a team who didn't really like her. Maybe she would apply for that job with Conroy's department she figured was open now. Wilcox had said she needed a partner. Mia could see what happened after.

He'd kissed her a couple of times and seemed to care. She could certainly say she cared about him. That crush had smoldered for years, and now it was alight again. Flames she hoped she didn't get burned by.

"Have a good life, Meena." Mia intended to do the same.

"Fine." Her sister hopped up to pace nervously. "I'm going. You'll never see me again."

"If I had my wallet, I'd give you my card so you'd have my number. You'll just have to get it from dad."

"So I can text you Merry Christmas, or Happy Fourth?" Meena rolled her eyes and yanked the door handle. Beyond the threshold stood a uniformed police officer.

Mia recognized him. "Basuto."

"Special Agent Tathers." He said nothing else. Didn't move, didn't nod.

Another cop content to let her take the lead? What did they put in the water in Last Chance County?

Meena skirted around the cop as though, at any second, he would pull out cuffs and slap them on her.

The door shut and she was alone again. Mia looked around. She didn't have anything, let alone her phone. How could she even call Conroy? She wanted to. The time to connect was now, since the bad guy was finally in jail. They probably even had evidence they'd be able to pin on Ed. Something to prove his participation in one of the many crimes he'd committed. Much like her sister, she didn't doubt that if Ed was still walking around town like he was above the law, she'd have a harder time with the whole forgiveness thing. Much harder than if he was sitting in a jail cell.

The door opened again. Basuto stuck his head in. "I've gotta go."

"What happened?" He was getting called out? What was that about? "Is it Conroy?"

"I'll tell him you asked about him." Basuto shifted. "They're sending a security guard up to this floor, and I have to go back to work."

The door clicked shut, loud in the empty room. Except for her. She was here, so it wasn't really empty.

Why had she thought that about herself, like she meant

nothing? Mia was self aware enough to know she had some work to do in order to get a complete grasp on who she was. She'd never thought about it before. Now that there was a possible relationship on the horizon, she couldn't risk bringing her baggage into it.

Even she knew that, though she'd never had a real boyfriend.

While she was waiting on her healing and discharge, Mia decided to go find her dad. Nothing wrong with her legs. She shifted them to the side of the bed. Even with the nice meds in her system, she could still feel the burn in her shoulder.

It took some teeth gritting, but she got her pants on. Mostly fastened. She tucked the hospital gown into the back of her waistband. Ready to go.

Mia pulled the IV bag stand with her. She let go of it to twist the door handle, the arm they'd put in a sling to take the weight off her shoulder tucked against her side. Her sister had been here. She hadn't apologized. Meena was starting a new life, and this one wasn't for her.

Meanwhile, Mia wondered if Last Chance County hadn't been the place she was supposed to have been this whole time.

Her home.

The door was suddenly tugged out of her hand. She took half a step back. A very male body tugged hers against his, steadying her so she didn't fall.

"Careful."

She lifted her chin and looked into his eyes. Experience... and not a small amount of pain resided there. Something very familiar to her, it was almost comforting.

He smiled. "I brought you a present."

She blinked, wondering what on earth it was. "Tate?"

## 35

C onroy stepped off the elevator, Wilcox with him.
"The doc said she's in four."

They'd escorted the chief in. Jess was still with his body. They had no other family that Conroy knew of.

He'd asked the desk nurse about Rich. Since Mia was here, he had to go through Mia to get the specific information about his condition. Beyond the fact he was stable at least.

Conroy stopped. End of the hall on the second floor of the hospital, he could see the door to room four. An open door, where Tate stood. His arms around Mia.

Neither saw Conroy, or Savannah, who both watched as Tate slid his arms back and lifted a brown paper bag.

Mia opened the bag he held with her good arm—the one with the IV tube snaked through the inside of her elbow. After a second peering inside, she looked up and beamed at Tate.

"He said he was running an errand."

Conroy didn't glance at Wilcox, he heard it all in her tone. "Guess he was."

"Hey." Meena sashayed to a stop in front of him, and he realized only then that she had been headed their way.

He tore his attention from Mia and looked at her sister. Eye level with him, her gaze shifted. She was on something. He expected her to be cocky. Took a few seconds, but then she got there.

"Guess you're here to arrest me." Meena lifted her wrists and held them together.

"I've been too busy." Did he need to explain that she wasn't all that high on his priority list? "You'll have to wait until I have a warrant."

Meena lowered her hands and sighed. "Maybe next time you'll be lucky."

*No, thank you.* His gaze strayed to her sister.

Meena sighed, long and dramatic. Conroy was pretty sure Wilcox snickered beside him. Conroy said, "It's been a long day."

"Right. You're busy."

Tate and Mia had noticed them now. Conroy wanted to wince. He looked like a total loser standing with his detective and Mia's sister by the elevator, watching her while she stood in a clutch with a man he sort of respected but didn't all the way trust. Maybe he should tell her that Tate wasn't as straight laced as any of them thought.

Which only made him wonder if she liked that. Maybe a little bit renegade was her thing, more than Conroy. Maybe all they'd shared was all they would ever have between them.

Wilcox looked at her phone. She didn't say anything, but it wasn't like they could stay long. There was still a host of paperwork to do and a million phone calls. It was late. Tomorrow would be another full day as would every day be for the next couple of weeks. Then again, did life ever really slow down?

He stepped aside and pressed the elevator button for Meena. "Don't let us hold you up."

She shifted, studied him.

Wilcox said, "Chief Ridgeman passed away earlier."

"The old man is gone?" Meena's painted brows lifted.

Conroy glanced between them. Why had Wilcox shared

that? He hadn't thought they were anything to each other, least of all friends.

Meena looked at her sister for a second, down the hall where Mia stood with Tate. Watching. Mia lifted her good hand. Seemed like she was about to wave him over, but she didn't. What was in that brown bag Tate had brought her?

Meena said, "She told me to do the right thing."

"Yeah?" He watched Meena's face. The war played out there, a battle over whatever she was trying to decide. What did 'do the right thing' mean?

He had enough evidence needed for a warrant to have Meena arrested, along with Ed's people who'd broken into the police department and shot one of his officers—once they identified every masked gunman. They'd kidnapped Mia and stolen evidence. Surveillance footage was ready for his people to go through. It would take time, but Conroy was sure they would get there.

The next step to bringing down Ed Summers.

What he really wanted was to tear the whole operation apart. Throw *all* the players in jail for good. No more Ed, no more illegal business. And not just illegal business—though that was bad enough—he just wanted his old friend to be out of play and off the street. For good.

With the break-in and his officer shot, he could bring charges against those who'd perpetrated the crime. But in order to get Ed as well, Conroy would have to be able to prove that he either participated in it or commanded it to be done. That he'd sent them in to target the police department.

Without looking at the evidence they had, and running down the leads to get a full picture, he didn't know what he could do.

The chief's death had stalled out his day. And with everything else that had happened—including getting shot and knocked unconscious again—he needed twenty-four hours of sleep, a pot of coffee, and three weeks to work through this case.

Finally Meena said, "Ed has a set of books. Transaction records between him and the group that supplies the guy he buys from."

"Drugs?" Conroy would probably have to call the DEA.

She actually rolled her eyes. "Among other things. There's a safe in his uncle's office, but the set of books in there is fake. Under the rug that the desk sits on, there's a loose floorboard. That's where the real books are."

"You're giving us Ed?" Wilcox shifted closer to the two of them. "By handing us his uncle?"

"No love lost between them," Meena said. "He didn't like the old man having that much power over him, keeping track of his accounts. So he sent me." The look she gave him indicated what that had involved.

Wilcox said, "So you entrap him. Ed uses that to blackmail his uncle. Leverage."

Meena smiled, sickly sweet and directed at Wilcox. "We all have our skills, sweet cheeks."

"Gross." Wilcox walked past Meena, toward where Mia stood with Tate. Conroy saw them start talking.

What about? He wanted to go over there, but the job came first. The chance to put Ed behind bars.

"Get the books." Meena had a knowing look on her face. "And I'll come back if you need me to testify or whatever. Otherwise, I'm gone. You'll never see me again."

Wilcox said, "Will wonders never cease? I was having a bad day up until now, and you go and cheer me up."

Conroy shot her a look, then pulled a business card out. He handed it to Meena. "Keep in touch. I'll let you know."

"Fine by me." She pocketed his card.

Conroy wasn't going to delude himself that she was doing this out of the goodness of her heart. She probably figured she'd handed him enough he could arrest Ed, and the source of her problems would go to jail. Meena wouldn't have to come back.

She wouldn't have to testify. She probably figured this was the clean break she'd been looking for.

Not that her sister had convinced her to act honorably. This was just in her best interest. Light a match and walk away. She didn't plan to stick around long enough to see everything burn.

"Don't drop off the map."

He didn't need her getting deeper into the things that had a hold over her life. She was the kind of woman who went all in, against advice. Usually the thing she went all-in on wasn't good for her. Or anyone.

"Maybe find a rehab center. Get in a program."

Mia's sister moved closer to him, lifted a hand and touched his cheek. "So sweet." She patted his cheekbone. "Make her happy."

Before he could respond, she breezed past him. Stepped into the elevator before the doors could close.

Conroy took longer than he wanted to rally. Meena didn't mean much to him, personally at least. Not aside from the standard care he had for anyone who lived in his jurisdiction. She was Mara's kid sister, too young he hadn't hung with her at all back then. Mia had been part of his life, though. At least on the periphery as she trailed after her sister.

He cared about her, though. Didn't like seeing her caught up in the junk Ed was doing. Even if it had been of her own volition. Conroy didn't think Meena walked into anything without her eyes wide open, even if it did often lead to her being in over her head.

It was the connection.

Mia—and her sister—had been part of his life for years. Despite the fact he hadn't hung out with either one. For different reasons. The two of them were an integral part of who he was. The man he had become. They had a connection, something he'd been waiting to feel for years, and he got it now? From Meena?

Beyond her, Tate stood down the hall with a disapproving look on his face.

Conroy didn't need that.

Wilcox shoved at the private investigator. Irritated, for whatever reason. The two of them wandered off in the opposite direction, leaving Mia standing at the door to her room. Black skinny pants under her hospital gown.

He didn't want her left alone, just in case she needed help.

Okay, so that wasn't the only reason he went over there. "Hey."

Her eyes smiled. "Tate brought me my badge and my gun."

"That's good."

Mia nodded. "I was feeling a little...naked without it." Her eyes flashed. "Uh."

Conroy said, "He got you out of bed?"

"I was going to see my father."

"I'll walk you."

"Thanks." She tried to set off, but with all the stuff she was carrying, it was difficult. She pulled her gun from the bag, still in its holster. "Look after this?"

He nodded and slid it on the back of his belt. Her badge she tucked in the front pocket of her pants.

"That's a good look with bare feet."

Mia chuckled, then sobered. "Is everything okay?"

"The chief..." He couldn't force the rest of the words out.

"Oh, no." Her voice was quiet.

He was about to brush off her concern, as though it wasn't a big deal. That was a lie, and she knew it. Mia moved closer and touched his cheek. Same as her sister had done. He wrapped one arm around her, the way Tate had done to her.

"Thanks."

He frowned. They had more between them than this.

Then she pressed her lips to his before she pulled back, so they were still close. "I'm sorry for your loss."

Conroy leaned in and rested his cheek against hers. "Thank you."

When the moment had passed, he walked her by the nurse's desk. The nurse shot them a disapproving look but didn't argue when he told her where they were headed. He went with Mia all the way to intensive care where she had to check in as a visitor.

Conroy wasn't allowed in. "I should get back to the office. Don't walk back to your room without help, okay?"

"I won't."

"I'm glad you're all right, and I'll be praying for your father."

"Thanks."

He didn't know what else to say. Conroy had to go. There was so much to do, but he wanted to stay there. Sit with her. Hug her. Wait for news about her dad. Make sure she got something good to eat and more medicine when her shoulder started to hurt.

Mia's expression softened. "Go."

He looked down for a second. "I'll be back."

"You'd better be."

Conroy walked away smiling. Until he pulled out his phone. Kaylee picked up right before he got into the elevator.

"Boss?"

"Get me a meeting with the judge. I need a warrant for Kenny Aggerton's office."

"The uncle?"

"I got a lead on a set of books. Ed's financial records." Conroy's grief lifted for a second. Long enough to say, "We have a shot at getting him."

# 36

---

*One week later*

M ia climbed out of the car, passenger side. Wilcox got out on the driver's side. She'd been keeping Mia up to date on the case since the last time she'd seen Conroy. He'd been busy all week. She'd been released after a couple of days and had gone home to shower. Then she'd come right back during visiting hours every day to sit with her dad.

Her hearing was much better—almost perfect. Sometimes her ears got overwhelmed, and she had to wait out the ringing. She was supposed to stay away from earbuds, or headphones in general, as well as loud situations like rock concerts. She was careful to wear ear protection when firing her weapon at the range.

If she got in a prolonged gunfight at some point in the future, she would likely wind up with permanent hearing loss. Scar tissue would build up on her eardrum, and there was no way back from that.

Over the past few days she'd been passing information on her father's prognosis back through Wilcox to Conroy. At least, she assumed the information got back to Conroy. He was busy.

Too busy to call, or even text, apparently. The latest information he didn't even know—that her father was awake finally.

All she knew about what Conroy had been working all morning was that he was unavailable. When Savannah explained why, Mia knew she wanted in on the operation.

"No." He strode over to them, shaking his head. "Absolutely not."

Behind him was a crowd of officers all dolled up in their SWAT gear. Vests. Helmets. Conroy had cargo pants on, a polo shirt under his vest. One of the few times she'd seen him in anything other than a suit.

"All hands on deck," Wilcox announced. "Right?" She strode past them, a knowing smile on her face that Conroy didn't see. Headed for the trunk.

Super loudly, Mia said, "What?" and glanced between them.

"You can't even…" He turned to Wilcox. "She can't hear?"

"Actually, that was a joke." Mia spoke normally this time. "I'm fine."

He didn't look amused. "Yeah. No."

"What's that supposed to mean?"

"It means go home, Mia."

"You're arresting Ed Summers and all his people. You think I'm going to miss that?"

"You are not here," he said. "You have no badge, and no authority to be here."

He knew. "Yes, technically I resigned from the ATF and quit three days ago. I'm no longer a fed. I'm also not a licensed PI even though I asked Tate about that. Apparently you have to have someone sign off on your hours. And it's a lot of hours."

That was when she'd made her final decision.

She'd talked to her boss, and he'd sent a local agent to pick up her badge and gun. She'd surrendered both. There had been a lot of paperwork, but she'd fulfilled her obligation to the ATF. It hadn't been nearly as hard to sever those ties as she'd thought it would be.

His expression darkened in a way that indicated she probably didn't need to have brought Tate into it. "So it's like that?"

"That I have a friend in this town? Because total right now, I have three. Besides you and Wilcox, Tate is one of them."

"You're trying to distract me."

She took the protective vest Wilcox handed her and lifted it over her head. Ouch. She took advantage that he couldn't see her face as she lowered it over her shoulders to wince.

"You're not fooling anyone."

"I'm going in with you." Before he could argue, she said, "I'll hang back. Out of the way. It's not like I don't know what I'm doing. I've kicked in hundreds of doors to serve warrants."

"You're not a cop right now."

Interesting choice of words. Not a cop right now. He could have said she wasn't a cop "anymore." But he hadn't.

"How's Jess?" She figured asking about the chief's granddaughter might distract him.

He didn't bite.

"I'll stay out of trouble."

He shot Wilcox a pointed look. "I blame you."

"Fire me later, Chief." She wandered off to join the other cops.

He called after her, "I'm not the chief yet."

Mia pulled the filled-out application from the back pocket of her pants. It was tri-folded and crumpled. If she was a boss and someone handed her this, she'd throw it away. But he had spots to fill, and if he took a chance on her then she would make sure he didn't regret it for even one second.

Conroy frowned.

"Wilcox printed me off an application." She rolled it up and slid it right underneath his vest, right at his shoulder blade.

His lips twitched, along with a muscle in his jaw. "I'm not allowed to read it?"

"There's no time. We've got an arrest warrant to serve."

"Do you even have a gun on you?"

"I could borrow one, right?"

"You'd really take a job here? You live in Seattle." Conroy said it cautiously, like he didn't want to get his hopes up that she would actually move back to Last Chance County for good.

Mia said, "Maybe you could go back with me, help me move." She shifted her shoulder. "I can't lift heavy things right now."

Basuto jogged over. "Chief, we're all set and ready to go."

He ignored her grin. "Thank you, Sergeant."

They considered him the chief, even if he hadn't technically been sworn in by the mayor yet. That would happen in a week or two, apparently. But until then, she figured he would be hard at work doing the job, the same way he'd been doing the job during the chief's sickness. Just not taking over the old man's now empty office. Not yet anyway.

"When's the funeral?"

He almost looked relieved she didn't razz him about the "chief" thing. "Tuesday."

No, she wasn't going to point out that his recent promotion was due to his boss's death. The mayor had signed off—Conroy Barnes would be the police chief soon enough. After the official ceremony, of course.

He yelled, "Sergeant!"

She started. He twisted around to where Basuto turned back. "Chief?"

Conroy said, "Lieutenant Tathers needs a weapon."

Took him a second, but Basuto figured it out. Mia said, "We might need to give everyone else a little longer than that to get used to it."

Conroy chuckled. "Time to go."

"Maybe I should be a detective, and Wilcox should be the lieutenant?" She didn't want resentment in the department.

"No!" Wilcox shook her head, vehemently. "Don't do that to me, Chief."

"Relax." He held up a hand to her.

Mia said, "Are you sure?"

"I like my job as is. Do not mess with me." Wilcox strode off. Again.

Mia frowned. Conroy tugged her onward. They set off but didn't get far before he said, "Be. Careful."

She nodded. "I'll be as careful with myself as I'd expect you to be."

She saw a flash of his teeth in the dark as he grinned.

Basuto said, "Ready for you."

"Fifteen seconds to 'go'."

"Copy that." Basuto turned and keyed his radio. "All positions, fifteen seconds. Mark."

Someone handed Mia a pistol, which she readied in time for the signal.

"Go! Go! Go!"

Basuto led the way. Conroy was to his right, angling out to swing around the flank. They ran flat out over the ridge to sweep down. She jogged, hanging back. As much as she wanted to be part of this, physically she was more of a liability.

Ed Summers and his guys seemed to be tailgating in their own backyard. Truck beds, folding tables. A bonfire in the center, flames licking high into the air.

Someone yelled.

People scattered. Men and women scurried. Cops descended, throwing down. Just as she was wondering if they would be able to pull this off without gunfire, the first shot rang out.

Then the answering shot.

It was far enough away it didn't hurt her ears and wouldn't compound the damage previously done. If she was to be a cop, then she'd have to be very careful with close-quarters gunfire.

Mia hung back to get the big picture, praying for the safety of every person here. Praying this didn't erupt into a bloodbath. Along with a couple of other officers, she watched for the rogue who would make a run for it. Slip through the cracks and try to get away.

There.

She raced to the east, across from what amounted to Ed Summers's front lawn. "Police! Stop!"

It was Summers.

She realized that as she ran after him, closing the gap as she'd done in many high school cross country races. He wasn't going to get away with this. The same way he hadn't gotten away with killing her sister.

Summers turned and fired at her.

He missed but she fell to one knee, got up, and kept going. Faster. Before he could fire again, Mia jumped and tackled him to the ground, pain reverberated through her shoulder. She pinned him down with a knee to his back.

"Drop the gun."

He didn't want to, but he let go of it.

The similarity between this and the day she'd killed Thompson Stiles couldn't be denied. It rolled through her like a flash of cold.

He twisted. Launching up, he flipped her onto her back.

Mia gasped, her ears ringing now.

Ed reached for her throat.

Then he was gone. His weight lifted off her and she saw Conroy, his face twisted with anger. He shoved Ed onto his front and cuffed the guy before she could even speak.

"Edward Summers, it's my great pleasure to tell you that you're under arrest for drug and weapons trafficking. Among several other things, including accessory to murder." Conroy continued, explaining his rights in a way they couldn't be argued. There would be no mistakes on this.

Mia laid there, trying to remember how to breathe—how to move—when she still had abject fear rolling through her, along with a mega dose of adrenaline. Bonus, her shoulder didn't hurt too bad right now.

"You okay?"

It took her a second to realize he was talking to her, given how her ears were ringing. Mia managed to choke out the word. "Yep."

Great. He was never going to hire her for real now. She'd just been bested by a suspect he'd been trying to bring down since forever. He'd had to come to her rescue. Ed could have gotten away because of it, and it would have been all her fault.

Conroy backed up past her, holding his gun aimed at Ed Summers. "I'd be more assured if you didn't look like you were about to pass out."

She climbed to her feet.

Conroy stood behind her, arm out with his gun pointed at Ed. His free arm slid around her, supporting her injured arm and taking the weight off her shoulder. She nearly groaned in relief. Her legs would have given out had he not been holding her up.

He tugged her back until she was against his chest. A hug. "Basuto!"

She jumped.

"Sorry." His voice was breathy against her ear.

The sergeant raced over, hauled Ed to his feet, and walked him off.

"We should go help with the clean up." She started to move.

He didn't let go of her, so she wound up just turning around while still in his arms. "Chief?"

He shook his head, an amused look on his face. "You really want to be my lieutenant?"

"What else would I do? I'm a cop."

"Yes, you are."

It wasn't a compliment, but boy did it feel like one. She grinned at him. Then she reminded herself she'd done next to nothing. Conroy was the one who had arrested Ed. "You got him."

He nodded. "We got him."

She didn't know about that.

"And until you're signed off to active duty by the doc, you're not working in the field. You're at a desk."

"So you accept my application? Even after that?"

Conroy said, "I accept." He gave her a squeeze. "You're a great cop, Mia. And I know that when you're fighting fit again you'll be an asset in keeping this town safe."

"I'll do the best job I know how to do."

"It scares me a little, but Wilcox needs a new partner."

"That scares you?"

He nodded. "Of course. You two are going to cause chaos. I'll be spending my days putting out the fires you two start."

"I wouldn't want you to be a bored chief."

"Mmm."

She grinned.

"One other thing I'll need."

"What's that?"

"Will you have dinner with me tomorrow night?"

She chuckled. "It seems like we've been through enough we should have done that already."

It had only been a couple of weeks, but her feelings ran deep. And from the way he was looking at her, she figured his did also.

"We did, I think. But we should start this off on the right foot, you know? Dress up and go somewhere fancy." His eyes lit with hope.

She hadn't even packed a dress coming here. And hadn't been home since. She was going to have to go shopping or she'd wind up "somewhere fancy" wearing jeans and sneakers.

Maybe Wilcox would want to hit some stores.

"Why do you look like I just gave you an idea for something I'm going to regret later?"

She laughed and leaned in to press her lips against his.

"There's absolutely nothing to worry about."

THANK you for reading *Expired Refuge*, I hope you enjoyed it! Please consider leaving a review, it really does help others to find their next read.

Turn the page to read the first 2 chapters of the next book in the Last Chance County series: *Expired Secrets*

U.S.A. TODAY BESTSELLING AUTHOR
LISA PHILLIPS PRESENTS

# EXPIRED SECRETS

## LAST CHANCE COUNTY BOOK TWO

# 1

Tate Hudson, private investigator, sat at the corner booth. Hotel bar. Thursday night. Most of the guests were at other hot spots, like the club two blocks over, so it was pretty quiet. Too few people, and he'd be spotted easily. Too many, and he'd never get what he came for.

He left the drink he'd ordered untouched. His phone kept his attention far more than the beverage, like so many other patrons. But what occupied him was not social media. He angled the cell against the edge of the table so its camera showed the man at the bar.

Blue suit. Brown hair, no discernible style. Middle aged. A few too many donuts around his middle, though not enough to indicate anything more than a bad habit. At least, Tate told himself, it was nothing a good New Year's resolution couldn't fix.

The subject glanced around. Getting the lay of the land. He turned to a woman as she slid onto the stool beside him. Red dress, blonde hair. A convention attendee, according to the badge hung around her neck. She flashed a white smile—dental health conference.

They were forty miles outside Last Chance County, where

no one knew the subject at hand. Not well enough to know he worked in management at the phone company. Or that he had a wife who'd hired Tate to find out whether her husband's night meetings were, in fact, him cheating on her.

The subject bought the red dress woman a drink. She laughed, though she was completely sober. The subject was into his fourth drink. If he got his keys and decided to head home, Tate might be tempted to intervene.

Most people would call the cops and report a drunk driver, or the bartender would take his keys and request that he call for a ride. The police department in Last Chance County had set up a text line, so folks could anonymously report the things they saw. Tate never used it. Probably never would, since he preferred a more *hands-on* approach.

Red dress was giving his subject the brush off. Too bad she couldn't see the potential there, because Tate would've been able to snap a couple of images, and then send his report to the wife.

Along with an invoice.

Tate got a couple of pictures, though it was plain to see, even from the cell images he took, that as hard as the subject tried, she just wasn't taking the bait.

*Better luck with the next one, buddy.*

Tate sighed. He sipped at his drink and watched the subject glance around, looking for someone else to try his lines on.

His phone screen flashed. It started to vibrate across the tabletop and a name illuminated on the screen. *Claire.*

Double sigh. He almost didn't answer it. "Hudson."

"I didn't think you'd pick up." Her breath crackled against the phone's microphone. But it wasn't Claire, it was her sixteen-year-old.

His body tensed in reaction to the tone of her voice. All thought of his subject was dismissed from his mind as he stood. "What's going on?" Tate pulled out his wallet, tucked a folded twenty under the glass, and headed for the lobby. He pushed outside. "Lex, talk to me."

She spoke again as he strode out to the parking lot. "It's mom. She won't wake up." Her voice tremored. "He hit her pretty hard this time."

Bile rose in his throat. "Call an ambulance."

"No. She said—"

"I don't care what she said." Tate hauled the driver's door open so hard he nearly pulled the thing off the hinges. "You know what? Forget it. I'll call Dean. Maybe he's close."

"He's on his way."

"Your first call?"

"Yes."

"Because your mom has the medic on speed dial?"

"Don't be like that." She sounded like an adult and a child, all at once.

He wanted to ream her for making excuses for her mom, as he would any of his peers who'd made a tough choice. But he didn't. She might look and sound like an adult, but Elexa was still a kid. A smart kid, independent and capable. Good grades. Held down a steady job at the ice cream shop. She might've been his kid in another life.

Tate hit the gas and tore out of the parking lot. "Where's your stepdad now?" His phone's Bluetooth connected to the car stereo, and he tossed the cell in the cup holder.

Her voice came through the car speakers. "He was gone before I got home."

"So you don't know for sure it was him who did this."

"Pretty good assumption. He was coming home for dinner." Elexa let out a long breath. "She was excited. They were gonna talk."

Elexa's stepfather, her mother's third husband, only talked one way. And it wasn't with words.

"A car just pulled up outside," she said. "That you?"

"Probably Dean but confirm that for me. I was working at the Sunrise."

She whimpered. "It'll take you an hour to get here!"

"No, it won't." He heard the doorbell ring. "Go answer it. Don't hang up."

"Okay."

He heard her talking, and then Dean came on the phone. "Tate?"

"What's the situation?"

"One sec." Dean spoke again, but Tate couldn't make out what the former SEAL said. Elexa answered a series of questions, then he came back on. "We're going to the hospital."

"Serious head injury?"

Instead of answering the question Dean said, "That's a good idea. I'm sure Lex will appreciate you meeting us there."

Tate pressed his lips together. He needed an answer, but if Dean didn't want to say while Elexa was listening…well. That was an answer in itself, was it not?

"Put her back on the phone."

A second later she said, "Tate?"

"I'm here." He said, "Text me when you get to the hospital. I'll meet you there. But you need to drive separate, and pack an overnight bag. Both for you and your mom. Can you do that for me?"

"Yes." She sounded relieved. "I've been halfway packed for weeks."

"Since volleyball camp." The teen had been gone four days over Spring Break.

"That isn't why." She paused. "I've gotta go. Dean is taking mom."

"See you soon."

He hung up and held tight to the wheel. So tight he wouldn't be surprised if it was warped when he let go. Tate had been Claire's first husband. After they divorced, she'd gone and gotten pregnant a few weeks later. Elexa's father hadn't married her, but up and left when he found out about the baby. All those years ago.

Claire and Tate had had a two year marriage and had agreed to disband it before things got too out of control. He'd been volatile back then. Fresh out of his short career with the FBI. At first, it had been a draw for her, his wild ways. Then she'd tried to "settle him down." That had been the beginning of the end.

Tate reached the gas station at the edge of town. He pulled over and loaded the app that would find Elexa's phone—something she'd willingly given him access to. She'd actually asked him to set it up. Just in case.

Maybe for some people, their relationship—whatever you might call them—might be weird. A forty-five year old man couldn't be friends with a sixteen-year-old girl. But he cared about her mom, and she knew she could always count on him if either of them needed help.

The little dot said she was on her way to the hospital.

He sent her a text to meet him in the lobby. When he walked in twenty minutes later, she said, "I kind of thought you'd have brought cops with you."

"Your mom decide to start filing police reports now?"

Claire never had before. She always said she could "handle" it, despite the fact he could see the pain she was in. Physical and emotional. Elexa didn't answer. "She should. If she wakes up."

"Come on. She's gonna wake up."

"You didn't see her."

"Dean knows what he's doing, and so do the doctors." He had to hold himself in check. "Besides, if Rob disappears later, I don't want my name involved in a police report. You know the first place they look at is the spouse, right? Second place is the ex who's still in her life."

Elexa rolled her eyes, but he didn't miss the edge of fear.

"She'll be okay."

"You don't know that," she said. "But thanks."

"Let's go find out."

She had to speak with the hospital staff, and fill out all the forms for her mom. While she did that, he made a call.

Tate wrapped up his call when she started towards him. "Thanks." He stowed his phone back in his jeans pocket. "All good?"

Given her look, he figured that was a "no."

She said, "They did an x-ray. She's still unconscious. The doctor said there's a fracture in her skull. She might not wake up for a couple of days, maybe longer." Tears gathered in her eyes.

Tate lifted a hand and squeezed the back of her neck, his forearm resting on her shoulder. She grasped it. Holding on for dear life while she got a handle on her emotions.

"I told her that she should leave as well."

He nodded. She'd been planning her exit for months, wanting her mom to go with her. Tate had encouraged them both to start a new life. He didn't know if Claire was just scared, or if she was so under Rob's thumb that she felt like she couldn't leave. Whatever it was, he was prepared to help Elexa get her mom to work through those feelings. Otherwise, neither of them would ever get free.

"I know you did." He let go of her neck. "Maybe this will convince her."

Elexa shrugged. "They said nothing's gonna change tonight. Maybe not for a couple of days. They said there's a spot where I can sleep, though. Cause I don't really wanna go home."

"You packed bags for you and your mom like I told you to, right?"

"I thought that was just for the hospital."

"You wanna sleep on an uncomfortable hospital chair, night after night, with the lights on and people everywhere?" The alternative was that she go back to the house, where she would be alone with her stepdad—after putting her mom in the hospital.

Fear washed over her face. "Can I stay with you?"

He shook his head. "That's not a good idea."

"Whatever. Everyone already thinks you're my dad."

He nearly choked. "What?"

Elexa made a face. "Literally *everyone* I know thinks you're my dad."

"And, of course, you told them that I'm not?"

"No way. Let them think whatever." She brushed at her hair, and he realized how exhausted she looked. "It makes me more mysterious. The town's super-hot, rogue private investigator might be my dad...or he might not be." She lifted her hands and wiggled her fingers. "Nobody knows."

"Tune in at ten for more fictional adventures."

She almost laughed.

"I'm not even touching that super-hot thing."

"You're old, but it can't be denied. All my friends think so, but I told them to quit talking about you like that because that's just gross. But even mom said it. Though, I think she still hates you for the umbrella thing."

Yet another thing he wasn't going to touch. "Let's go. Tomorrow you can get an update before school." Before she could move, he said, "I do need to know if he's ever touched you. Or hurt you in any way."

"Because you'll kill him?"

He would certainly want to.

"He's never even touched me. I already want you to kill him. That would just give me even more reason." She studied him. "I have money saved up."

He gently shoved at her shoulder. "Come on."

"Where are we going?"

"A safe place for you to stay."

Tate drove, and she followed him in her car across town. Set up as a shelter, Hope Mansion now took any single woman—children, too—on an application basis. They also had empty rooms for occasions like this. The owner, Maggie, was going to meet them at the door.

Anytime Tate called, day or night, Maggie picked up.

He got Elexa's bag off the backseat. "Maggie said she was going to make tea for you."

As they approached the side door, it flew open. A woman ran out. Tate caught the flash of a police shield on her belt right before she slammed into him.

"Easy." He grasped her biceps to keep her from knocking him over, and the bag banged against the side of his leg.

She looked up at him. Those blue eyes, blonde hair. Flustered. Breathy, as though they'd just kissed.

"Savannah." He sounded like they'd just kissed.

"Seriously, Dad? You're gonna flirt with a woman right now?"

Any other time it might have been funny.

With literally *any* other woman.

## 2

S avannah pulled up outside the victim's office thirty minutes later. She shut off the police lights and siren before also turning off the engine. The black and white car she parked behind was dark, but the gentrified office building was lit up and the officer was at the front door.

*Don't think about Tate.*

She climbed out and shoved the door closed. It slammed. Savannah pulled on her jacket like there was nothing wrong. Nothing but frigid spring night air, and the fact she hadn't seen the beach in far too long—or even a warm day, for that matter.

Her brand new partner, Mia Tathers—formerly ATF—winced. "What's so wrong that you gotta take it out on your car?"

Savannah said, "Sorry. What've we got?"

Mia didn't didn't begin to explain the situation at hand—a dead man. "He's not getting any deader." Mia folded her arms over her wool coat, and Savannah noted she'd curled her hair. "So explain."

Savannah looked down at her partner's red skinny pants, and her eyes continued down to the white-soled sneakers on her feet. "Were you on a date?"

"I changed my shoes. And you're avoiding the subject," Mia said. "But while we're talking about it, Conroy wasn't super happy he didn't get to the 'walking me to my front door' portion because of the murder I had to come investigate."

"So I hope you reminded him it was his idea you become his new lieutenant, and my partner. Which means, as the chief of police, he can't really complain, right?"

The whole situation was hilarious. Mostly because her boss had been uptight for so long. She was enjoying his game being thrown by his newfound emotions. The former chief had passed away a few weeks ago after an uncharacteristically long, drawn-out battle with pancreatic cancer. The interplay between Lieutenant Mia Tathers and new Chief Conroy Barnes was like watching a soap opera happen at work.

There was a police department poll circulating the office to correctly guess what month they would get married, even though Conroy hadn't asked her yet.

Savannah had her money on July.

Mia said, "He's uh…working on dealing with the fact me being his lieutenant means I actually have to be a cop sometimes."

Savannah grinned. "I'm sure."

Mia was taller than her, lanky like a volleyball player. Savannah felt like the sidekick—five-four and curvy. Older, by nearly ten years. On top of it all, her new partner was also a former ATF agent. Talk about an inferiority complex. A fed? Savannah loved her job, and she loved Mia. But if you took away either of those, she'd be back with the town shrink and something new to talk through.

Mia had also grown up here in Last Chance County, so people all over town knew her. They knew her story; how Conroy had dated her older sister—before she'd been killed in an automobile accident. Mia had forgiven Conroy for what she'd believed was his responsibility in the tragedy, while he'd worked to keep her safe from a crazy guy with a career terrorizing people.

Savannah, on the other hand, had been here two years, which meant she was about twenty-eight years from officially qualifying as someone "from here." She was a newbie in town, and she would always be the detective not born and raised here. An outsider.

Savannah said, "How's your hearing?"

"Some ringing on occasion, but generally good."

A dangerous man had fired a weapon next to Mia's ear only a few weeks ago. She was recovering better than the doctors expected from having a perforated ear drum. Still, she would never be back to full capacity. Mia had to wear ear protection to safely fire her weapon, which meant that in the event she had to draw—and fire—her gun on the job, she would be stuck with permanent hearing loss. One that would confine her to a desk indefinitely.

Savannah had already had the hard conversation with Conroy about Mia's hearing. She'd tried to convince him it wasn't worth it for Mia to take that risk. One incident was all it would take for her partner to wind up disqualified from field work. But, and for good reason, he wanted her to make the choice herself.

In the meantime, that meant Savannah had to report directly to him, regularly, on how Mia was doing. Loud noises were going to be a problem. Gunshots. Explosions. Maybe they'd had their fair share of those before Mia's injury—when that dangerous man had targeted her—and things were back to normal now.

Whatever that meant.

Though, she figured it at least meant no more Tate Hudson.

"What?"

Savannah said, "We should get inside."

"Yeah, no. Spill."

She decided to rip off the bandage. "I ran into Tate on my way out of my place—where I live." She turned to head for the scene. "That's all. No biggie."

"If you're using the word 'biggie,' then it *is* a big deal." Mia snagged her arm. "What?"

Savannah sighed. "I literally ran into him. As in, slammed right into him. My face hit his chest, and he grabbed my arms."

Mia's dark brows angled together. "He grabbed you?"

"Not like that." They'd had a moment. As hokey as that sounded, she'd stared up into his eyes and just paused. "He was nice about it. There was this girl with him."

"A girl?"

"She called him 'dad.'"

"*No.*"

"So now you know, let's go. End of story. Time to work."

Tate Hudson, private investigator and one time FBI agent, had a kid. A full grown, beautiful teenage daughter.

Savannah made a beeline down the sidewalk at a strip mall in the low-rent end of town. The dead guy was a CPA, Kenny Aggerton. Well known in town as the owner of two businesses. One legitimate, and the other one that resided…under the table. Where he kept a second safe, literally, in the floor beneath the rug under his desk.

They checked with the officer stationed on the door. "You found him?"

Donaldson nodded. He was young, but he'd proven himself recently when he'd helped save Mia and Conroy's lives and detain the dangerous man. He said, "Call came in from a neighbor who works at the clothing store next door. She heard shouts and called it in. By the time we got here, the guy was DOA."

Mia said, "You ID'd him?"

"Photos on the walls, name on the door," Donaldson said. "It's him."

Mia nodded.

"Checked his pulse, but it was pretty clear he's dead. I didn't touch anything else."

The reception area was clear. Single desk with a computer and phone, a faux leather couch and coffee table. Side table and coffee pot. Water dispenser. "Donaldson, get the receptionist down here."

He said, "Copy that."

Savannah stepped into the office and saw what he meant about it being "pretty clear" he was dead. Her partner wasn't going to like this. "Mia, you—"

She nearly slammed into Savannah's back, though not like Savannah had slammed into Tate. "Good gravy."

"Yeah." It was gruesome. Just what Savannah needed to get Tate out of her head.

Sure, they'd worked together a bit during the time Conroy had been protecting Mia. They'd brought down Ed Summers, a local guy who'd been selling drugs—and other things—for years. She still didn't understand everything Tate had going on. It had been clear he worked according to his own rules.

Still, they'd finally gotten enough evidence to topple the empire, which then created a power vacuum in town among the criminal element. They weren't a big town, but big enough; the highway connected them between two major cities. Ed Summers had controlled what went through town, charging taxes on things transported across the state.

"Kenny Aggerton."

"Yeah." Savannah said, "Ed Summers's uncle, via his mother." She pulled paper booties over her shoes and moved to the body, donning rubber gloves. "Got your camera?"

"In the car."

"Once we have the preliminary look done, we'll get down to processing the scene." It was going to be a long night. She crouched. "Multiple stab wounds."

Up close and personal. Someone was angry.

Aggerton had been holding leverage over his nephew, Ed Summers. Now that Summers was in jail, pending his court case, could be he'd taken out his anger on his uncle for the man's part in the charges against him. Or he'd ordered it done.

He still had loyal friends on the outside. Even after a lot of his crew were swept up with him.

Then again, Aggerton wasn't exactly an upstanding guy.

Stabbings didn't just happen. Sure some people carried knives with them everywhere, especially in more rural communities like this. But it wasn't usually the top choice in weapons for a premeditated murder.

"Look around for a knife. If it's not here, we can widen the search to the surrounding area. Maybe the killer dumped it on the way out."

Trash cans. Streets and side roads. Storm drains. If they knew which direction the killer had fled, they'd be able to narrow the search.

"Okay." Mia's voice sounded funny.

Savannah glanced at her partner. "If you're gonna hurl, you should do it outside or you'll contaminate the evidence."

Mia glanced around, her face pale. "He certainly enjoyed staring at images of himself. This wall is covered with photos of him with all kinds of people." She wandered to one framed photo. "That's the governor."

The victim was a power player in town. A guy with known criminal ties, who made money through those connections. She stared at his body. Then she stood and looked around.

Who had he angered, and did it have to do with the case being brought up against Summers?

She turned around slowly, taking in the room as a whole. "The safe is undisturbed."

Because the desk was still where it always stood. Something Savannah knew from the last time she was here. It had been a few weeks ago since they'd served a warrant and removed evidence from the safe under the rug. Part of their case against Ed Summers—removing account books from Kenny Aggerton's office

On the wall, behind a painting, was another safe. The one his clients saw him use on occasion. That was also undisturbed.

She muttered, "He wasn't looking for something."

File cabinets were shut; the key turned so it was locked. Computer intact, switched off. His phone lay on the desk.

"But they argued, and he or she pulled a knife and killed him." Savannah pressed her lips together while she thought about it. "Means they brought it with them. Unless they grabbed a letter opener, or something else, and used that. But when you stab someone multiple times, things get slippery. Your hand slides down the weapon, and you usually end up cutting yourself and leaving DNA on it. Or prints if you don't get cut yourself."

Mia said, "So we really need to find it."

Savannah glanced at her partner. "I'll make notes if you get the bag."

Mia nodded, leaving Savannah alone with the dead guy. Too bad all she could think about was Tate. Last in a long line of things, and people, she didn't want to remember. Or dwell on.

Working cases was the only thing that made sense. Pieces of a puzzle she dug up that fit only one way. Solving crime was what she had been born and raised to do. *Thanks, Dad.* Not much she could be grateful to her father for, but that was something at least. After her mom had died, he'd done his best. She hoped he had, at least. The thought gave her only a sliver of comfort.

Her thoughts drifted again, to a different man.

*Seriously, Dad?*

The girl had spoken to Tate with obvious affection. He could have a family he'd never told her about, though she knew he wasn't married. Why did she care, anyway? They had sparks, but it wasn't a thing.

She was a cop. Just a cop, with no room in her life for complicated anything.

A man was dead, and she would figure out who did it. Then she would arrest them. After that, there would be another case. Another victim, with their own suspect. That was about all the complicated she could handle. Adding in emotions and drama because she found out Tate had a daughter and he hadn't even—

"Whoa." Mia stepped into view in front of her.

Savannah realized she hadn't even noticed her friend and new partner had walked back in. "Just checking your reaction, regardless of circumstances. You passed."

Mia shook her head, smiling. "Yeah, sure."

Not fooled, but that was no surprise. Savannah needed to get her head together. If Tate wanted a relationship, or even had feelings for her, then he'd have said something. He hadn't, and that was fine. Because Savannah needed procedure. She needed investigation.

What she did not need, was more secrets.

Officer Donaldson appeared in the doorway.

"Security cameras?"

"Oh. I'll look." He came back a couple of minutes later. "One over the front door, another at the back."

"Call Ted. Have him come down here and find us the footage." Their tech guy was a genius, and Savannah had about as much patience for technology as she did for the US Postal Service.

"Copy that." Donaldson disappeared.

Two hours later, her hunch paid off. Ted called out to her from over at the receptionist desk. The woman had logged him into the computer, then she'd been escorted off the premises by the officer who had driven her here so she could answer some questions.

Savannah strode over from the CPA's office. "What is it?"

Ted shoved back the thick, dark hair that had fallen over his forehead. "I've got something you're gonna need to see to believe."

———

Continue the story, find it on Amazon now!

# OTHER BOOKS IN THE LAST CHANCE COUNTY SERIES

Find ALL of the books at:

LastChanceCounty.com

In this Series:

Book 1: Expired Refuge

Book 2: Expired Secrets

Book 3: Expired Cache

Book 4: Expired Hero

Book 5: Expired Game

Book 6: Expired Plot

Book 7: Expired Getaway

Book 8: Expired Betrayal

Book 9: Expired Flight

Book 10: Expired End

Also available in 2 collections!

Books 1-5

Books 6-10

# ABOUT THE AUTHOR

Follow Lisa on social media to find out about new releases and other exciting events!

Visit Lisa's Website to sign up for her mailing list to get FREE books and be the first to learn about new releases and other exciting updates!

https://www.authorlisaphillips.com